a Spiral

INTO Marvelous

LIGHT

a Spiral
INTO Marvelous
LIGHT

A NOVEL

Michael Gryboski

AMBASSADOR INTERNATIONAL
GREENVILLE, SOUTH CAROLINA & BELFAST, NORTHERN IRELAND

www.ambassador-international.com

A Spiral into Marvelous Light

© 2019 by Michael Gryboski

All rights reserved

ISBN: 978-1-62020-864-9
eISBN: 978-1-62020-885-4
Library of Congress Control Number: 2019932343

Scripture taken from the King James Version. Public Domain.

Cover Design & Typesetting by Hannah Nichols
Ebook Conversion by Anna Riebe Raats
Edited by Katie Cruice Smith

AMBASSADOR INTERNATIONAL
Emerald House
411 University Ridge, Suite B14
Greenville, SC 29601, USA
www.ambassador-international.com

AMBASSADOR BOOKS
The Mount
2 Woodstock Link
Belfast, BT6 8DD, Northern Ireland, UK
www.ambassadormedia.co.uk

The colophon is a trademark of Ambassador, a Christian publishing company.

"We don't get religion.
We don't get the role of religion in people's lives.
And I think we can do much, much better."

—Dean Baquet,
Executive Editor of *The New York Times*

CONTENTS

HERBERT SPIKER

IT WAS A SURVEY OF his labors. Shelves covered most of the walls. Books filled up each row. Diverse in their origins and content, they varied in age, color, size, and intellectual merit. Some were paperback, others hardback. Many were worn, stiffened and yellowed with the passage of the decades. Others were fresher, with crisp pages and clear lettering. The oldest dated to around the Second World War, while the youngest came in just a few weeks ago. Several had informal bookmarks of scratch paper marking important quotations. A petite library, a collage of anthologies.

Yet from this surface diversity came ideological cohesion. The authors and their arguments were of one mind on many issues, seldom dissenting from the grand narrative. For the owner of the room, the worldview was obvious. Books refuting the errors of evolution, denouncing sexual debauchery, and bashing secularism filled the shelves. Other works nitpicked the arguments for the Social Gospel, the latest wave of feminism, Islam, the New Age, and socialism. Less contentious volumes included devotionals, theological contemplations, and sermon compilations. There were several editions and translations of the Bible, though the King James was the most beloved.

He had authored a few of the published texts. Many of them drew from past homilies, speeches, and opinion columns. A couple of them were best-sellers, purchased and consumed by the like-minded masses.

All, save two, were nonfiction, centered on matters of faith, politics, or faith *and* politics. The fiction works covered similar themes, though one of them was very conspiratorial, with a plot that included Freemason villains, secretive bankers, unjustly accused Christian fugitives, and the Antichrist. Critics were quick to pounce on that one, seeing it as proof that the author was a crazed individual, fomenting hysteria. There were always critics. It was a hazard of the occupation.

Several framed images dotted the white walls. They hung above the tops of the shelves. There were two degrees, suspended side by side, to the right of the desk. Each one was from a religious school founded in response to the dreadful tide of modernist thinking. They had fancy cursive writing and the emblem of their respective accredited establishments. One of them had just recently named a new on-campus building in his honor. It was a controversial move, with several hundred protestors signing an online petition. Still, it happened, with the board of visitors seeing little threat of boycott.

The rest of the framed items were photos. Spanning the decades, a third of them were in black and white. All of the suspended photographic images were from his public career—speeches for political initiatives, messages at revival meetings, cordially shaking hands with a host of prominent figures, including three Republican presidents. Intimate visuals were located on the desk, facing the plush chair. Smaller than those on the walls, these rectangular photos showed family and good friends. One framed image did not show people or places, but rather the text of First Peter 2:9—his favorite verse.

Occupying the desk was a flat computer screen with a mouse, a case, and a keyboard—all black. It was only a few months old, having recently replaced a bulkier beige machine. He had held off getting a new one, believing that his older system worked just fine. However, as it became increasingly sluggish, he conceded defeat and purchased the present set. Younger subordinates were quick to transfer his files and documents to the new motherboard, and all returned to normal. The mouse rested upon a pad that featured a red cross at the center and various linguistic variations of the name Jesus. At that hour, the computer was warming up for the forthcoming work day.

He was seated before the moaning machine, awaiting its resuscitation. A deeply wrinkled man with blue eyes, his once-dark hair was a thinning white. His frame was slim; but for much of his adult life, he had been heavier. At his peak, the average-height man passed the 250-pound mark. Within his possession were many clothes, mostly due to his fluctuations. That morning, he wore his usual drab attire. Black suits with white button-up shirts and faded black dress shoes were typical. Only the tie, a red one with thin blue stripes, gave color. He tended to dress well, rarely wearing blue jeans, shorts, or sweatshirts.

As he waited for the computer to finish loading, he took to reading his personal Bible. A black leather-bound book, its once-prominent gold letters on the front cover were faded to the point of being invisible. The opening pages included personal records, listing the date of his one-and-only marriage, the births and baptisms of his kids, and then, later on, their marriages and their children. He was running out of space for recording the milestones. The Good Book was open to a passage in the Psalms. Reading through the verses of praise and adoration, he felt a tinge of pain in his left arm.

The spurt was initially disregarded. He was an old man, after all, and well-acquainted with the aches of a frail corpus. Then the pain got sharper. It was enough to dislodge him from his Scriptural focus.

Putting the Bible on top of the keyboard, he grabbed at his left arm. The pain coursed through the left side of his chest, causing panic to enter his mind. He knew what was happening. Pushing back the office chair as he rose to his feet, he expressed muffled pain as he staggered in a failed attempt to get help. Stumbling around, he soon fell to the carpeted floor, lying between the left side of the desk and several shelves of books. He glimpsed the bright ceiling fan light above him before his eyes shut.

A minute later, the office door was opened, and a woman entered. She was in a business casual dress and had a mop-top haircut. With one hand, she opened the door, while she held several papers with the other. The balancing act was a common practice for her. Looking down at the pages, she entered the room talking as though another person was present to listen.

"Okay, so I got the copies of the speech printed just as you . . . " Her words died away at the moment she looked away from the pages and saw the body.

* * *

Behind glass doors, the newsroom was starting to buzz. There was a growing symphony of typing fingers, ringing phones, talking heads on television screens, and face-to-face conversations. There were exchanges, personal and business, informal banter between official affairs. An hour earlier, few were around: a custodian, an early riser, and a couple of editors. By the following hour, there was a crowd of people, each with their own contribution to the spread of information.

The Kensington Post was a mixture of online and print media, of written news stories, opinion columns, and in-depth pieces. Last year, they added a video team, which produced man-on-the-street interviews, live coverage of events, and in-studio reports. Periodically, prominent public figures and celebrities came to the office. They were interviewed on camera for the digital world to behold. Social media carried the live feed, especially if it involved a presidential debate or a massive protest. They lacked a good international bureau, so seldom was there something bloody to record.

The exterior and interior of the *Post*'s headquarters were bland. They did not control the entirety of their Northwest DC high-rise, sharing the ten-story building with a few other businesses and two nonprofits. Yet they were the largest tenant, taking up five floors. Two of them were for archives, one for the print journalists and their editors, one for the video team, and a fifth for various purposes, including large group meetings or holiday parties. The floor with the print reporters featured groups of cubicles separated by department. A collection of islands, they were in the same archipelago yet separated by space from being linked as one. Each department had its own editor.

The wall bordering the outside world was glass with black frames. It overlooked a horizon covered by other edifices. No clear view of the Washington Monument or the Capitol Dome from their floors. The opposite wall was also transparent, but visual access to it was obscured by the interior walls for the editors' offices. A third wall featured four large flat screen televisions that were constantly turned to cable news. For a time, each TV had a different station tuned in. However, it was decided that this was too confusing. Now, it was the same channel on all four screens. The final wall was the entrance, which was several feet behind another transparent wall that bordered the outside world. It was also comprised of glass. This wall halted before a hallway that had an external wall of glass on the other side.

Scott Addison was in the general news department. As such, his cubicle and the cubicles of his peers were the nearest to the four flat-screen televisions attached to the interior wall. A thirty-something blonde was on the screens, receiving little attention from Addison or the three other reporters whose cubicles bordered his own. Each adhered to the business casual dress code. Every morning, save rare alternative circumstances, they pitched their stories to their editor-in-chief, Michael Phillips, who personally oversaw their department. Phillips was an energetic fellow, unphased by the fact that he was in his sixties.

Sometimes, they pitched their stories on instant chat. This morning, the story ideas were given in person. The team gathered at Katie Nicholson's cubicle, which was the one of the four stations closest to their editor's office. A woman of slender figure and olive skin, she began her journalism career as a broadcaster but came to prefer the literary wing. She sat in her chair, its broad back turned away from her computer to face the editor. Scott was beside her, leaning on the desk surface. To their left was Mandy Salver-Jones, a bespectacled woman who was the only married member in the department. To their right was Tyrone Spearman, who joked that he was assigned to general news for the chief purpose of integration. He was in the process of finishing up his pitches.

"And for your second story?" inquired Phillips, shirt sleeves rolled up to the elbows.

"There are reports that ISIS is training chickens to be used as suicide bombers," said Tyrone, getting amused glares from his peers.

"Really?" laughed Phillips.

"I checked; the sources reporting it are not satire sites."

"Then definitely write that one," said Phillips, who stroked his chin for a moment before adding, "and make sure our cartoon team hears about this."

"Yes, sir."

"Okay, that should keep you out of trouble for the next several hours," said Phillips as he directed his attention toward the seated Nicholson. "Okay, Katie, you're up to the plate. What do you have?"

"Well," began Katie. "House Democrats are planning to introduce a bill to make Planned Parenthood's federal funding permanent."

"Hmmm . . . ," contemplated Phillips, stroking his chin once again. "A story only about a bill being introduced, especially from the minority party." He shook his index finger at her. "That might not get many hits."

"Well, they claim they will get enough Republicans to vote for it. You know, the ones from swing states and all that."

"Okay, okay," nodded Phillips. "That might work. What else?"

"Well, I would think that if they have enough moderate Republicans, then that is the story, right?"

"Maybe, maybe. Right now, I'm thinking about how we can grab people's attention. Most of your story is still just conjecture. Speculative."

"A way to grab people's attention."

"I have an idea," interjected Tyrone. "How about you title it the 'Perma-Fund Planned Parenthood Bill'?" The others, especially Phillips, were amused by the response.

"You know what? I like it," replied Phillips. "For once, I actually like your title idea."

"I try."

"So, yes, you can write that one," said Phillips to Nicholson. "What else do you have for me, Katie?"

"Benny Hinn claims that the death of Billy Graham will bring forth some big huge religious revival in America."

"Really? What's the source?"

"Some rightwing Christian site, so obviously a sympathetic source."

"Okay, okay," pondered Phillips. "That sounds possible. Sure, why not? You can have that as your second for today."

"Hold on," spoke up Scott, prompting the others to turn to face him. "I'm pretty sure I wrote that story a while ago."

"Really?" asked Phillips.

"I'm pretty sure. At least, it sounds like something he said a couple years ago."

"Hmmm, I wonder," said Phillips. "Katie, can you show me the link to your story source? I want to get a good look at this."

"Sure," replied Katie, who swung her chair around to face the computer screen. Phillips approached, with Salver-Jones making space for her editor to get a good view of the Internet. "Here's the story." Katie clicked on the link she had saved and up popped the story. She pushed a little to the side as her superior took control of the mouse and scrolled down the page, studying the printed information.

"Okay, the date of the story is from yesterday," Phillips thought aloud. "And they have a link to the video." Phillips placed the pointer upon the dark blue underlined text, distinguishing it from the black letters all around. A left-click and a new webpage emerged. The video automatically played on the page; however, the audio was mute. Each computer had its own headphones for private listening. Soon, Phillips saw the problem with the video. "Uploaded July of 2012. July 2012!"

"Whoops," said Katie.

"Yeah, definitely not timely."

"Nope."

"Five years ago," pondered Phillips. "That's not news . . . that's history!" Katie and the others smiled. "Anyway, what other stories do you have for me?"

Before Nicholson was able to muster a response, a loud gonging noise emanated from the one unmuted television. In most circumstances, the reporters and their editors ignored the audio signal. After all, most of the breaking news being heralded were things already posted to the *Kensington Post*'s website. Other times, they were not viewed as sufficiently newsworthy. However, since it was the time for assigning stories, Phillips and the others gave it attention. The anchor's announcement was of great interest for the editor-in-chief—indeed, one that granted him even more vigor.

"We are just now receiving confirmation that the Rev. Sammy Milton has died. A spokesman for the Milton family provided a statement to media explaining that the eighty-six-year-old fundamentalist pastor suffered a fatal heart attack on Monday morning. A controversial figure, Rev. Milton spent several decades in the public light and is credited with mainstreaming the Christian Right movement . . . "

"Oh boy, oh boy, oh boy," stated an excited, yet composed, Phillips. "Oh boy, oh boy. Okay, okay. This is a big one." Phillips drew his focus away from the televisions and toward his team of millennial-aged online journalists. "Okay, team. We have to really get on this one. This is a top priority. Tyrone."

"Yes?"

"I need you to write a quick little obituary. I'd write it myself, but it might look like gloating." He and his small audience smiled at the comment. "Anyway, nothing too detailed, just something we can post on the site asap. I have a basic outline with some points, which I'll email you shortly. Find the Milton estate's official announcement and quote what you can."

"Okay," said Tyrone, giving a faint salute before returning to his cubicle to begin work on the assignment. Phillips turned to Nicholson.

"Katie, for your second story, go on social media and find some reactions. I'm thinking the crueler, the better. Doesn't have to be anyone famous; just look for ones that are biting, ones that are funny. Basically, anything that puts Milton in his place."

"Okay," said Katie. "How many should I find?"

"Fifteen to twenty will do," replied Phillips, who pointed at Salver-Jones while he kept talking. "Amanda can help you find some." As Katie nodded and turned to her computer, Phillips looked at Salver-Jones. "After you help Katie find social media responses, email the video team and have them whip something up."

"What should be in the video?"

"Just spotlight a couple of his more ridiculous public statements. You know, when he called some kids' TV character gay, blamed liberals for 9/11, stuff like that. And be sure to write up a companion listicle."

"Sure thing."

"Good, good," said Phillips, directing his focus to the last general news reporter lacking a specific assignment centered on the recently deceased. "Scott."

"Yes," Scott replied, snapping to attention.

"I have a special assignment for you," the editor noted, pointing his index finger at the reporter. "I want you to interview one of Milton's old enemies. We need to remind people just how over-the-top crazy he was. And I have just the guy for you. And the best part is, I think he's in town."

"Okay. Who?"

"Follow me to my office, and I'll get you the details. If I can get something scheduled, it would be best to do it in-person, okay?"

"Sure," agreed Scott as the two rushed to Phillips' office, while the other three reporters were focused on their individual tasks.

Their walk was an expedient one, with Phillips in front and Addison close behind. The office door was already wide open. Entering the quarters, Scott saw the office accoutrements. There was the bachelor of arts degree hanging on the wall, the photos of famous people Phillips had interviewed over his career. More partisan homages were also on display. This included the front page of the editions celebrating the United States Supreme Court's nationwide legalization of gay marriage and the 2008 election of Barack Obama. Phillips added bumper stickers to his desk, with messages like "Democracy Not Theocracy," "COEXIST," and "Deficits Are For Republicans" plastered on his work space. Scott had seen them before and was not surprised by their presence.

Addison sat down opposite the desk with its two flat-screen computer monitors facing away from him. Phillips quickly got to emailing Tyrone the paragraphs for the breaking news story and then checked his inbox for any new information. Quickly shooting off another email, Phillips directed his attention to a notebook containing scores of phone numbers and email addresses for interviewees. They were accrued over years of reporting and editing, periodically updated for new contact information or death. Addison patiently waited for his editor to do what was needed to set up the interview. Phillips found the correct number after turning a few pages and dialed. A few purring rings were heard in the receiver. Then a voice answered. Scott could only make out Phillip's end of the dialogue.

"Hello, Herb? Yes, it's me, Michael," said Phillips, who briefly laughed. "Sorry, Michael Phillips. Yes, that Michael. Two L's and two P's. How are you? . . . Good, good. Anyway, you're in DC right now, right? . . . Okay, I thought so . . . Of course, you would be, no question . . . Is it the same studio I interviewed you at years ago? . . . Okay, good . . . Well, I am calling because I need to send over a reporter to interview you . . . No, no, nothing scandalous." Phillips laughed a little more. Apparently, the other fellow told a joke. "No, no, like I said, it is not about you *per se* . . . Yes, it's about that . . . So, can I send over a reporter to interview you? . . . Good, good . . . Yes, he should be able to make it . . . His name is Scott Addison. He'll have ID ready . . . Yes, yes good to hear. I will tell him myself. He should be there soon." Phillips laughed even more. "Well, maybe next time. Anyway, bye!" Phillips hung up the phone and then looked at Scott. "Are you familiar with Herbert Spiker?"

"The porno guy, right?"

"Yes, the 'porno guy,'" said Phillips, nodding. "He and Milton hated each other. They battled each other in the courts in a major free speech case. After that, they debated each other on TV and on college campuses. Lots of antagonism. I bet he's thrilled Milton is dead. And you are going to get him to say that on the record."

"Okay."

"He expects you to get there in about an hour," said Phillips, who was looking down at a piece of paper, which he wrote on with a blue pen. Then he returned his visual attention to Scott, handing him the paper. "Here is the address to Spiker's studio. Like I said, he expects you within the next hour. Be sure to be punctual."

"Sure thing," said Scott as he took hold of the paper.

"Just a warning," began Phillips. "Spiker can be very sensitive about how his words are used. When I first interviewed him back in the eighties, he demanded to see an advance copy of the article. I eventually talked him down to seeing just the part where I quoted him. I won't be surprised if he treats you the same way."

"Thanks for the warning."

"Now if you don't mind, I would like to quit doing your job," jokingly stated Phillips, eliciting a smile from Scott. The reporter rose from his seat and began to leave the office when he was stopped by his superior. "By the way, one more thing."

"Yes?"

"While you're at the studio, don't get, you know, too happy," said the editor.

"I think I know what you mean."

* * *

Scott Addison saw a bronze reflection of himself on the elevator doors. Moving up the lofty structure, he was of a normal disposition. Five years ago, there would have been nerves. He acclimated to the process through performing hundreds of interviews over the phone and in-person. Sometimes it went without problem; sometimes the interviewee commended him for the coverage. In rare occasions, he received a vicious response via email or a blog post. They would claim his piece distorted what they said. He tended to be in the right on those matters, and Phillips knew it. Experience granted him comfort.

The lifting stopped, and the doors pulled open. Before him was a simple hallway and from there, an entrance with a bulky bodyguard. There was a stool to one side of the portal, presumably for the man if he ever became tired of standing around. He was dressed in all black, having the feel of a bouncer from a night club. Muscles bulged out of the tight t-shirt. As Scott walked off the elevator platform into the hallway, he approached the man, who was at least one foot taller and two feet wider than the journalist.

"Hello, I'm Scott Addison, and I have an appointment to interview Mr. Herbert Spiker," spoke Addison in formality while holding up his press lanyard. The bodyguard studied the identification.

"Wait here," he grunted before leaving the hallway and going into the studio. Scott did not expect him to fit through the doorway. He waited for a few moments before seeing the guard return. "Go ahead."

"Thank you," nodded Scott as he walked passed the hefty gentleman and into a studio with white walls and blaring music.

Couches and chairs of basic colors dotted the room he entered, a clean hardwood floor under his feet. There were a few other rooms in the office. People here and there going about, including a pair of statuesque young women wearing high heels and little else. Scott, the tempted man, naturally turned a fleeting gaze at the attractive creatures as they walked by. The techno instrumental music got louder as he got closer to the adjacent room, as did barked orders and the clicking of cameras. The door to the next room was open, and a few people were inside. From his vantage point, Addison beheld the backs of fully clothed men. Seeing no one else standing in the space he was in, he wondered who the guard talked to so quickly to grant him permission to enter the studio.

"Can I help you?" asked an assistant, a normal-looking woman in her late thirties. She was dressed in modest attire and wore thick glasses. Her hair was in a bun.

"Yes, I am a reporter who is scheduled to interview—"

"Oh, of course, Sid just told me," she said, taking turns looking at Scott and a notebook she held with her left hand. She pointed at a smaller room to his left as she continued, "Just wait in that room, and Mr. Spiker will be with you shortly."

"Sure, thanks," said Scott as the woman rushed back into the space where the photo shoot was taking place. Another model walked past Scott wearing just enough to cover her private parts. She gave him a perfect smile, prompting the reporter to smile in return. He was disciplined enough to not look back as he entered the room. As with the first space, it had ivory painted walls, a hardwood floor, and basic furniture. There were two pieces of modern art, bizarrely shaped sculptures that were each about two feet tall. They occupied their own small tables, placed between three couches, positioned in a U-shape.

Scott sat down, leaning back into the plushy couch that faced the entrance. He waited for a few minutes, seeing the occasional scantily clad woman or fully clothed photographer going by. The techno music blurred from one track to another, as though guided by a turntable-manning DJ. One long continuous stream of beats. Then he heard a raspy, profane voice. Through the door, he saw a wheelchair-bound man rolling along, speaking a few comments with a man walking beside him. It seemed that the duo were both going to grace Scott with their presence; but right at the threshold, the seated man gave a final comment; the walking man nodded; and then the latter returned to the source of the music. Only the disabled person rolled into the chamber.

"Hello there, my name is Scott Addison," he began as he rose from the couch to shake the hand of the newcomer. "I'm a reporter with *The Kensington Post.*"

"Ah, yes," cackled Herbert Spiker as he shook the journalist's hand. "Phillips called me and said you were coming. Sit." Scott returned to the couch.

"Thank you," said Scott as he took out his digital voice recorder and placed it on the short, white coffee table positioned within the middle of the three couches. He turned it on but did not push the record button. Spiker wheeled around to be situated at a corner of the table. "Anyway, what I am hoping to do is ask you a few questions, on the record, about your experiences with Sammy Milton."

"Fair enough," replied Spiker, who gritted his teeth as he talked, as though clinching an invisible cigar in his mouth. "You know, I used to be a reporter back in the day." He smiled when he saw the recording device on the table. "My recorder was way larger. Of course, when I started my magazine, the cameras were larger, too. Man, I was one arrogant little jerk, too. But yeah, you wanted me to talk about Milton."

"Yes."

"Well, fire away your questions," said Spiker. Addison nodded and pushed the record button on the slim, silver device. A bright red light came on, and the small square screen displayed a track number and slowly changing digital black numbers.

"Okay, first question: when did you first learn about Milton?"

"Well," began Spiker, shifting in his wheelchair. "It began back in the seventies. Probably before you were born. Around the time I was your age. I was just starting to spread my magazine out to the East Coast. I got the investment from my father's will. Pretty much the only thing he ever did for me. Anyhow, I kept hearing from folks in Virginia that they were getting some heat from a fundy preacher. I didn't think much of it, at first. I told them, 'If you don't annoy some preacher, you're not doing your job!'" Spiker paused to laugh, while Addison smiled in amusement. "But it turned out this preacher was different. He was political. He campaigned for stuff. He got a bunch of ordinances passed banning my magazines. He was a threat, not a nuisance. He was Sammy Milton."

"So, what did you do after you realized Milton was a threat?"

"I struck back, that's what," responded Spiker with a boost of enthusiasm. "I had our publication run a few cartoons showing that fanatic in some, well, let's say, not family-friendly positions with a donkey. And then a cow." Spiker laughed a little more, recalling the gross imagination of his staff. "Man, we really had some guts back then. But yeah, Milton didn't particularly enjoy our sense of humor, and he sued us. He wanted five million dollars in 'emotional damages.'"

"That's a lot of money."

"You got that right. Especially back then. Back in the seventies, five million dollars could have bought all the casinos in Vegas. So, you bet your sweet behind we fought him tooth and nail. In the end, we won. Everyone knows that. But in the seventies, all the other courts ruled against us. First, there was the district court judge. We brushed that off because he was friends with people who went to Milton's church. But when the appeals court ruled the same, it was getting scary. We were thinking of throwing in the towel. Maybe reach a deal. But one of my lawyers urged me to keep going. So, we did." Spiker's eyes sparkled. "And we won. We won. The Supreme Court sided with us. Even the rightwing nut jobs on the bench joined the majority. A great triumph for free speech and nice-looking flesh."

"I see," lightly laughed Scott. Returning to a professional composure, he continued his query. "And then what happened after that? As I understand, you and him had several debates."

"Uh-huh," affirmed Spiker. "We went all over the country, debating each other on college campuses and forums and local TV. If some town was planning to ban my business, we'd both show up and argue our points. Sometimes he won; sometimes I won. If we had internet back then, we would have just done it all once online and called it a day. But yeah, lots of battles over many years."

"So, then, would you say that, with Milton's death, you feel a sense of relief?"

Spiker quit gritting his teeth, his shark smile mending itself into confusion. Scott was becoming a little uncomfortable with the silence. The pause was too short to be too awkward, yet long enough to disrupt the previous climate of the on-the-record conversation. Spiker started to analyze Addison with his eyes, and then spoke up. "You know, I used to be a reporter. Long ago. Probably would still do it if I didn't make so much money off of smut. I can still hear my editor and how he always gave me an angle. 'Don't forget the angle! Don't forget the angle!' What's your angle, Mr. Addison?"

"Well," said Scott as he moved in his seat. He looked down before responding. "Well, um, Phillips wanted me to interview an old enemy of Milton's to get their views on him now that he has died. Someone who . . . who wouldn't mind seeing him go, so to speak. Someone who hopes that Milton's cause died with him. That . . . that sort of thing."

"Ah, I see," said Spiker, grinning again. "You want to know how I feel about that man? Am I happy to see him die?"

"Um, basically, yes," stuttered Scott.

"Well, then," began Spiker, pushing his wheelchair to get a couple of inches closer to the reporter, "you're in luck, young man. Because I will tell you exactly how I feel about him. Are you ready?"

"The recorder is still working," Scott replied.

"Then I will tell you," began Spiker, a deeply interested Scott ready to jot some notes as the recorder continued. "Sammy Milton was one of the greatest men I ever knew. He was civil, kind, and a very good friend." Addison laughed, thinking his interviewee was joking. Then he looked up from his notepad and saw a serious expression.

"Wait, you're serious?" asked the journalist, who quit his notetaking and stared at the wheelchair-bound older man.

"Very. Do you want me to repeat it? Because I will," stated Spiker. "Sammy Milton was one of the best men I ever knew. He was kind, civil, and a very good friend." Spiker gave a big smile. "Now, how is that for a bombshell?"

"Well, um, well, it's a big one, that's for sure," responded Scott, regaining his prowess. "So, when did you become good friends? How did that come about?"

"It began back in the eighties," recalled Spiker. "We had just finished off another debate at some place—I think it was in Montana or North Dakota. Some piece of junk place. But yeah, we both took our private jets to get to the spot. Milton would call it Divine Providence. I think it was dumb luck. But whatever force was at work that day, it just so happened that our planes were scheduled to dock at the same gate."

* * *

It was still daylight. The debate had taken place a couple of hours earlier. They shared a stage and an audience. Their views were not shared. A long table with a beige sheet covering was on the elevated space. There were three microphones placed on top of the table. One for him, one for his opponent, and one for the moderator. Between seventy and eighty people showed up for the argument. The amphitheater had many empty seats. Both adversaries attributed the attendance to low population.

Herbert Spiker found the view beautiful. Gripping a smoking cigar with his teeth, he peered out of the large glass wall that separated him and the tarmac. Occasionally, he took the nicotine object out of his mouth to blow smoke. His clothing was fairly formal: a tie, collared shirt, and dinner jacket. Yet he wore them in fatigue, with the tie loosened and the shirt untucked. There were few people around, so he did not care. Two stern young men flanked his wheelchair, their heads slowly turning back and forth to survey the surrounding interior. Dozens of other people were in the large open space, yet they were seated elsewhere, waiting for different planes or different visitors.

Occasional intercom messages blared; the static making them borderline unintelligible. Some people walked to, and some walked from, indifferent to the presence of the celebrity. Another stream of smoke billowed out of his mouth, jetting forward before gently rising above him and his guards. More smoke exited his nostrils as he held the cigar between his index and middle finger. Contemplating nothing in particular, he examined the bright blue sky. It was a grand horizon, since few manmade structures obstructed it. Clouds and the occasional plane glided along the natural background.

Spiker calmly returned the cigar to his mouth, securing it between two rows of teeth. He jumbled it around to get it just right for optimum pleasure. His ride was coming soon. A few more minutes and he was leaving the state. His third wife was probably not going to be home when he arrived. She loved the night life. A lot. For a time, he put up with it; after all, she was several years younger and a liberated soul. Her leisure being a deal-breaker came later. During that time, he was simply enjoying the view, with the arrival of the aerial transport being the sought-after prize.

Then some rustling, then some noise. It was not hostile; no audience member from the debate had followed him in anger. None had followed at all. The conversations were a mesh at first, but the individual portions became coherent as the talker neared, and then, far too familiar. They were uppity, and he knew why. His stomach twisted, the nerves peaked, but his outward self remained relaxed and disheveled. Taking the dying cigar out of his mouth and holding it with his left hand, he used both hands to move the wheels, turning his line of sight to confirm who he thought was approaching.

"You did a great job there, Sammy. You really did," commented an older fellow with mostly gray hair and a touch of dark brown. He was average height and wearing business casual, like most of the entourage.

"So, you believe I won?" inquired the center of the entourage, his blue eyes directed to the older gentleman to his left, unaware of who was ahead of him. He was slightly taller than his friend and a few sizes stockier.

"Definitely," he replied, the others nodding and offering terse agreements. "In fact, I think your performance was so good . . . " The sentence remained incomplete as each man in the small group looked forward. Their progress to the waiting area was halted. They were no more than twenty or thirty feet from the disabled man and his detachment.

"Tim, are you sure this is the right gate?" asked the older man to a freckled youth standing behind the Rev. Sammy Milton. For his part, the young man took out a notebook and turned to the proper page, quickly finding the agenda for that day.

"Yup, number ten."

"Well, um..." trailed off the older fellow. A couple of them looked at the ground, the others at Milton. Dinner jacket draped over his left arm, Milton raised his right hand to assure the entourage. Mouthing some words of assurance, Spiker saw him come toward him as an individual. The security studied the man, unsure how to deal with the coming personality. Both looked with sunglassed eyes at their employer. Giving a look of assurance, Spiker calmly brushed them off. The two took a few steps away from Herbert, who put out his cigar by jamming the smoking end onto a metal bar on his chair. Milton walked up to the glass wall, standing six feet away from the seated counterpart. There was silence while Milton looked outside before turning his attention to his opponent.

"Mr. Spiker," stoically uttered Sammy.

"Rev. Milton," replied Herbert in like manner.

"Waiting for your plane?"

"Yes," he said. "Same for you?"

"Yes."

"Same gate," observed Herbert.

"You know, Herbert," began Milton, correctly assuming he could address his adversary in a less professional manner, "I always use my private plane to get to these debates in faraway places. You use your private plane to get to these debates in faraway places. We always go to the same debates. This is just an idea I have—feel free to disagree—but how about we take the same plane?"

"Hmmm," pondered Herbert. "That does make sense. Who goes first?"

"Well, it was my idea. So, I guess, on that level, I should go first."

"Hogwash," replied Herbert. "Your idea is a good one. In the spirit of cooperation, I will volunteer my plane for the next debate."

"Okay," agreed Sammy.

"Shake on it?"

"Why not?" consented the preacher, who walked up to the seated pornographer and grasped his extended hand, generating much chatter among the members of his entourage.

* * *

"And that was how it happened," explained Spiker to Addison, the young reporter still recovering from the twist. "We alternated jets every time we went out to debates. It was awkward at first, but over time, we got used to it. While we didn't agree much on politics and religion, we had a lot of other things in common. We're both from the South; we both had drunks for dads. Stuff like that. From there, we paid each other visits. Whenever he was in Nevada, he came over to my office. Whenever I was in Virginia or DC on the weekend, I'd go to his church."

"Wait, you went willingly to Milton's church?"

"Of course, I did," exclaimed Spiker. "Many times. He puts on a good service. Whatever I thought of his views, I always respected his speaking abilities. Pretty good singer, too. I think he thought he could save me. Truth be told, a couple times, he came close. Also, I take credit for helping him slim down later on."

"Really?"

"Well, maybe," Spiker explained. "You see, I had put on some pounds myself, and a fitness guru put me on a diet that worked. When he asked me for advice, I gave him the regimen, and he did it. So, I guess I helped him stick around that much longer."

"Very interesting stuff," commented Scott after a few seconds of pause.

"I'm glad you like it. Scoops were a big thing in news years back. I think they still are."

"Well, anyway, thank you very much for the interview," said Scott in a mixture of sincerity and ritual. He stopped the recorder, rose from his seat, and shook Spiker's hand. "The article should be up online sometime tomorrow."

"So, I'm it?" asked Spiker, his grin removed.

"Well, yes. Phillips wanted me to interview only you. He wants something out soon. Anyway, thanks again for the interview."

"Hold on a moment," said Spiker, his hand raised to further convey his point. Scott stood still, listening in patience and awkwardness. "I used to write obituaries for people. Morbid stuff, let me tell you. But I remember that my editor always wanted me to get as many perspectives as possible. He believed that you couldn't really get a good understanding of a man from just one source. It had to be many." Spiker straightened in his wheelchair and took a commanding tone with Addison. "Sonny, I do not want you to use my words in your article unless you get more people for your story."

"Okay," replied Scott, a little nervous from the statement. He played along. "Who do you believe I should talk to?"

"Beverley Clayborne, for one. He knew Milton for decades. The man's as old as dirt. He lives in some retirement home in Richmond. He'd be a good source."

"Okay," said Scott, wanting to exit the room. "I will look into it."

"I am serious," stated Spiker, pointing at the journalist. "If I see my words online or offline in an article written by you, and no one else is quoted . . . well, just remember: I won at the Supreme Court." He gave a sinister-looking grin following the remark.

"Okay, I'll remember that."

"Attaboy," noted Spiker. "Take care now." Before Scott could add to the conversation, the modestly-dressed female aide entered the room to discuss some business regarding the photo shoot. Addison saw his own way out of the office, pondering how he was going to explain this to his editor.

* * *

Physically, the trip back to the office of *The Kensington Post* was not unpleasant. The metro line was punctual, and the weather was welcoming. Mentally, it was an annoying venture, as Scott Addison struggled with how to deal with the demands of the interviewee. He had dealt with obstreperous sources before. There were those who demanded to see his article in full before publication, others who called back multiple times to add corrections to their earlier comments. None of them were as notable as Herbert Spiker. Getting on the wrong side of a nameless activist was more preferable.

Going up the elevator, Addison loathed the possible responses from his superior. He objected to the idea of having to find and write up another story, especially at so late an hour in the morning. Scott felt it was more challenging to get timely responses from sources who were contacted long after 9:00 AM local time. He tried to comfort himself with the assumption that there was no way Phillips was going to have him endure all this just to kill a story. Least of all a story Phillips probably thinks will paint Milton in a negative manner. Then again, when he finds out that Herbert Spiker actually showcased a positive side of the fundamentalist leader, that defense will disappear.

Going past the opening doors, Addison walked down the hallway until he saw the glassy wall of the office. He veered left to face the door, grabbed the handle, and pulled it toward himself to enter the active space. There he saw his editor standing over Tyrone Spearman, who was at his desk in the cubicle group. Phillips' sleeves were rolled up more so than earlier that morning. As Scott got closer to his editor, he took a breath. For his part, Phillips briefly glanced upward to see the approaching journalist. He congratulated Tyrone, patting him on the shoulder, before turning to speak to Addison.

"Hey Scott, did the interview go well?" asked Phillips with optimism.

"I got the interview, but there is a minor situation," said Scott who, without stopping his walk, followed up with his request. "Can I talk to you in your office?"

"Sure, sure," replied a concerned, yet confident, editor. The two men left the cubicles and entered the office. Scott closed the door while Phillips went to his seat, arms resting on the top of his desk.

"What's the problem?"

"Well, I don't know how big a deal this is, but first the good news."

"I prefer the bad news first," stated Phillips. "I like to get it out of the way."

"Okay," conceded Addison. "Well, Spiker doesn't want me to write the article until I get other people to comment."

"Alright, alright," responded Phillips, who began to stroke his chin and look down at his desk. "Who did he have in mind?"

"He mentioned one name—Beverley Clayborne."

"Oh yes, I know him. Not personally, but know of him. For a long time, he was Milton's righthand man. Like a second-in-command almost. Anyone else?"

"No, but he was adamant that I have other people. Otherwise, well, he kind of threatened me. Said that if I ran the story, I'd be going up against a man who won at the Supreme Court."

Phillips laughed. "That sounds like Herb, alright."

"Well, what do we do?" asked Scott, dreading the assignment of a new story for the day. "If necessary, we could still run the story, right?"

"You know what? I'm starting to think here," said Phillips, his hand gripping his chin. "Yes, yes, I think that might actually work."

"What will work?"

"Yes, I think that Herb has a good idea going. I approve it," said Phillips as he looked at Scott. "If nothing else, plenty of other sites already posted stories where they interviewed old enemies bashing Milton. We need something more detailed, more in-depth. You follow me?"

"I think so."

"So, yeah, yeah, I think this will work," thought Phillips aloud. "Get many people to talk about Milton. All the sour parts. We will do that."

"Would this be for the weekly edition?"

"Yes, definitely," said Phillips, who raised a finger. "However, it won't be on the main page. By next week, Milton's death will be old news. And Congress dealing with all these new bills, yeah, definitely not main page. But still in it."

"Okay," began Scott. "So, what's my lede?"

"Pretty much the same one you had when you left the office, only this time get a bunch of people to talk about Milton. Especially people who resisted him. Clayborne will, of course, be an exception, but hey, we all know he's going to defend his friend."

"Yes, true."

"I know some people who you can talk to," said Phillips, a jump in interest coloring his voice. "Ones that come to mind for me . . . hmmm, let me think . . . " The editor leaned back in his office chair, his eyes directed toward the ceiling. Fingers danced around in the air as he recalled the information. "Let's see. There was a black pastor named Henderson. Jabez Henderson. He'll be a good source on Milton's racism. Friedman is another one. She's a women's rights activist based in Richmond. Years back, she signed this widely circulated manifesto denouncing Milton as a hardcore misogynist. The manifesto called for a boycott of all of Milton's ministries, political and religious."

"Should I be writing this down?"

"No, no, I'll email you the info. Just thinking of a couple of others," pondered Phillips. "Oh, I just thought of two more. I don't really want you talking to family, but I think these two will do if you can get them."

"Okay. Who would they be?"

"Well, the first is Milton's grandson. He's an evangelical pastor, but, he gained a lot of headlines a few years ago for bashing his grandpa's public career. Good stuff. And the other, well, is a bit complicated."

"Complicated?"

"Yes, yes, it is," said Phillips as he changed his seated position to bend forward, hunching over his desk as though to whisper a secret to

Scott. "This is going to sound like a conspiracy theory, but there were always rumors that Milton had a gay son stashed away somewhere, shamed out of the family and all that."

"For real?"

"Well, I don't know. I mean, I know, I know," said Phillips as he waved his hand at Scott. "I know that every conservative Christian out there gets the allegation of being gay or having a gay son, or something like that. It's just that, this one had a little more evidence to it. Nothing concrete, but more smoke than usual. You following me?"

"Yeah."

"Back when I was still a reporter with my Religious Right beat, I tried to make a story out of it. But my predecessor told me that I didn't have enough solid evidence for it to run. So if you come up empty like I did, no big deal. But if you do find him, try and get some comments. It will be pure gold; I guarantee it."

"Alright. I'll try," said Scott as he turned to exit.

"Scott, one more thing," interjected the editor. Addison turned around to face his determined superior. "Your article is a very important piece. There are people who want to lionize Milton. Make him out to be some positive contributor to society. You must remind the American public that Milton was a racist, sexist, homophobe, whose legacy is only bigotry. Do you understand what I want for this story?"

"Completely."

"Good, good," said Phillips with a pearly white smile. "Now get back to your desk, so I can send you the contact info for your sources."

"Will do."

* * *

Old Town Alexandria was a common place for them to meet after hours. This historic quarter of the Northern Virginia city had its own metro stop and free trolleys. Sometimes, the team went all the way to the waterfront. There, they saw vessels gliding along the Potomac with the lights and spires of the District of Columbia in the background. Other times, they stayed closer inland, not far from the imposing George Washington Masonic National Memorial. Simply called "Masonic Temple" by locals, it was perched upon a hill, its lighthouse-inspired top jutting over three hundred feet.

Old Town was lively at night. Several bars and restaurants along King Street offered a wide range of sustenance, with brick shops and stores leading all the way to the cobblestone roads near the water. During certain months, the trees planted on both sidewalks had their branches covered with sparkling lights. A beautiful sight was where King Street went alongside the city government, whose property included a large, square-shaped fountain. The plaza area had various outdoor gatherings like concerts and, back in 2011, a sesquicentennial anniversary celebration of the Civil War. To that point, at the intersection of Prince and Washington Streets was a Confederate statue called Appomattox. While residents were divided about its presence, all agreed that driving around it was a pain.

The grid format of Old Town made for simple navigation, even if parking was a trial barely assuaged by the small number of parking garages. Finding the King Street tavern for their little gathering was easy. They had been there before. Like most buildings off that major route, its front was unpainted brick. It had outdoor seating, with a waist-high iron fence sectioning off the tables. While the weather was nice enough to be outside, those places were all taken. No matter, the four preferred an indoor booth anyway.

"This again?" asked a playfully annoyed Katie Nicholson. She and coworker Mandy Salver-Jones had arrived at the tavern first. They came through the Yellow Line, getting off at the King Street station. When they left the office, both men in their department were still finishing up assignments. The women walked by the bizarre piece of artwork few realized was supposed to be a giant tricorn. Instead, for most it seemed like a bunch of connected black poles of random sizes and lengths. Having a hasty sojourn on the brick sidewalk did nothing to achieve their goal of beating the evening rush.

"Yes, this again," firmly stated Mandy, holding a sweaty beer bottle, whose fermented contents had the same bronze shade as the item her colleague was drinking from. "It just seems so ridiculous."

"Let me try and explain it, since Michael does such a bad job," replied Katie. "When you end a quote with a comma or a period, the comma or period goes *inside* the quote. And that is the style we must use for stories. It's that simple."

"But it doesn't make sense," insisted Mandy after finishing a swig of her beer. "The comma or period wasn't in the original quote. So, we're adding to the quote something that wasn't there. That does not sound right."

"But we do that all the time," countered Katie. "Whenever you insert brackets to a quote to add a word that wasn't there before, you're adding something to the original quote. Bracketed words never bother you."

"That's because we've always done bracketed words," said Mandy, who kept an eye on the entrance to the tavern. She and Katie were seated on stools at the bar, waiting for a booth to empty. "Besides, British media put the commas and periods outside of quotes."

"The British spell jail with a G."

"That's different," Mandy stated defensively. "Besides, when Graham was our editor-in-chief, he wanted us to put commas and periods outside of the quotes."

"Mandy," said Katie with a smile, "when Graham was editor-in-chief, same-sex marriage was still illegal in most states."

"Has it really been that long?" sarcastically pondered Mandy. She took another drink from the bottle, while Katie talked.

"How about if you try it for a week. One week. And if you don't like it, we'll see about getting you a job with the BBC."

"Thanks," laughed Mandy. Her laughter stilled when she saw Tyrone Spearman enter the front of the bar and restaurant. After searching for a few moments, he turned his eyes to just the right angle to see the two familiar faces at the bar. He gave a smile and walked toward them. "The man of the hour is here!"

"Hey there, ladies," he said as he approached, putting a hand on Katie's right shoulder and the other hand on Mandy's left shoulder. "You are looking at the man who will be on THE front page of next edition."

"Congrats, again," said Katie as Tyrone gave her a quick kiss on the cheek. As he turned to do likewise to Mandy, she held up the hand which included her wedding ring. Getting the message, Tyrone nodded his head and backed off. "Have you been celebrating before you got here?"

"A little bit, here and there," confessed Tyrone with a smile, gradually ending his grip on both shoulders. "But I have plenty of party left in me. I only get to be featured on the front page for the first time once in my life, you know?"

"I know they shot down your first title idea," said Mandy with lighthearted cruelty. "What was it going to be called again?"

"Oh, c'mon Mandy, like he remembers every—"

"'The Unholy Crosses Still Burn Bright,'" recounted Tyrone with ease. "Yes, dearest Katie, I remember every one of them."

"And that's him drunk," said Katie to Mandy, pointing at the chest of Tyrone with her thumb. All three laughed at the comment.

"Still, in all seriousness, it was a good story. It's scary to think how many hate groups have sprung up since the election," said Mandy as Tyrone walked in between the two seated coworkers and asked a bartender to open a tab. After an ID confirmation, he got his first beer at that particular location.

"So, where's your boyfriend?" asked Tyrone to Katie, making her faintly blush.

"I thought you saw him last."

"Yeah, when I left the office. But then I went to a place a couple blocks away. I thought he'd beat me here."

"Looks like you bested him again," said Mandy with a smile as she drank more of the bronze liquid.

"What good it did me," said Tyrone as he took a swig from his newly acquired drink. "When are we getting the booth?"

"The waiter said in a few minutes. So not long."

"Okay, I think I can wait. Until then, let me show you some funny stuff I saw online," said Tyrone as he pulled out his smart phone. With a quickly punched password and a few touches of the small screen, he got to where he wanted to be. "Check it out."

He heard them laughing as he got near. No one was watching the entrance, so Scott Addison slipped in unnoticed by his coworkers. They were gathered around the phone screen, amused by the many posts throughout social media insulting the recently deceased. He temporarily wondered how to introduce himself, as they were so beholden to the profane images mixing humor and hatred. A tap on the shoulder, a shout of greetings. Scott decided instead to go for the smart remark.

"You showing them your nude photos, Tyrone?" declared Scott, turning the heads of all three of his friends. They greeted the late-comer.

"Did you miss the metro train or something?"

"Oh no," Scott assured them. "Just had to deal with some details on a big assignment I have. Anyway, congrats. I guess this means we pay for your meal, right?"

"Sounds good to me."

"Now, now, I didn't agree to that," stated Katie with both hands raised. Scott patted her on the back in response.

"What's this big assignment you're talking about?"

"I get to write the long piece on Milton."

"Oh, that guy," muttered Mandy. "Was one interview not enough?"

"Nope," agreed Scott. "Phillips gave me some people to talk to. I'll be driving down to Richmond tomorrow to work on it. Might be gone for the rest of the week."

"And in Richmond of all places," said Tyrone with disdain. "I heard they have more Confederate flags than American ones."

"Hey, hey, only some parts of the city," interjected Katie. "Downtown was pretty awesome. Except at night. That's when people get stabbed."

"Wow," declared Scott. "I'll try to remember that."

"Oh, Tyrone," said Mandy. "Can you show Scott the photo you have for his Milton piece?"

Tyrone smiled and showed him the image on his smart phone. The others laughed anew as their peer was exposed to the graphic cartoon poking fun at the late reverend. While he had not seen the specific animation that Herbert Spiker told him about during their interview, he was pretty sure, based on the description, that this was probably it. "What do you think, Scotty? Perfect?"

"Stick to titles, Tyrone," said Scott with calm amusement.

"Alright, I can do that," he replied, pausing to tap his chin a few times and look upward before continuing. "You know, I even have one for your piece."

"Oh, really?"

"Yeah, man. Picture this," began Tyrone as he directed his gaze outward. His hands were both raised, palms facing beyond him as though placing some long board upon the wall. "'A Tunnel Into Darkness.'" Scott shook his head.

"Oh c'mon, Scott," said Katie as she held his arm, "that one doesn't sound half bad."

"And that's exactly what you'll be entering when you get those interviews," added Tyrone. "That man was horrible. The world is a better place without him."

"Exactly," chimed in Mandy. "I mean I'm Jewish, and I know he liked Israel. But still, that man was a jerk."

"And the world will remember him as a trashy hate-monger when my piece gets published," added Scott, getting agreement from his peers.

"You want a beer, Scotty?" asked Tyrone. "I think we need to make a toast to my success and your safe travels."

"Thanks, but I'd rather wait until we get a booth."

"That might be a while," remarked Tyrone, whose timing was impeccable as the waiter arrived and informed them that they could be seated.

BEVERLEY CLAYBORNE

HE PITIED THOSE ON THE opposite side of the highway. Scott Addison went his usual five to ten miles above the speed limit. He was going south on Interstate 95, while a swarm of motor vehicles crawled northward to the District of Columbia. Their plight was familiar. When he first moved to the area, his apartment was in Woodbridge, and his job was in Georgetown. Neither the start nor the finish had a metro rail. This forced Addison to endure the starts and stops of the morning rush hour. An upside of that former post was that he got to leave in early afternoon, beating the crowds.

This morning was the beloved reverse commute. Only a handful of cars were going his way, and many of them departed his presence once they arrived at the mixing bowl. Things got pleasantly scarcer once Scott drove past Quantico. From there, even fewer automobiles veered onto the three-lane route to Richmond. Things picked up a little bit in the Fredericksburg area, though, again, nothing as soul-crushing as one typically experienced in the DC area. Addison had his worst adult tempers while stuck in that grueling traffic—when all is stopped and no discernible reason manifests. Journeys like the one he had that morning reminded him of the joy of driving.

Addison's sports car handled the road well. At one point, he was going in the low eighties, but when he saw what looked like a police car up ahead, he was shrewd enough to decrease his velocity. While it was a false alarm, he decided to refrain from such speeds for the duration. Still, he was well above the posted limits until he neared the exit. Scott left the highway miles before he would have gotten to Richmond proper. With his electronic GPS screen guiding him by image and voice, he made the correct turns. He soon found himself on an elegant piece of property. Well-cut green grass, perfectly paved roads, large spreading trees, and a massive brick building modeled in the Adam style.

The grand structure was constructed as a mansion, a status symbol for the rising suburban area. It was a sign of the early post-Reconstruction growth for the southern city. After the original owners had passed away, the facility became a retirement home. Generous donations led to expansion, with new wings emulating the brickwork, the balanced rectangular windows, and the pillared entryways. They also added a greenhouse, an indoor pool, a few exercise and physical therapy rooms, and offices for staff.

Addison found a space in visitor parking. He finally turned off his car. Happy to escape the driver's seat, he stretched his legs before making his way to the main entrance. A few gray-haired folk in bright-colored sweats were walking by. A few others were dressed in slacks and sweaters, going about on canes or sitting down, kindly socializing with their neighbors. After all, it was a pleasant morning. Next to the entrance was a short, white van, a shuttle used to ferry people to and from various locations. In this case, the trip was to a nearby shopping center. Scott got onto the pristine sidewalk and then entered the building. It felt more like a hotel than a retirement home. This was the intention of the owners. A fifty-something, frumpish woman sat at the receptionist desk. A sign-in sheet with pen was located on the countertop between her and those approaching the front desk.

"Can I help you?" she asked.

"Hello, my name is Scott Addison, and I am a reporter with *The Kensington Post*. I believe we talked over the phone about my interviewing one of your tenants."

"Oh yes, I remember," she smiled. "Go ahead and sign yourself in. Mr. Clayborne is in room thirty-seven. It is just down that hall." She pointed to the hallway to the left of her desk, Scott looking up from the sign-in sheet as she did so.

"Thank you," said Scott.

"No problem," she uttered as she went back to facing the computer screen.

Scott walked down the corridor. It was a nice space. A light green paint job with white trim for the walls, spotless flooring with ornate neoclassical designs. Each door was painted white and had a bronze knob, a small peeping hole near the top, and black digits noting the number of the unit. Addison walked past an orderly who was wheeling an elder resident. He eventually located number thirty-seven. Ignorant of the proper protocol, Scott raised his right fist and pounded a few times on the door. A voice from inside told him to go ahead and enter. Scott obliged and turned the knob.

* * *

"Paul!" exclaimed the old man with great happiness. Scott felt awkward. He did not know how to respond. Standing on the opposite side of the living room space, the elderly gentleman had a hopeful smile, displaying a lower row of crooked teeth. A shaky hand went closer to his wrinkled face, pushing the thick lenses closer to his weak eyes. "Oh, I'm sorry; you're not Paul, are you?"

"No, I am Scott Addison with *The Kensington Post.*"

"Pardon?" he asked, wobbling closer to the young visitor. He lacked a cane, but his steps were iffy enough that he seemed to need one. As he got closer, Scott noticed that the man had a hearing aid covering the interior of his right ear.

"My name is Scott Addison," said the reporter, leaning forward and projecting his voice. "I was told you can talk with me for a news story."

"Oh, that's right," he realized. "I forgot. Yes, the newsman. A pleasure to meet you. My name is Beverley Horacio Clayborne. The first." Standing hunched over before Scott, Clayborne stretched out his hand to shake his visitor's. The reporter obliged. Scott noticed the skeletal-looking paw, its knuckles visible and bearing many dark spots. His hair, which seemed solid at first, was very thin. The grayish white color scheme blended with the pale skin, giving, from a distance, the inaccurate portrayal of fullness.

"Pleased to meet you," began Scott.

"Likewise. Forgive me for thinking you were Paul. You look a lot like him. He's my grandson. A good kid. Have you met him before?"

Scott was a little confused but kept his obvious critiques to himself when responding to the elderly man. "No, I haven't."

"Anyway, he's a good kid. Looks a lot like his father," he said while hobbling to a plush chair not far from a television set. Scott followed him, stopping when he stopped. "Did I ask you if you wanted any tea or coffee?"

"No, but that's okay," said Scott, who realized that he might not have said it loud enough. "No, but that's okay."

"Oh, okay," nodded Beverley as he returned to walking to the chair. "Go ahead and have a seat on the couch." Scott agreed and sat down. He watched Beverley slowly descend into his chair, expressing a sense of relief once he settled into the cushioned place. "So, what did you want to talk to me about?"

Scott had explained these things on the phone the day before. While the conversation was between himself and the front desk, the receptionist heavily implied that Clayborne was privy to their conversation. Nevertheless, he was aware of the mind he was working with.

"I am working on an article about the life of the Rev. Sammy Milton."

"Okay," noted Beverley.

"I talked to Herbert Spiker the other day, and he told me I should talk to you. He says you knew Milton from long ago."

"Yes, I knew Milton. Long ago, too," said Beverley.

"I assume you know about his passing."

"Oh, yes. I saw it on the TV. Someone from his office came here later on," said Clayborne, whose sentiment never truly entered the territory of the dour. "He was a good man. He did a lot of good things."

"I was hoping you could tell me more about him. How he was like when he was young, when he became a preacher, things like that."

"Well, let me just begin by saying I didn't know Milton when he was a kid. I'm not from Virginia. I met him when he was an adult."

"Okay," said Scott, who realized that he might finally need to turn on his recording device. "Is it okay that I record our conversation to get exact quotes for my story?"

"I don't see why not."

"When did you first meet Rev. Milton?" inquired Scott as he turned the device on.

"I met him before he was a reverend."

"Okay," noted Scott. "When and where was that?"

"You know, when I was a kid, I used to work at a livery stable. And my boss—Hickory was his name—he taught me everything I knew. He always made me learn it the hard way. When I asked him once why he did it that way, he said to me, 'Dear boy, showin's better den tellin'.'"

With that comment, Beverley slowly rose from his chair. Like a rocket readied for launch, he gradually got to a proper posture. He then slowly hobbled away. Scott was confused as the elderly man went into the adjacent room. Lacking any social cue, Scott sat there, pushing the pause button on his recorder. A minute or so later, Beverley returned with some photos.

"Sorry about that. I just remembered that they were in my bedroom."

"That's okay."

"Anyway," began Beverley as he showed a small photo of himself to his guest, "this is a picture of me from my heyday." The man in the black-and-white image did bare a resemblance to the hunched-over ancient in that living room. He had a stern face and was wearing a suit and tie. Before Scott could study the photo for long, Beverley took it away from his view and replaced it with another larger photo. "This is me when I played professional baseball."

Scott was genuinely interested in this image. The photo showed Beverley in his pinstriped team uniform, hands on hips in the dugout. "Interesting," said Scott, who had the photo taken away once again before too long.

Finally, Beverley showed a third photo. It featured two men in baseball uniforms, each holding a bat.

"The one on the left is me," noted Beverley, pointing with a bony finger. He started to laugh as he continued, "And do you know who the fellow is on the right?"

Scott studied the countenance of the photographed figure. It clicked for him quickly, in part because he had a feeling about the direction Beverley was taking. And yet, it was still an unforeseen context. "Wait, that's Rev. Milton?"

"You bet," said Beverley. "Shocking, isn't it?"

"I'll say," agreed Scott as the photo was taken away and the old man limped over to his seat, taking several seconds to firmly plant himself onto the cushion.

"My stable boss was right."

Scott turned the recorder back on before continuing. "So, you and Sammy Milton were both professional baseball players?"

"Yes, we were," stated Beverley. "Don't let my current stride fool you. I played for twelve seasons in the American Baseball League. First with the Bears, and then with the Wolves. Sammy got in after me. He started in 1951; I started in 1949. We both quit in 1960. We first met in 1953 when we were both drafted to the Wolves. That was a good team."

"How good was he?"

"Very good. Did you know he actually held the career record for stolen bases? He was amazing. Took ninety-two of them in one season alone. I think that was the one where we won the championship. Yeah, that was the one. Good ol' 1957 series. I remember the last game. We were facing off against the Ospreys. It was the kind of game that made you think of the movies—all tense and down to the last inning . . . "

* * *

Dozens of large, glaring lights illuminated the diamond, its points covered by four dirtied bases. While most of the field was green, the white lines of the formation were atop brownish dirt. Within the core of the formation was the mound on which the pitcher stood, glove covering one hand while the other held the white ball with red stitching. Like his teammates guarding the bases, he had a light brown shirt with black lettering, leggings with black pinstripes, and black socks. These were the hues of the Ospreys, who had won the last two games in the series, tying them with the other team. They were attentive, yet confident; after all, they were ahead by two in the bottom of the ninth.

Up to bat was one from the other side. White shirt and knickers, dark red socks, dark red pinstripes, and a hard batter's helmet that did not offer protection for the ears. Standing to the side of home base, the member of the Wolves focused all his concentration on the invisible line between himself and the man with the ball. He channeled out the monotonous droning of the patient crowd. He ignored the stands—the roguish male juveniles with their greased hair and black jackets, the trendy women with their poodle skirts, the higher society with their suits or sweaters, or the awkwardly high number of empty chairs signifying the lull in interest for the national pastime.

Cameramen filmed the game from multiple angles, which broadcasted live for those in the Eastern and Central Time Zones. The rest of the country would either have to wait a few days or experience the lower quality of the kinescope process. Many took to the radios, patiently sitting around their screenless venues of entertainment in anticipation of the next pitch. Some preferred the exclusively audio means, for it allowed for either greater imagination or less distraction when working on other tasks.

Sammy Milton thought only of the ball. He gripped his bat with both hands, narrowed his eyes to better see the orb, and readied as the pitcher finally lifted his leg, cocked back his throwing arm, and hurled the white dot quickly to the catcher's mitt. The confirmed call and the mixed crowd reactions fueled Milton's annoyance. In frustration, he squinted his blue eyes closed, circling around for a few moments before returning to the plate. He tapped the top of home base with his bat before raising it again. Spitting as he waited, Milton tensed and focused once more, and the white sphere was struck.

The crowd roared as the ball darted between second and third base, slowing as it tumbled along the greenery. An Osprey player rushed toward it, lifting the ball with his glove before giving it a short toss into his right hand and then throwing it to second base. No matter, Milton had no plans to go beyond first for the time being. Breathing hard, he rested his hands upon his knees, bent over while waiting for the next batter to emerge from the dugout.

The arrival was one of the growing number of African-American players. When Milton first played for the team, blacks were prohibited from joining. However, by season three, the first two had been drafted. Some on the team were supportive; some were opposed. Milton only cared if they could play well. They were met with some boos and slurs from the almost exclusively white crowd, but those crude opinions were drowned out by other noises. Between the two strikes, Milton defied the watchful eye of the pitcher and rushed to second base, getting a nice pop from the audience for his craftiness.

The successful advancement on the part of Milton may have delivered a psychological blow, as the pitcher struggled to concentrate on the next pitch. Sure enough, the speed was low enough that the batter struck the orb with ease, hurling it between first and second, bypassing two Osprey players in the process. Milton got as far as third, while his teammate made it to first. Both caught their breath as the next player came to bat. Milton smiled at the arrival of the teammate, for he knew his capability. His white shirt and shorts stained with dirt from an earlier scoring slide, he was a few years older than Milton. Indeed, he was actually the second oldest member of the active roster.

He looked with determination at the pitcher. Aware of his teammates' positions on the field, he sought to go for the big strike. It was a common practice. Both teams had already attempted the strategy of filling or mostly filling the bases before one of the sluggers did their utmost to send everyone home. The pitcher sent the first throw. The umpire declared it a ball. The next was labeled a foul. The one after that, a foul. All the while, the studious veteran was feeling out his counterpart on the mound. He read him well; and when the next ivory sphere was thrown his way, Beverley Clayborne successfully hit it with all his power. Like a mortar round, the ball went upward in an arc, well above the other team, and then beyond the walls. Outfielders ran in vain to catch up to the projectile that landed several feet behind the dividing barrier between grass and walkway.

Thousands rose to their feet in exuberance as the three men jogged down the bases. Their teammates stormed out of the dugout to greet them, especially Clayborne, the man responsible for the triple header. He was lifted shoulder-high by the roster and the coaches. Several of the men did likewise for the African-American player. While getting a bunch of pats on the back, Milton was in the throng of the team. Clayborne soon noticed his friend below him and shouted at the others to raise him up. At first, he begged them off; but they insisted, so he relented. Soon enough, he was above the others on an unstable throne.

An hour later, the Wolves were out of their pinstriped uniforms and into suits and ties. These items became ruffled as the night of celebration continued. A large portion of the roster went to an Irish-themed bar one of them had heard was the best in town. While the bottles were a split type, and thus much smaller than average, many of the players compensated by drinking a larger number of them. A few ordered dishes for the others, the boosters and coaches present happy to foot the bill. Some harmless ethnic jokes were made when some of the food turned out to have potatoes in them.

Given that the series was held in a fairly progressive northern city, the business allowed the African-American teammates to enter and be served. To be sure, some customers were hesitant at their presence. However, all cooled down when they learned that the championship came to the city because of their efforts. Maybe sport was the great equalizer after all. They talked and laughed, drank and ate, the merriment of victory filling them all. Clayborne lived it up like the others, toasting and chugging.

Milton drank little and talked little. He was not an introvert by tendency. Indeed, at other gatherings he was as loquacious as any. Alcohol was never consumed by him in great amounts. This was the byproduct of an upbringing that featured a father who was woefully beholden to the bottle. Yet through the raucous talking and rapid-fire Gaelic tunes, he was solemnly looking down at his drink. Occasionally, someone would tap him on the shoulder, causing him to break out of the trance to smile and banter. Yet when basic interactions were completed, he returned to seriousness.

Clayborne took note of this behavior, seeing his teammate and friend finally get to a second pony bottle. It was late and only getting later. Most of the team peeled off from the festivities and headed back to the hotel. They left in groups, making sure that no one walked the vesper city streets alone. The pub itself was dying down, the employees finally outnumbering the patrons. Music was softer and slower, like a lullaby for the weary partiers. Then it was just Beverley and Sammy. Expenses were paid for, and the two men slowly rose from their seats, giving their regards to the man at the bar. Both men pushed at the door to get outside, neither fully capable of walking straight.

"Hey, hey, hey," cautioned Clayborne, who was a little more inebriated than his teammate. "The hotel is that way." He threw his arm with pointed finger to the other end of the sidewalk, opposite the way Milton was starting out. Sammy gradually turned around to see where his friend was pointing. While Milton drank less than Clayborne, he also had a lower tolerance. "Don't want to get lost on the big day, right?"

"Perish the thought," Sammy said, putting his hands in his pockets and lowering his head to look at the night ground. Beverley studied him.

"You okay?"

"I guess, maybe," he responded, kicking the ground a little as he passed by Beverley. The two kept going down the sidewalk. To one side, there were closed shops and restaurants, with a few very dark alleyways between them. To the other, the occasional wide, bright-colored car with a menacing grill and dual fins in the back drove by. Their path was lit by street lights perched high upon green poles. Some of them had posters taped to them, advertising for local events and gatherings.

"Not buying it, buddy."

"What are you . . . what are you not buying?"

"You saying you feel good," said Beverley, stopping a block away from the hotel. "You've been acting really sad today. I mean, shoot, you'd think we lost or something."

Milton looked up at his teammate and then looked back down to the ground. He tried to start walking again, but soon found Beverley in his way, arms folded. "Come on, Sammy. It's just us out here. You can tell me all about it."

"Well," hesitated Milton, his hand rubbing the back of his neck before he continued. "It's just that . . . I don't know . . . this is stupid . . . "

"No, no, not stupid, not stupid," insisted Beverley. "Just tell me what it is. The best you can."

"Okay," nodded Milton, who paced around for a few seconds before speaking up. "It's just that I won. I won the championship. We won the series. You and I, we worked years for this. We left home; we shied away from girls. We shied away from everything. All that work, and we finally won."

"I'm not seeing any problems so far," countered Beverley, who briefly lost his footing while standing with arms folded.

"But now what?" Sammy declared. "Now what? So, we won. We made it. I mean, I'm twenty-seven years old. What do I do now? The rest of my life?"

"Win another one," flatly stated Beverley.

"But then what? I got, maybe, what? Five, maybe seven or eight seasons more until I got to hang up the cleats."

"Oh, you at least have another ten."

"Ten, then. And you, probably less," said Sammy, who upon seeing the unamused expression on his older friend's face immediately followed up with a "no offense."

"What's your point?"

"My point? My point. My point is that, it's so hollow. It feels so... brief. And so, it feels so pointless. I guess I expected more happiness when I won."

"You'll feel better tomorrow."

"I'll feel a hangover tomorrow."

"So, you want to quit baseball or something?"

"No."

"You want to join another team?"

"Definitely no."

"Then what do you want?"

"I don't know!" shouted Sammy. "And that's the worst part." Sammy put his hand to his head, meandering in front of his friend. As he struggled to walk properly in light of his fermented-influenced status, he rested a hand on the nearby light pole. Rather than feel the predicted coldness of the pole, his hand rested on the flat surface of a cardboard sign. It led him to look up in curiosity. "What's this?"

"A sign with words."

"I know that, smarty pants," replied an annoyed Milton. He looked at the poster, its letters and format looking like an ad for a prize fight. Except instead of a fight, it was a revival meeting; and instead of a boxer pictured, it was a preacher. "Hey, Beverley, have you ever heard of a Pastor Fisher?"

"I think so," pondered Clayborne, who stumbled over to where Milton was standing to see what his friend was seeing. "I think I heard him on the radio a few times."

"It says he's in town tomorrow."

"Yeah, some auditorium. I guess we bring in better crowds," quipped Clayborne, whose friend seemed to ignore the comment.

"The bus doesn't leave until tomorrow night. This is early afternoon. I think we can make it."

"You want to go?"

"Why not? Neither of us have been to church in a while. I'm sure this will compensate."

"Yeah, true," said Beverley, who smiled when he added, "and best of all, it's not happening in the morning."

* * *

Hastily going down the sidewalk, annoyance filled both men. They did not tackle the distance as they would on the diamond. Nor were they in their athletic attire. It was a fusion between walking and running—too fast for the former, not fast enough for the latter. They donned suits and ties and slacks. Similar to what they had worn last night for their alcoholic revelry. However, those specific items still smelled of the evening before, so both thought it prudent to have on fresher clothing.

Sammy Milton and Beverley Clayborne were both culpable in their tardiness. The two men went to bed late, and both awoke later than expected. Clayborne slept longer and took longer to get ready. By the time he met Milton in the lobby, the meeting had already begun. Apologies were accepted, and the two went on their way. The problem is that neither one of them was adept at navigation, causing a few wrong turns here and there. Minutes were added to their pedestrian commute. Finally caving in to asking for directions, they received the correct path and neared the auditorium where it was happening. The venue was smaller than the stadium where they played, seating no more than five hundred.

"Next time, get a wake-up call scheduled or something," Milton ordered Clayborne.

"I thought I did, sorry," shrugged off Beverley, still feeling the traces of a hangover headache. The two calmed down their tone and their pace as they neared the main entrance. Beverley pondered out loud, "You know, some day, they'll invent a map that tells you where to go, so you don't get lost."

"I bet they will," replied Milton as they were kindly greeted by a pair of ushers who flanked the opened doors. Entering the lobby area, Sammy and Beverley were handed bulletins. They could hear the booming voice of a preacher.

"I'm very sorry, but we have run out of seats. You will have to stand in the back," said the usher who handed them the programs.

"That's okay," replied Milton. "That's what we get for being late." The usher smiled and gently opened the door for them. The two baseball players quietly entered a space where all attention was centered on the stage.

"Just as well we're late," whispered Beverley to Sammy. "We might cause a lot of folks to ignore the preacher and ask for our autographs."

Milton simply nodded as he listened along with the others. There were a couple dozen others leaning against the red wall of the auditorium. Sammy saw that, indeed, every seat was taken and presumed the same to be so in the balcony above. It gave extra shadow covering for the two athletes. The rest of the house portion was dimly lit, the major lights concentrated on the stage. In the background was a choir in white robes with blue trim. Above them, a large banner read "JESUS SAVES!" Four chairs were downstage from the choir. Three of them were occupied; the fourth was empty. The man who sat there was at a podium topped with a microphone, proclaiming the Gospel. In confidence and candor, he projected his voice with such force as to question the need for the audio amplifier. Sammy and Beverley reverently listened to each profound point.

"And what of it? What of all the human accomplishments? They all fall away eventually. All eventually is destroyed. Empires collapse; cities are destroyed; food rots; monarchs die; even the great pyramids are slowly eroding away. If the Lord does not return soon, even those grand structures will decay into dust. Friend, let me stress all the stronger that putting your trust in earthly things and in earthly victories is foolishness!

"Think of those who have won honors and titles, who have conquered nations, raised up great buildings all to their own vainglorious desire. Think of those who win medals, championships, or finals in professional tournaments. Do you believe these things are truly lasting? No, I tell you, they are as filthy rags. In time, the athletes age; the trophies rust; and the people forget.

"So, what then can we do? Who can save us from these meaningless pursuits? I know of only One, the One Who came down from Heaven and promised life everlasting. The One Who died and rose again, proving that His love and His power outlast all worldly things. 'Heaven and earth shall pass away,' He said. 'But my words shall never pass away.'[1] Friend, nothing can destroy the Kingdom of God. No earthly power can overcome Jesus Christ our Lord. Nothing. The Communists could conquer Western civilization tomorrow, and the Kingdom of God would still endure perfectly for all time!

"Friend, I implore you. I say to you now, believe the Good News. Put your efforts not in these temporary pleasures and fruitless pursuits, but put them to the service of the Gospel of Jesus Christ. If you have not yet put your trust in Him, do so now. If you know Him, then do all in your power to serve Him. Preach the Gospel; do the work of an evangelist. If you dedicate your life to Christ, you will be part of a glory that never dies! That never rusts! That never passes away! Death itself cannot contain Him.

"In serving our Lord Jesus Christ, you will find a glory that lasts forever. You will find satisfaction beyond any short-lived carnal desire. You will have peace transcending all understanding. So, as we sing that beloved, timeless hymn, 'Amazing Grace,' I ask for you to come. If you do not know Jesus, come. If you seek to do more with your life than mere vanity, come. Come and worship. Come and believe! The altar is open; the Bridegroom calls. Do not delay; do not waste another moment."

The choir began the familiar sacred song, with the audience following. Several did not sing, but rather left their seats and went toward the stage. They were met by ushers, who prayed with them. They gave their confessions and professions. Beverley was moved by the words; however, it was the awed Milton who started walking forward. Beverley tried to grab his arm; he was not opposed to the spiritual ecstasy, but rather was concerned about the two high-profile baseball players drawing undue attention from those in the auditorium. His efforts failed, and he saw Sammy get smaller as he walked along the downward slope of the aisle and then to the ushers gathered at the base of the stage. For the first time since they had left the stadium, Beverley saw joy in the face of his friend.

"I want to become a preacher," said Sammy to his friend a few hours later while they sat in the team bus. The two sat near the back, with Milton taking the window side, while Beverley took the interior. None of the other passengers paid him much attention, as they were either talking to one another, looking out the windows, or sleeping. The statement grabbed Clayborne's full attention, as his friend had been quiet for most of the time between the meeting and the departure of the bus.

"Are you sure about that?"

"Surer than anything in the world, Beverley," said Milton as he turned from the window to face his friend. "I want to travel the country as a preacher. I want to save souls, build up faith. All of that and more."

"Sammy," began Beverley. "You got a few more years on your contract."

"I know," he replied, turning his eyes to face back to the window. "And I have to go to seminary, so I can know what I'm talking about." In passionate earnest, he returned his gaze back to Clayborne. "But I want to do it, Beverley. I will do it. And there is nothing that will stop me. Not baseball, nothing."

"Well, alright."

"And I want you to help me."

"Excuse me?" asked Beverley.

"You're a great singer. God can use that."

"I don't know."

"Come on, you know you're a great singer. And if I'm going to do this, I need people to bring music to the meetings."

"I still don't know."

"Just think about it, okay?"

"Well," conceded Beverley. "It is a long bus trip back. That should give me plenty of time to think about it."

"Great," Milton said with a smile.

* * *

"By the time the bus pulled up at the stadium, I had made my decision," said the ancient Beverley, his wrinkles becoming even more pronounced as he grinned. "It was the third best decision I ever made, behind accepting Jesus as my Savior and marrying my wife."

"So, did Milton quit being a baseball player?"

"Oh, not at all," replied Beverley, waving his pale arms around. "He stayed in his contract. Sammy found a seminary that allowed him to take correspondence courses. And in the off season, he took classes on campus. It was on campus that he met the sister of a classmate—Ginny, that is. They got married after graduation."

"Okay, alright," noted Scott, taking some notes while the digital recorder's time kept moving upward. He took note of the place in the recording, jotting a comment or two. That way, it was easier to find the important information and quotes later on. "And you sang at his, um, church meetings?"

"Sammy liked to call them 'Salvation Meetings.' Yes, I was lead singer. I did solos, quartets. Sometimes, I led the crowds in hymns. Not that new stuff, but the good old hymns. You know the ones I mean, right?"

"Like 'Amazing Grace'?"

"Exactly," Beverley affirmed. "Anyway, we did a bunch of small meetings at first. You know, after he became ordained." Clayborne became more animated as he described things. "The big one came in 1961. That I'll never forget. We had a few thousand at that one. And there were television cameras. A bunch of reporters. A really big deal."

"Was he nervous?"

"Not really, no," said Beverley, whose eyes turned upward as he thought about the question. "Maybe he was, but remember . . . remember, he was a professional baseball player. This was not his first rodeo, as we say. Heck, we'd seen bigger crowds during the series games. So if he was nervous, he kept it hidden."

"And you? You weren't nervous, were you?" asked Scott with a faint smile.

"A little bit," conceded Beverley. "But singing and baseball, they have one thing in common. Once you get started, it never feels that bad."

"So, what happened at the 1961 meeting?" asked Scott. Beverley rocked back, remembering that evening. He was caught in the pleasant dreamy nostalgia of that bygone time.

* * *

The movie theatre was filled to capacity. Outside in the lobby were signs beside each door. Using nothing but capital letters, they proclaimed that this was the "SALVATION MEETING!" with "THE REV. SAMMY MILTON" giving the message and featuring "THE DOWNTOWN CHOIR" and "MR. BEVERLEY CLAYBORNE" as singers. They resembled ads for prize bouts, with each name featuring a cutout photo of their respective subjects. Hundreds of similar promotional materials were scattered throughout the cityscape, posted to poles, taped to bus stops, and handed out on sidewalks.

Crowds funneled in, a mixture of men and women, aged and youth, proper attire and casual dress. Some were connected to the local choir, friends or family coming to bring encouragement. Others were clergy and lay leaders from assorted denominations, offering moral support to the spiritual endeavor. Many were curious; some were seeking; others were unaffiliated. A few were downtrodden and wondered what this event and its holy message was all about. Some drove; others walked.

It was an elegant space. Bright red cushioning for the seats, golden-hued balconies and railings, large dark blue curtains for the stage. Above those on the elevated platform, the choir, the speakers, and the lead singer, there were fanciful paintings of actors long passed. An homage to the previous eras of performance. On either flank of the stage were special seats, which on this occasion were filled with all sorts of folk. Entry was free, and seating was unassigned. Droning conversations ebbed off as the introductory speaker gave his remarks. Then the choir began a tune. Soon Clayborne followed. He was confident and showcased his three-octave range to the applauding approval of the still-increasing audience. Some familiar songs came from those on stage, ones that most in the house had heard since childhood. Many sang along, hymnals not required.

Sammy Milton sat in one of a few folding chairs set up on upstage right. As Clayborne continued his musical medley at downstage center, Milton clasped his black, leather-bound Bible tighter. He was given the copy of the Good Book upon graduating with his masters in divinity. Its thick, applied gold lettering was visible from a good distance. Having received it after his youthful days, the pages for personal milestones was almost fully empty. The only two entries dated receiving his clergy credentials and his marriage. Milton recognized the hymn that his friend was singing. By the lyrics, he knew the melody was nearing its conclusion. He had to wait a little longer as another fellow rose from his seat and approached a podium placed downstage right. He gave brief remarks, mostly introducing Milton. He asked for them to welcome Milton, which they did with gentle applause.

Sammy got up from his chair and walked to the podium. He and the introducer exchanged smiles and nods when they passed by each other. Milton placed the Bible on the sloped platform of the podium, turning its hallowed pages to the passage he intended to preach from. As the audience sat in relative silence, he carefully turned the pages to the New Testament. From there, he reduced his focus on the Gospels. Pulling away another collection of pages, he found the book of Matthew. Turning a few pages thence, he came across the specific verses from that book which he was to preach about.

"The Scripture I have in mind for today," began Milton, breaking the quiet, "is a passage familiar to many here. It is the conversation between the rich young ruler and Jesus. If you brought a Bible with you, this can be found in the Gospel according to Matthew, chapter nineteen, verses sixteen through twenty-six. Hear now the Word:

> And, behold, one came and said unto him, Good Master, what good thing shall I do, that I may have eternal life? And he said unto him, Why callest thou me good? there is none good but one, that is, God: but if thou wilt enter into life, keep the commandments. He saith unto him, Which? Jesus said, Thou shalt do no murder, Thou shalt not commit adultery, Thou shalt not steal, Thou shalt not bear false witness, Honor thy father and thy mother: and, Thou shalt love thy neighbor as thyself. The young man saith unto him, All these things

have I kept from my youth up: what lack I yet? Jesus said unto him, If thou wilt be perfect, go and sell that thou hast, and give to the poor, and thou shalt have treasure in heaven: and come and follow me. But when the young man heard that saying, he went away sorrowful: for he had great possessions. Then said Jesus unto his disciples, Verily I say unto you, That a rich man shall hardly enter into the kingdom of heaven. And again I say unto you, It is easier for a camel to go through the eye of a needle, than for a rich man to enter into the kingdom of God. When his disciples heard it, they were exceedingly amazed, saying, Who then can be saved? But Jesus beheld them, and said unto them, With men this is impossible; but with God all things are possible.[2]

"This is God's Word," concluded Milton once the reading was completed. The theatre house fell to a hush; the choir reverently sat silently behind him in white robes. Clayborne was seated behind Milton, upstage right with the other speakers. He looked at those in the audience in the same manner as he did those in the stands and those on the field. He paused intentionally, bringing forth the temporal tension before erupting into his sermon.

"He was a good man! He was a good man. Have any of you heard that? You probably have. It is what many say of those who do not live an active Christian life. It is how they are justified in the eyes of our fallen world." Milton leaned his left arm on the top of the podium as he continued to speak, lacking any written notes to guide his remarks. One of his professors at seminary had discouraged the practice, believing that only the heart and a Bible were necessary to give a sermon that inspires those who hear it.

"When walking down one of your streets, I recall hearing a preacher giving the Good News. At one point in his message, I heard him say, 'How do you know he was saved?' A heckler, likely trying to justify himself, blithely retorted, 'Because he was a good man!'

"In the Scripture read today, we see Jesus dealing with the same reasoning two thousand years ago. The rich young ruler—this worldly, privileged man. He comes to Jesus, hoping to be justified by his works. He begins his fallacious reasoning at the very onset when he calls Jesus good. And Jesus, our Savior, He challenges this rich young ruler with a declaration that echoes and indicts our modern society."

Milton paused, lifting an index finger upward as he looked down and re-read the verse: "'Why callest thou me good? there is none good but one, that is, God . . .'" Milton returned his passionate focus to the audience, who in turn were deeply intrigued by what the preacher was going to say next. "Why callest thou me good? Why call me good? Only God is good. Only God is good.

"In saying what Jesus said, He affirmed statements in both the Old and New Testaments. 'There is none righteous, no, not one.'[3] 'For all have sinned, and come short of the glory of God.'[4] God said He would spare Sodom if ten righteous men could be found. Did He find ten?" Some in the audience openly uttered no, while Milton smiled and then affirmed their answer. "No. He did not. Jesus' words here are powerful, more powerful than many have understood. He is saying that there is no way, NO WAY, that there can be a good man. There are no good men. There is no way you can be good without God. This is a message that was not just powerful then, but remains powerful now in our wicked age. An age of juvenile delinquency, an age when godless Communism continues to conquer more and more of the world; an age where Darwin's 'theory' is taught in our schools; an age where a small group of people in New York are right now suing to get prayers taken out of our schools." Many in the crowd nodded in agreement with his concerns. "Jesus is telling all of them, they are not good. They can never be good. No matter what they do.

"This is the message He gives the rich, young ruler. He asked the ruler—and I find this very interesting—He asked the ruler if he follows the Commandments. For those of you with Bibles handy, look at the ones Jesus mentions. Do not murder; do not commit adultery; honor your father and mother; do not lie; love thy neighbor as thyself. What is missing? The religious ones! Jesus does not mention the commandments of no idols, of no other gods before Thee, or of not taking the Lord's name in vain, and of honoring the Sabbath. Just the non-religious ones. I mean, let me tell you, if these were the only ones, the atheists wouldn't be so hard-pressed to remove them from courthouses. Am I right?" Some in the crowd laughed; others nodded. "It is almost as though Jesus knows that the rich, young ruler is not following these commands. He mentions only the secular commands so as to drive home His point of there being no good without God.

"So when the rich young ruler responds that he follows these, that he is a 'good man,' Jesus takes His conclusion a step further and tells him that if he wants to gain eternal life, he must sell everything he owns, give it to the poor, and then follow Him. Jesus is telling the rich, young ruler and us—definitely us—that if you want to try and get to Heaven with good works, then you're going to have to take this all the way. You must sell everything. You must give everything. You must spend every waking hour, EVERY WAKING HOUR, doing good things. And if you don't, then you aren't going to make it. And sure enough, the rich, young ruler walks away, saddened, for he had many things."

Milton paused to let the point sink in, looking down at the opened Bible on the podium top. And then he continued, those in the house ever more attentive to his words, his poses, and his emotion. "We—we modern Americans—we judge the rich, young ruler very harshly. We have this bad tendency to separate ourselves from him, as though he was somehow more in need of God's grace than we. But, friend, let me warn you. Let me tell you about these words Jesus says about the rich. He says that 'it is easier for a camel to go through the eye of a needle, than for a rich man to enter into the kingdom of God.'

"Now there are some modernist theologians who will claim that what Jesus really means is that some gate in some town was named 'Needle Eye'; and for camels to enter, they had to bend down to go through. This is all liberal compromise and has no place in sound doctrine. There is one meaning here, not many. Jesus was not being metaphorical. He was being literal!" declared Milton, eliciting a few cheers from the crowd. "There is NO WAY a rich man can enter Heaven!

"And yet, remember, friend, that this rich man, who is clearly condemned, was not nearly as rich as us. Whatever wealth he may have had, he did not have a television. He did not own an automobile. He lacked a refrigerator, superglue, or any modern medical advances like penicillin or the polio vaccine." Many contemplated his words; some laughed at the thought of ancients having televisions. All were impressed as Milton continued, "So if you think that rich young ruler was doomed, just imagine how doomed all of us are, for we are all richer than he could have ever been!

"At this point, the disciples, and hopefully all of you, are realizing just how helpless they truly are. They realize that no amount of good deeds can save them. Or you. Or me. That being a 'good man' is not enough. And so, likely in exasperation, they ask, 'Who then can be saved?'" quoted Milton with arms outstretched and in a theatrical tone. His arms went back to the podium; and after a pause, he calmly continued.

"Jesus answered them. He answered them with that famous declaration: 'With men, this is impossible; but with God all things are possible.'⁵ But with God. BUT WITH GOD! With God! 'With God, ALL THINGS ARE POSSIBLE!' Glory!" shouted Milton, with many shouting "glory!" back.

"'All things are possible' with God. You don't have to worry, Jesus said. Yes, you can never do enough. But you don't have to do enough. I've done enough, the Lord says. I have done what needs to be done. I have overcome the world! That is Jesus' message to His disciples and to us. Friend, never take comfort in the works-based salvation. There is no comfort there. You should be as terrified at the idea of works-based salvation as I am. Because it is a terrifying concept. You'll never know if you've done enough. You don't know how many good works you have to do, whether it be a number or a quota. You don't know if you're too late to finish them, if they have equal value, or if what you did was even good.

"But with God, you know. With Jesus Christ, you know. You can boldly say that you are saved. Friend, why do we call Jesus good? Is it because He did a bunch of good things? No. We call Him good because He is our Lord; He is our Savior; and if you accept Him into your heart, you will be saved! YOU WILL BE SAVED!" The crowds echoed his passions, cheering, shouting "Amen!" and "Glory!" Milton concluded, arms resting upon the podium, "Friend, if you have not asked Jesus into your heart, please come forward. Do it privately in your heart, but then let this assembly know. Let this fallen world know. Let your life be a testimony to God's transforming love. If you feel called to this new life, I would ask you to come here to the front and be counted."

The music began to play a good, old hymn with the choir and Clayborne performing together. Milton and the other speakers waited with confidence. It did not take long for a few to come forward. And then more. They left seats; they sauntered forth from the back of the house. They came in growing number, walking down the faintly sloped aisles and then up to the stage. Prayers were spoken over them. A final song was performed; applause was given to God and all those in His ministry. And the throngs, inspired by the music and the message, entered a world of hurt and uncertainty.

* * *

"From there, everybody wanted to see Sammy. The press, the television stations, the crowds, everybody," recalled Beverley, with Addison intently listening. "He used to do this thing. This thing, where he would, you know, pose for the cameras." Beverley attempted to mimic the postures that Sammy did, folding his fingers into two open fists and bending his arms as though holding a baseball bat. "Something like this. Or maybe like he was a pitcher. You know, with his leg bent up and facing the camera to the side." Beverley repositioned his arms to emulate the pitcher pose. "The press loved it. They used it for magazine covers."

"I see."

"He stopped doing it after a while. Not sure why. Maybe he thought his baseball career was too distracting." Beverley laughed a little. "He once told me, it was all 'vainglorious.' And . . . and that it would 'be for naught.' That is what he told me once. I guess he was right. I mean, who today even knows he played?"

"So, he did a lot of these, you called them 'Salvation Meetings'?"

"What now?"

"Salvation Meetings?" reiterated Scott with projection.

"Oh yes, he did those. But he also did baptisms, church services. For a long time, if a town had a river, he would baptize folks there. Preach by the water, and then people would show up and get baptized. He did that until he got too old for it. And let me tell you—because a lot of folks don't realize this—but when we did rallies up north, we had integrated events. Negroes were there, alongside whites." Beverley stopped, an awkward expression on his face. "Oh, I'm sorry, that's not the right word anymore, is it? Blacks. Blacks is what I mean. There were many blacks who would come, and Sammy would pray over them. He did it just as well as when he prayed over whites. No difference."

"Interesting," noted Scott. "So, when and why did Milton become more political in his messages? Was there a specific event?"

"I am sorry; my memory doesn't recall very well. I am not the best to talk about those days. I was there, but not really in it. You would do better talking to Pastor Johnny Canker. He's the one who encouraged him to do politics. Before that, he stayed away from politics like a cat stays away from water."

"Johnny Canker?" pondered Scott for a moment. "Oh, I remember. The eighties TV preacher?"

"Yup, that's him. If he's still around, you should talk to him."

"Okay, then," said Scott as he pushed the button to end the recording. He and the interviewee rose from their seats, the latter taking more time. "Thank you very much for talking with me. This was very interesting stuff."

"No problem," Beverley replied. "Again, I am very sorry I said that word. I meant to say 'blacks,' but you know sometimes it just comes out."

"No big deal; I won't quote that in my story," said Scott. "For what it's worth, when I was a kid, I remember when everyone, including me, used the term 'mentally retarded,' but now it's totally bad."

"Wow," said Beverley with a grumbling laugh, "you're starting to sound like an old man."

"Maybe," laughed Scott. "Would it be okay if I got a copy of this photo of you with Milton in your baseball uniforms for my article?"

"Of course, go ahead and tell Betsy at the front desk. She can do it," said Beverley as he escorted Scott to his unit door. "Oh, and if you see Paul around, let him know he's running late. He was supposed to drop by yesterday."

"Sure," humored Scott, his pity concealed. Exiting the room, he walked down the corridor and quickly made it to the front desk. "Hey there, could you make a copy of this photo for me?"

"Yes, I can do that," the receptionist replied pleasantly. "I can scan it in and print it out."

"You don't need to print it," said Scott as he handed her the old photo. "If you could just scan it in your computer and then email it to me, that should work." Scott took out his wallet and gave her a business card. "This address."

"Sure thing. Shouldn't take long."

"Thank you."

"And I can get Mr. Clayborne's photo back to him when I am done."

"Okay," agreed Scott as the bright laser of the machine went along the surface of the image, copying the image and showing it on the nearby screen. The receptionist saved the file, opened an email window, typed in Scott's contact information, attached the photo image, and then sent it off. Addison checked the internet on his smartphone.

"Did it go through?"

"Yes, yes it did," said Scott while still looking at the small screen. "Thanks, again."

"No problem," smiled the receptionist. "Have a good day!"

"You, too!" said Scott as he turned and walked away. He narrowly missed running into a young man walking past him. Addison noted that he was about his height and bore a vague resemblance. He thought little of it as he continued toward the automatic doors at the front entrance, until he heard the conversation going on behind him.

"Hi Paul! Long time, no see!"

"Hey, Betsy."

"Your grandfather's been wondering where you are."

"Busy work week. Hope he's okay."

"Oh, he'll be so thrilled to see you."

* * *

"How can I help you?" asked a kindly, middle-aged woman behind the counter. She had a rounded face and a rounded body, as well as curly, dyed hair. She wore comfortable clothing and a pair of thick-lensed glasses around her neck on a string.

"I would like a room, please," responded Scott Addison, who had parked his car in the lot a minute ago. After leaving the retirement community, he had eaten lunch at a fast food restaurant situated in a shopping center. From there, he ventured down the Midlothian Turnpike until he found a simple roadside inn to spend his time while down there. The superiors preferred as few travel expenses as possible, so motels were preferred over classier habitations. The place he found had two floors, white walls, and green doors. Its marquee sign promised a cheap rate on a micro fridge. "A one-bedroom should do the trick."

"Okay, then." The woman smiled as she looked at her computer screen, putting on her glasses to check for vacancies. The large sign located at the parking lot entryway indicated that there was room. She quickly searched the listings to find something. "Okay, we have a few one bedrooms on the first and second floors. Do you have a preference?"

"First floor should work."

"Okay," she said with a jovial attitude. "One moment while I punch you in." She typed a few strokes to process the pending transaction. "So, what brings you to the Richmond area, if you don't mind me asking?"

"I'm a reporter working on a story."

"Uh-huh," she replied, finishing up some typing and then turning to face the customer in serious curiosity. "You're not with the Clinton News Network, are you?"

"Oh no, no, I'm with a news site. *The Kensington Post*," replied Scott, vaguely nervous about how his response would be accepted.

"Hmmm . . . never heard of them," she said, returning her ocular attention to the screen. She typed a little more. "Did they endorse Hillary?"

"Nope," answered Scott, being shrewd enough to not mention that his editors instead endorsed Bernie Sanders.

"Then I might check them out."

"That you should."

"Okay," she said slowly. "You'll get unit number eight on the first floor. It has free Wi-Fi, cable, and a mini fridge, but nothing's in there now. Vending machines and ice will be in the corner to your left. Cost will be fifty bucks a night. First payment due now."

"Do you take credit?"

"Doesn't everybody?" she said as Scott handed her his credit card. She swiped it through a machine located next to the computer. It took a few seconds for the processing to finish up. A thin roll of paper came up, with her ripping it off before another thin strip emerged. She handed the first strip and a pen to Scott. "You can sign here, please." Scott obliged and then handed both items back to her. She proceeded to give two key cards, each bearing the name and address of the motel. "Okay, then. Have a nice night."

"Thank you," said Scott, getting a parting smile from the woman manning the counter. Addison pushed open the door and returned to his car, where his bags were. He brought a week's worth of clothing just in case. He also brought his laptop and a battery, as well as plenty of pens and two notepads. Dragging the wheeled luggage behind him and with the laptop case strapped around his shoulder, he made his way to the appropriate unit and unlocked the door with one of the keycards.

As the day closed, he habituated to his new surroundings. It was a queen-sized room, with light pink wallpaper and a large bed in the middle. Near the one large window was a small, round, wooden table with two chairs. The television and cable box were located opposite the bed, with a remote laid out horizontally in front of the entertainment device. Next to the remote was a channel guide and a piece of paper listing the Wi-Fi name and password. The service was decent, much better than he assumed it would be. Logging into his work email, he saw over twenty unread messages.

He got a confirmation email from Jabez Henderson regarding an in-person interview the following morning. Henderson explained that he was unavailable the day that Scott came into town because it was his Sabbath, since he worked Sundays. Scott found a phone number for the archives department of the American Baseball League. They were quick to confirm Milton's sports career and accomplishments, with the young voice as surprised as Scott was to learn about it. Scott also found contact information for Johnny Canker. He sent out an emailed query, requesting an interview. Before having dinner, he spent the remainder of his time transcribing the interview with Clayborne.

The conversation with the elderly singer was an interesting one. Finding out that Milton had once had a successful baseball career added depth to the man he was supposed to destroy. While the words about Milton were kind, they were also suspect. Addison expected there to be niceties and rose-coloring on the part of his subject. Had Herbert Spiker not been so insistent, Addison would have dodged that interview altogether. But then again, he realized, if he had not talked with Clayborne, he would not have learned about this part of Milton's life. Something that many readers, even those who hate Milton, may find interesting. Perhaps even ironic. Addison did not let the positive press provided by Spiker and Clayborne trouble him. Tomorrow he expected a harsher critique.

That night, Addison decided to do some additional preliminary work. He had already transcribed the Spiker and Clayborne interviews, respectively. Going to his documents folder, he created a new Word document. He clicked on the title to edit the document title, deciding to name it "A Tunnel Into Darkness-01." Upon finishing the title, he clicked elsewhere on the folder background to solidify the appellation. Then Scott double-clicked the small word icon, and his screen was filled with the blank page. He went ahead and typed in the working title Tyrone Spearman had suggested. Somewhat inspired, he began to type up a few things at the start: "Bigot. Racist. Homophobe. Sexist. Hate-Monger. All these are words associated with the recently deceased Rev. Sammy Milton. Those who fought against him the longest share their stories about the worst of his actions."

Scott's phone rang. He was not expecting a call, but also was not that shocked to hear it go off. The screen showed the name Katie Nicholson. Scott pressed against the answer button and then dragged his fingertip to begin the conversation: "Hey, Katie."

"Hey, Scott," said his friend. "Did you have a safe trip down to Richmond?"

"Yeah, it went fast."

"Got to love the reverse commute," agreed Katie. "So how is Richmond?"

"It's okay," began Scott, slightly lowering his voice as he added, "the woman at my motel asked me if I worked for the Clinton News Network."

"Wow, that's . . . I can't even," laughed Katie.

"But otherwise, nothing too scary."

"Well, if you feel homesick, I suggest going to Carytown. It's a lot like Old Town Alexandria, except not as old."

"You mean shops and stuff?"

"Yeah, a good place to walk. Just go down Cary Street between Nansemond and Boulevard, and you'll be there. Lots of good restaurants, too."

"I'll keep that in mind. I'm pretty sure I'm going to be here all week."

"Well, anyway, just checking in. If you have any other questions about the RIC, just let me know," said Katie.

"Alright, will do."

"Good night, Scott."

"Good night, Katie."

JABEZ HENDERSON

SCOTT ADDISON DID NOT EXPECT the church to be so busy on a Thursday morning. Coming from a Christian background, he remembered going to worship on Sundays and doing nothing much for the other six days. In hindsight, his childhood church probably had plenty of events going on from Monday to Saturday. The worship bulletins did include a bunch of paperwork. It was the stuff that he threw away or let slip from his grip when traveling from the entrance to the pew. He never bothered to read them, and his parents made little effort to encourage him.

So, to see several families coming to the entrance was a surprise. Most were walking; a few had older automobiles. Not an antique old, but a worn old. Most of the adults were female, and all were African-American. Grownups and kids came in, but only the former exited. As he got closer, Scott was able to read a sign by the entrance explaining that this was the place for the preschool and kids' care programs. The display included an illustration of four happy stick figures, with two having faces colored in brown and one with a face colored in yellow. A crossing guard prevented any potential accidents by helping car and man navigate around each other.

A few adults, specifically those overseeing the children's programming, were outside monitoring the situation. They also socialized with those who were not in a rush. All but two of them were female. The two men standing around were sharp contrasts. One was heavy-set, with dreadlocked hair and a thick beard, clad in blue jeans and a white t-shirt. The other was broad-shouldered but more proportional, with short gray hair and a clean-shaven face, glasses, and a well-polished suit. Addison was quick to recognize this man as the Rev. Jabez Henderson. While Addison was still about twenty feet away, Henderson looked in his general direction and immediately made eye contact. A smile came over the elder clergyman, and he waved at the reporter.

"Mr. Addison, am I correct?" projected Henderson in a deep voice. Scott smiled and quickened his step to approach him.

"Yes," replied Scott. "And you must be Rev. Henderson."

"Your conclusion is correct," said Henderson as the two shook hands. He then addressed the sexton and other church employees around him. "I have an appointment to speak with this nice, young journalist. I am fairly sure y'all can handle things without me."

"We'll manage," deadpanned the sexton, laughter coming from the others. With a wave, Henderson left for the inside of the church building, Addison walking alongside him.

"It is one of the very few flaws of the English language," began Henderson, speaking to the reporter. "We do not have an effective plural for 'you.' Thankfully, being a Southerner, I was well educated in the word 'y'all.'"

"Whatever works," said Addison as they went inside the complex. The largest part of the sacred edifice was the sanctuary, a simple, yet grand, rectangular structure with a triangular top and white-painted steeple. It appeared to stretch into the parking lot, as though shielding the blacktop from that side of the world. They were in the adjacent hallway, going toward the offices.

"So, you drove all the way down from DC to come here?"

"Yes."

"I thought reporters tended to do things through email and phone."

"Usually, yes," began Scott as Henderson pulled open the office door. The reporter nodded in gratitude as the clergyman let him enter first. "However, sometimes it is best to be on the ground, so to speak. My first interviewee is pushing ninety, and so email and phone wouldn't really work for him."

"I see."

"And since there were other people I needed to interview who also lived and worked around here, it just made the most sense to come down."

"Can I assume that getting away from the office was another factor?" Henderson lightly inquired, Scott not disagreeing. The two entered the reverend's office, which had wood-paneled walls and a carpeted floor. Both men sat down in two chairs facing opposite each other, an oak desk between them. Behind Henderson were shelves attached to the wall, filled with books and a handful of VHS tapes and DVDs. They were recordings of sermons and worship services at the church.

"Yes, leaving the office can be fun sometimes," conceded Scott.

"I interned in DC for a summer. I can still recall how crowded it was. And that was when the population was far, far smaller."

"Yes, I guess it's always been that way," nodded Scott. He then changed his tone and topic. "Well, if you don't mind, I would like to get to business. As I mentioned in my email, I'm working on a story about the life of Sammy Milton. My editor told me you would be a good person to talk to—you know, because you knew him for decades."

"Your editor is Michael Phillips, am I correct?"

"Yes, that's him."

"I thought so. Yes, I have known Phillips since he was a young reporter like yourself. I knew the Rev. Milton even longer."

Scott took out his digital voice recorder and placed it on the desk. He had asked in advance if it was okay to record their interview, to which Henderson agreed. "So, when did you first meet Milton?"

"1962," replied Henderson, slowly blinking his eyes in remembrance. "A time of struggle. A time of pressure. I had just turned eighteen. Already, I was an activist, trying my best to create that beloved community. My father was head of this church at the time. He was also involved in the movement. I did my part with my fellow college students and campus radicals. Pops went through the more traditional routes. We respected each other's work, even when we did not always agree."

* * *

He was a tall, gangly figure. During grade school, he was known to stand taller than most of his peers and even a couple of his teachers. The growth spurt came early and rapid. His afro added another few inches. He was combing through it that morning when his father told him about the day's agenda. There was nothing else scheduled for the day, so he did not mind going, per se. He had other issues about the meeting—least of all having to wear what he considered "old clothes." Looking through the mirror in his bedroom—a long reflection that showed him top to bottom—he was almost done. Slacks, shoes, and the buttoned-up shirt were on. What remained was a checkered tie. A long line, he began to wrap it around his neck, which was covered by a popped collar.

"You about ready, son?" asked his father. He was wearing a pin-striped suit and had shorter hair. Like his son, he once wore his hair long. However, a brief stint in the navy before the Second World War drew him to the crewcut. And since the missus liked it, there was no debate.

"Almost, pops," he replied, struggling with the fashion item. Another loop and a pull, he initially assumed victory. Yet as soon as he stopped tying the knot, Jabez Henderson realized that he had failed once again. His father took a deep breath and approached him from behind, his frame filling the background of the mirror.

"Turn around," he ordered, the son obliging. The father took hold of the knotted tie and undid it, straightening out the fabric. "Now, try again. And this time, focus."

"Yes, sir."

"A real man knows how to tie a tie. Only fatherless boys don't know that; and you, my boy, are not fatherless."

"Yes, sir," said Jabez, as he turned around and focused on the reflection. He mouthed the words of the instructions, the looping here and the crossing over there. The bulk of the tie was cautiously tucked behind the front knot and then dragged down. Pulling the knot to his neck, Jabez grinned in accomplishment.

"Better," noted the father, while his son put down his collar, covering the part of the tie that wrapped around his neck.

"Why are we doing this, Pops?"

"Because I said so."

"But, Pops," protested Jabez, while he nonetheless went to his closet to find a dinner jacket that matched his dress slacks, "this Milton guy—"

"Rev. Milton, Jabez. His name is the Reverend Sammy Milton."

"Rev. Milton," conceded Jabez as he found a matching jacket in his closet. "He's never done anything. No marches, nothing. Why do you think he'll help?"

"Maybe he will; maybe he will not. I know that in past conversations with him, he expressed an openness to working with our church. And he has yet to openly express hatred for other races."

"I don't know, Pops," stressed the son as he fitted the jacket upon his person. "I don't like the idea of going cap-in-hand to a white man."

"Boy," said an angered father, who seriously considered slapping his son, "this is not a 'cap-in-hand' approach. We are coming in power. The movement is gaining strength. This is about inviting Rev. Milton to be part of the movement. This is about building a coalition—a diverse group of brothers and sisters who can come together to bring about change to our society. A man like Milton, a national figure, a popular preacher with a growing church. That is the kind of man who can be a powerful ally. So, quit this stupid talk about cap-in-hand, you hear?"

"Yes, sir," Jabez agreed. As the two exited the house and made their way to the car, the son still had his dissent. "But why do you need me to come with you?"

"Because, son," explained the elder Henderson as he opened the driver's side door, "there will come a time when you will be leading my church. And you need to begin forming these relationships with other community leaders."

The father unlocked the passenger door for his son. Jabez opened it and got in. "But Rev. Milton is so old. He'll probably die soon."

"And if he does, it would be good to know his family. I bet, in time, he will start grooming his eldest for the ministry."

"I guess so," said a somewhat annoyed Jabez as the motor turned on and the car went onward. The trip was a quick one, thanks to traffic on the Midlothian Turnpike being sparse.

Mere minutes went by before the vehicle containing pastor and son turned onto the small road that led to a progressing future. There were construction vehicles, bright orange-and-white cones, and a large number of men in highlight green shirts and hard hats working along the beams and bricks. The growling engines, the beeping of reversing mechanical behemoths, the screeching of motorized blades, the virile shouts ordering workers around, and so much more added to the coordinated chaos. Turning to the unused parking lot for the small building containing offices and a sanctuary, Jabez eyed the message of a humble, painted sign near the border of cones: "Coming Soon! The New Building For Into Marvelous Light Ministries!"

Until that coming, the church that the Henderson family members entered was considerably smaller. A growing congregation, mixed with increased donations, gave them reason to expand. For the time being, they had to do three services each Sunday morning and one in the evening to accommodate their attendees. The Hendersons walked side-by-side upon approaching the front desk. Each one signed in, noting the time of their arrival. It was a short walk to the office. They were told to go right on into the office. Jabez saw a man in business casual attire writing an entry into a black, leather-bound Bible. He looked up with blue eyes, in a mood that switched from contemplative to pleasant.

"Rev. Uriel Henderson, a pleasure to see you at last," said Sammy as he got up and shook hands with the guest.

"Likewise, Rev. Milton," responded Henderson, who directed Sammy to the young man to his right. "This is my eldest son, Jabez."

"A pleasure," greeted Milton as the two shook hands. "Do you know the significance of your first name?"

"Pops tells me about it all the time," replied Jabez with feigned annoyance. The two older gentlemen laughed at the remark as they took their respective seats in the office.

"By the way, congratulations on your second child," noted Uriel.

"Thank you," smiled Milton. "It was a baby boy. We named him Wallace."

"He's not named after *that* Wallace, is he?" inquired Uriel.

"Oh, no, no," laughed Milton, who had not realized at first that he might need to clarify the origins of the appellation. "Not at all. My grandmother's maiden name is Wallace."

"Ah. I see."

"Although she was from Alabama, so I guess I'm doomed," added Milton, laughing along with Uriel while saying the second part of the sentence. A moment passed, and business entered the discussion. "Well, you called me about cooperation. Possibly sponsoring events and the like. I definitely like the idea." Uriel and Jabez both had their expectations raised. "Especially in times like these, when it seems like everything's falling apart; the Church, black and white, needs to come together. And I think worship and fellowship—what the Methodists call 'holy conferencing'—are always good for the soul."

"I am happy to hear that, Rev. Milton."

"So, what did you have in mind?"

"Well," began Uriel, "we were thinking of something along the lines of a march." Jabez studied Milton, seeing the white pastor's expression change from pleasant to cautious. The big smile melted with each sentence his father gave. "As you know, even with the *Brown* decision, there's still a lot of hostile resistance to integration. Protests, violence, and only token efforts to desegregate Richmond city schools. Even worse is what's happening in Prince Edward County. It's been three years since they shut down their public schools, which is forcing black children to either travel outside the county every day for classes or simply not get an education."

"And you're thinking a march?"

"Yes," affirmed Uriel. "I already have a few local clergy on board. The Unitarians, a Baptist church. The Catholic Diocese said they were interested. And I would like it if you could join us. Again, this is the perfect time for clergy of all churches to come together and send a message of justice."

Milton looked down, to the growing concern of Uriel. Taking a breath, he returned his focus to the father and son seated before him. "Forgive me, Rev. Henderson. I believe I must have misunderstood you when you first contacted me. I assumed that you were planning a revival event for the area. I apologize deeply. If I had known that this was your intention, I would not have wasted your time."

"Rev. Milton," inquired a disappointed Uriel, "are you saying that you are opposed to the struggle for civil rights?"

"Not necessarily. What I am opposed to, Rev. Henderson, are efforts that do not understand that a pastor's place is in the pulpit, not on the soap box. Our obligations are for sacred matters, matters of eternity. This is not an eternal matter."

"Justice is an eternal matter, Rev. Milton."

"It is, and I am not saying that there shouldn't be some effort against the evils of racism. I am saying that this is the job for secular figures. Our job is to save souls. Destroying Jim Crow doesn't save a single soul."

"It might save the soul of a nation," countered Uriel, projecting to the point of shouting.

"Old Europe persecuted plenty of good, Bible-believing Protestants because clergy didn't know their place in society. Our country has greatly benefitted from the separation of church and state."

"It's not in the Constitution," firmly replied Uriel.

"But it's there in spirit," Milton reiterated. "Again, I am sorry I wasted your time. But I remain unmoved on this matter. That said, whenever you want to coordinate an outreach service, something to convert the heathen and renew spirits, please let me know. It would be a pleasure to work alongside you."

Milton rose from his chair. The two Hendersons understood the implication. The father and son both grudgingly shook hands with the white pastor and left.

* * *

"My father was greatly disappointed," recalled the once-young Henderson, the reporter recording his every comment. "He made other attempts to get Rev. Milton to join the cause. All of them, most unfortunately, failed." Henderson leaned forward as he continued. "You see, Rev. Milton was never an openly hostile figure to the movement. He never advocated for segregation or supported Klan violence or anything of that type. No, unfortunately, he was a different kind of enemy: the indifferent friend. He offered no opposition to racial equality, but he also offered no help, either. And on borderline issues like busing and Affirmative Action—issues where many harboring hate could colorblind their views—he stood strongly against our efforts to equalize society."

"I knew that he had a troubled past on race issues," began Addison, "but I didn't realize it was so blatant. To actually say to your father's face that he refused to help. Dare I say, that's seriously messed up."

"His words, though hurtful, were significantly less vicious than those of more committed supporters of the racist status quo," noted Henderson, softly adding an antithesis to Addison's point.

"Still, I can imagine it had to be disturbing to be in the presence of a famous figure who turned out to be racist."

Henderson bowed his head, closing his eyes and offering a little smile. An eager reporter awaited a response to the declaration. After a moment, he returned his attention to the journalist before him. "Young man, can I assume you know about Frederick Douglass?"

"Yes."

"If you would allow me to engage in history, I would like to tell you an interesting piece of trivia regarding Douglass."

"Sure."

"When Douglass was older and after his first wife had passed away, he married a white woman. The woman in question was the child of an abolitionist couple whom Douglass had known for many, many years. Rather than be happy that their old friend was going to be part of their family, the abolitionist couple was horrified. Their longstanding friendship with Douglass was ended. Other white abolitionists likewise expressed their outrage. You see, these enlightened white liberals who supported freeing the black man nevertheless opposed him marrying their daughters."

"I think I see what you're getting at," said Scott, his interviewee nodding.

"In my time, I have worked alongside many Northern white progressives. Most of them are decent folk, whatever that may mean. However, nearly all of them had their hesitations, their reservations, their lines of comfort. It could be the idea of a black family moving into their neighborhood; it could be the idea of sending their children to a predominantly black school; or it could be their daughters bringing home a colored boyfriend," said Henderson, leaning back in authority. "Every American struggles with racism. It is, as the late Rev. Dr. King once said, our original sin. I refuse to judge Rev. Milton for his shortcomings. Unlike so many who conveniently forgot their past failures as time progressed, at least Rev. Milton stood before a large audience of blacks and whites and offered up a sincere, heartfelt apology."

"He did *what?*" asked Scott, his gaze immediately flinging from the notepad to the seated Henderson.

* * *

Sammy Milton looked over the crowd gathered in the main worship space of his megachurch. Into Marvelous Light's primary campus had been in operation for nearly two decades at this point. The sanctuary featured three long columns of pews, with four aisles that came toward the main stage at angles. There was a balcony supported by columns and rows of seats for the choir placed behind the pulpit, separated by a short, solid barrier. In front of the barrier was a row of seven seats reserved for clergy, the worship leader, the Scripture reader, and anyone else involved in the service. Closer to the pews, where attendees sat on downstage left, was the pulpit. On the opposite end of the stage was a drum set, which had a transparent fiberglass layer between it and the worshippers. Next to the drum set there was an organ and a piano.

The décor was not particularly elegant. There were no stained-glass windows or statues. No intricate carving work. Simple brick walls, small windows, a white ceiling, and a basic stage. A large, white cross was affixed to the wall behind the choir seats. The central point of the sanctuary lacked candles or an altar. The stage where the pulpit and chairs were located could be approached at any point from the house, as the entire stage had four short levels, like a step pyramid. Just below the bottom step was a removable railing that went along the whole stage, save the very center, which was left open.

It was a summer evening, so beams of natural light went through the small portals left on either side of the sanctuary despite the hour. It was a Wednesday—a time known to host church socials, yet seldom something this vastly attended. This night was different. Row after row of pews were filled with people. Many were congregants of Into Marvelous Light. Many more were visitors. Nearly all of the members were white, and nearly all of the visitors were black. Of the visitors, most came from other churches, situated in places like downtown Richmond, the Southside, and along Midlothian Turnpike. Many of the older whites and blacks kept to their own when sitting in the pews. This was not a mandate, but conditioned tendency. Younger members of both races were more likely to sit beside one another, even together in community.

Jabez Henderson and his wife were prominently seated, sharing the stage with the man who oversaw Into Marvelous Light Church and the overall Into Marvelous Light Ministries. The Rev. Sammy Milton and his wife were also seated onstage. With them were two more folks. The first was Beverley Clayborne, while the other was the music director at Hendersons' church. They coordinated the music. First Clayborne with the megachurch's choir. Then Hendersons' church did a number. And then, in profound symbolism, both choirs performed a number together. After that song was finished and the crowd celebrated the musical movement of the Spirit, Rev. Milton took a deep breath, rose from his seat, and approached the pulpit.

Henderson watched the older clergyman. The gray of his mane was gradually conquering his hair. Lines crisscrossed his face. His clothed belly hung over his belt. Still, he possessed an energy, an undying enthusiasm. Those blue eyes were vibrant and determined. Even when his task was an unpleasant one, he sought nothing more than to do the task properly. With admiration, Henderson watched the older, Southern gentleman adjust the microphone and speak. This was no ordinary message of salvation. To be sure, there was preaching of the Word, a call for salvation. These things were expected by all those in the holy place that night. Then came the hard part.

"Friends, this evening I must come to you as the publican of antiquity. He came to the temple, so afraid and guilty that he was unable to raise his head toward Heaven when giving his pleas for mercy. At this hour, I struggle to make eye contact with many of you gathered here. Those of you who had to struggle to get basic human rights years ago. You who fought injustice, bigotry; you who fought intolerance, violence; you who showed a great Christian example. You are the ones I can barely raise my head to look at, who I plead to for forgiveness. You are the ones I wronged."

Milton paused, overtaken by the emotion welling up within the space. He looked down at the pulpit, where often bullet points were printed to guide him through a sermon. Not this time. "Years ago, the late Rev. Henderson and his son—here with us tonight with his beautiful wife—came to me for help. They wanted me to stand for justice, for civil rights. They wanted me to help fight the good fight, to stand with fellow believers against an obvious pervasive evil." His head bowed again, his composure buckled but did not break. He looked at those gathered and described his actions in disgust. "And I said no. I refused. I told them it was not the job of a pastor to be involved in politics. I told them I was about saving souls and saving souls only.

"I was so, I was so . . . short-sighted. I was ignorant. I was ignorant of the plight of my fellow Christian brothers. I was ignorant of the clearly anti-Christian nature of Jim Crow. As my brothers in Christ choked on oppression, I lectured them about church and state separation." An eye began to become glassy, the speech reaching its catharsis. Milton felt the moral support around him, especially from Henderson. "I was worse than an enemy . . . I was apathetic. Or maybe just plain pathetic." That one comment got a few laughs from the audience. Another pause, another bringing forth to penance. "I ask you now. All of you who suffered from my indifference. I implore you as brothers in Christ. Please . . . please forgive me. Please accept my apologies for these years of sitting on the sidelines. Please forgive me for my ignorance.

"I know better now. Pastors do not just belong in the pulpit; they must shepherd their flocks in all matters: religious, political, and social. They must be there, standing against all forms of oppression. They must 'speak truth to power,' as Henderson so loves to stress." Milton turned briefly, pointing with an open hand at Jabez, who nodded in affirmation. "We must take back this country. We must create that blessed community. And we must fight for biblical principles in all affairs—national, local, political, social. We cannot afford to let our nation collapse into godlessness. And I cannot afford to go any longer without your forgiveness for my past wrongs. Before I take the speck out of my brother's eye, I must remove the plank from mine. So, if my good friend Henderson could please come forth and other church leaders from the congregations that witness to the Richmond area, please let us join hands and pray for all of us here tonight."

* * *

"And that is what we did," recalled Henderson, Addison surprised at the happening he described. "Rev. Milton prayed for a little while; I prayed over him; and the congregation joined and prayed with each other. It was a truly beautiful scene."

"Do you believe it was sincere?"

"There were those in my flock who questioned it. A few who came up to me later to say that it was 'too little' and of course, 'too late.' However, I later learned that a couple of the more, let us say, recalcitrant members of Rev. Milton's church left his congregation in protest over his apology. They thought it was sincere."

"But I seem to recall you two arguing from time to time on television," said Scott, pointing at Henderson with the top of his pen.

"Yes, we had disagreements over certain political issues. Yet, there were plenty of common threads outside of those television appearances. For example, while I accept our LGBT members as being fellow human beings of sacred worth, for me marriage will always be between one man and one woman. Therefore, both Rev. Milton and myself advocated for the passage of the Virginia Marriage Amendment in 2006. Also, later on, Rev. Milton spoke out against Confederate flag displays."

"He did?" asked Addison. "When was that?"

"A couple of years ago. Before a large group of Southern, white pastors, Rev. Milton implored them to pass a resolution encouraging themselves and their congregations to consider not flying the old, Southern swastika. I was present when he talked about his ancestors who fought for the 'Lost Cause,' how he saw it as a hindrance to spreading the Gospel. He closed his remarks by passionately declaring that 'the most expensive Confederate flag in America today is not worth the value of one black soul.' The resolution passed overwhelmingly. From there, our churches jointly held events on racial reconciliation, community involvement—things of that nature. He showed improvement in word and in deed."

"Interesting," acknowledged Scott, tapping the top of his pen against his chin. "I had never known all these things."

"You should," responded Henderson. "After all, I contacted your editor about each one, from the apology to the Confederate flag speech."

"You did?" asked a perplexed Scott.

"Michael Phillips is your editor, is he not?"

"He is, yes."

"I contacted him about the 1985 apology event. Phillips declined to attend. I asked him to pass the word to his editor."

"And did he?"

"If he did, it was not evident. No one from *The Kensington Post* showed up. Not for that event, not for the flag speech, none of it. He never came, and he never sent anyone." Scott did not know how to respond to this revelation. He looked down at his notes, grasping the bizarre information as Henderson kept speaking. "I was surprised about the refusal to cover the apology. After all, I thought the event would put Rev. Milton in enough of a negative light that Phillips would be thrilled to report it."

"Rev. Henderson," interjected the church secretary, breaking the thought pattern of Addison and prompting both men to face the open door. "Pastor Freeman is on line one for you."

"Oh yes, I almost forgot. I told him to call me now," Jabez said to his secretary. "I will take it momentarily." Henderson returned his attention to the reporter. "This is an important call. Do you have any other questions?"

"Um, no, I don't," said Addison as he turned off his recorder, got up from his seat, and nodded at Henderson, while shaking his hand. "Thank you very much for taking time to talk with me."

"No problem, Mr. Addison. Good day, and Godspeed."

"Take care."

* * *

Katie Nicholson was at her desk awaiting a phone call. Her computer was on, with the webpage showing her work inbox. There were two additional tabs open on the internet. The tab to the right of the inbox was the office instant chat. It included a general news chat, a department chat, a chat restricted to editors, and the option to communicate directly one-on-one with any coworker who was online. To the right of that tab was a personal email, which Katie preferred to check on throughout the day, just in case. Some of her coworkers had fixed their business email so that it forwarded to their personal email account. Katie was uncomfortable with the idea, so the two remained separate.

Most over-the-phone interviews involved her calling the person of interest. However, the interviewee specifically requested a phone number from Katie. Knowing what her source went through a couple of weeks ago, the journalist was willing to respect the demand. She was not working on a gleeful story. Indeed, the situation resembled a recurring nightmare that Nicholson had had since she started having articles published. It was not a frequent fear, though it did meander in the far corners of her conscience. The woman gave her a thirty-minute range for when she planned to call.

Katie was not nervous about the upcoming on-the-record conversation. Unlike most, she asked in advance if the person was okay with the call being recorded. She said yes. Not that Katie was unable to keep up with a normal speed of speech. While not as effective as a professional stenographer, she was well ahead of hunting and pecking. Recording was nevertheless preferred for better accuracy. Her source was more concerned about how much of their conversation was going out to the world and if it was an on-air communication. Katie assured her that it would be just the two of them on the line and that vocal fillers would be edited out of any quoted sentences.

The phone began to ring. Katie noticed that the caller ID conveyed the message "UNKNOWN NUMBER." This was not the first time an interviewee had phoned in with this identification. Celebrities were known to do that. Her recorder already on, Katie pushed the red button to begin the digital chronicling as she went for the receiver. It was the only landline she used in daily life.

"Hello?"

"Hello, this is Jessie Steary," said the calm voice on the other end. There was a little static, but it diminished as the call continued. "Is this Katie Nicholson?"

"Yes, it is," replied Katie. "Good afternoon."

"Afternoon."

"As you know, I am writing up an article about what you and other feminist bloggers have been through online. So, I guess, to begin with, could you give me a basic overview of what happened?"

"Okay," said Jessie, pausing before she continued. Katie had an idea of what took place, but she needed to learn the specific details from the person who endured it all. "Well, it began two weeks ago. I used to blog on women's issues once every few days. Politics, entertainment, choice, sexism. Two weeks ago, I wrote an essay about the presence of patriarchy even in movies with female leads. These films, billing themselves as pro-woman, still had things like the male gaze and Victorian constructs. I am, like, one hundred percent certain that was the one that stirred up the cyber-lynch mob."

"What leads you to believe that that post was the one?" asked Katie, a little concerned that her query might have been too pushy. "Because it all began the very next morning. And it was the one that got all the traffic, according to my blog stats."

"Okay, that makes sense," Katie agreed. "So, tell me what happened next."

"Well, the next morning, I woke up and turned on my phone. I had, like, three hundred text messages. Literally, message after message of rape threats, death threats, slut-shaming, and more. I went to my laptop and turned it on. More hate messages, more threats. They filled my inbox; they were all over social media. Message boards . . . post after post after post. There were photos, too."

"Photos?"

"Doctored ones. A few people put my head on the bodies of porn stars, naked women, BDSM. They posted those on message threads, posted them on my account walls, the comments sections for all my blog entries. It was everywhere."

"That must have been horrible. I can't even imagine how awful you must have felt."

"Yes, it was horrible," Jessie replied, pausing to give herself strength to continue the description of past events. "I felt so violated. They kept sending messages, posting things. Someone had taken my contact info and plastered it all over the web. I wanted to, like, crawl into a corner and lay there. But I had to do things. I contacted boards and sites that had the pictures and my contact info. Some of them took it down; others claimed First Amendment and left them up. I changed my email address, my phone number. I closed down my social media accounts and my blog. I just had to, like, get away from it."

"That must have been a tough choice," noted Katie. "Do you regret stepping away from all those things?"

"I mean, I didn't want to leave," said Jessie. "You never want to run away. You don't want them to get the last word. But there's, like, only so much abuse and humiliation you can take. Especially when you know that you literally cannot change their minds. I knew I could never reason with them. I could never convince them that no woman should be treated that way. No person should be treated that way. I want to think this is temporary. Maybe I will start a new blog. But I don't know. I really don't."

"Did you let the authorities know about your situation?"

"Yes, I did. The death threats and rape threats were definitely something they needed to investigate," she replied, then sighed. "But the detective I talked to told me that there was little chance anyone was going to be punished. The way the internet works, with screen names, pseudonyms. They said it was literally impossible to pin stuff down on people."

"Okay, thank you for your time, and again, I am very sorry for what you went through."

"Thank you. Bye."

"Bye."

Katie heard the click on the other end of the line. She felt it proper to let the interviewee leave the conversation first. With the silence assured, Nicholson hung up the landline and then detached the recorder from the phone. She took the headphones attached to the computer and gently pulled on them. She plugged the headphone cord into the top of the recording device so that she could hear the previous exchange without disrupting those working in the neighboring cubicles. As she was about to start transcribing the dialogue, her landline phone rang once again. This time, a familiar number came across the light green screen. Katie removed the headphones from her ears, lowering them to hang around her neck. Picking up the phone, she heard a familiar voice.

"Hey, Katie."

"Hey, Scott. How's Richmond?"

"Pretty good," he began. "Could you look up something for me?"

"Did you lose your internet access?" Katie jokingly replied.

"Very funny. No, I need you to go down to archives, because I'm pretty sure the older editions were not posted online."

"Yeah, I think you're right," conceded Katie. "So, what do you want me to look for?"

"Look in the 1985 editions for anything about an event where Sammy Milton apologized for being a racist."

"He did?"

"Yes," noted Scott. "Call me back when you've finished looking."

"Actually, you hit me right when I was between things. I'll go ahead and look now."

"Thanks, Katie."

"No problem, hold on."

"Sure," said Scott, whose voice sounded smaller because Katie was in the process of putting the receiver on the desktop as he spoke.

At the motel room, Addison had finished transcribing the interview he did earlier that day. He also talked with other sources for his story. Eileen Friedman confirmed that she was able to speak with him in person the following afternoon. Things had been hectic over the past several days with a renewed debate over the federal funding of Planned Parenthood. They were scheduled to talk at her Museum District office. Through a brief email exchange, he confirmed a time for his interview with Johnny Canker. It was going to be on a Saturday, which was the same day he was scheduled to meet with Frank Moore.

"Scott?" asked a female voice over the phone.

"Yes?" he quickly replied, only partly paying attention as the wait led him to draw away his focus from the call.

"Okay, I looked through the '85 editions, and there was nothing about Milton apologizing for racism. Are you sure it happened?"

"It happened."

"Well, we didn't cover it."

"Okay. Anyway, thanks, Katie."

"No problem. Will you be back in town for the weekend?"

"I'd love to, but Saturday I've got to talk to more people."

"Hmmm . . . sounds like you're avoiding me," she said with insincere suspicion.

"No, seriously. I have a couple interviews slated for Saturday. Trust me, I would much rather be up there with you."

"I bet. Anyway, back to work."

"Back to work."

EILEEN FRIEDMAN

SCOTT ADDISON STRUGGLED TO FIND parking. Townhouses crowded together along narrow streets, with cars hugging each curb. Many of the buildings were constructed in the early twentieth century, following a similar model of domicile that included a porch, three pillars holding up an awning, and a few stairs to get to the first floor. Scott's destination resembled this trend, with two square windows on the first floor and three on the second. On the yard in front of the structure, there were two small signs planted in the grass. One explained in English, Arabic, and Spanish that all neighbors were welcomed regardless of their origin. The other declared its support for science.

Addison could not find a gap between the parked vehicles large enough for him to squeeze his sports car into. Again turning right, he gave up and decided to go back a couple of blocks to a parking garage. It meant more blocks to walk, but at least the weather was mild. Driving up a flight, Scott was able to find a handful of empty spaces marked with thick, white paint. He selected one and turned off his automobile. His various journalistic tools were carried in the pockets of his light jacket, save for the press ID, which swung along his neck on a lanyard.

Scott turned the corner he had previously driven alongside and again beheld the structure with the two signs. The screen door was propped open, while the main door was ajar. Before he could knock, a young woman in jeans and a t-shirt pulled back the barrier. She and another millennial-aged woman were leaving the townhouse. They did not expect Scott's appearance, but they were not shocked. Both smiled as they walked past him onto the porch and then down the stairs. The door remained open, with Scott able to see the buzzing activism within. Some were manning phones, while others were pounding away on laptops. There were coffee and snacks scattered all over, two televisions tuned into two different news stations, and various progressive-leaning political posters taped to the walls. In an odd way, it reminded him of his office back in DC, albeit as a domestic setting with informal attire and a more overt bias.

Scott quickly discovered the person he was scheduled to interview. She reminded him of his editor. While Addison knew she was sixty-two, she masked it by being an energetic figure who made the rounds amongst the different youthful folks. They gave her updates; she gave feedback. The head of this pulsing hub of woke activists was, at times, strict in her orders and, at others, light-hearted and encouraging. She had few wrinkles, and some of her hair had yet to gray. The inconsistency of the coloration led Scott to conclude that it was authentic. Taking a few steps deeper into the first floor, he overheard parts of the discussion between her and a forty-something who looked related.

"So, I think we need to make sure we send two more folks to the Southside. Make sure they know that minority communities are the hardest hit," said Eileen Friedman to the younger woman. Both wore glasses and stood about the same height. The younger had thick-rimmed glasses and a detailed tattoo visible along her left arm. Scott noticed the elder of the two women wore a pink shirt with some writing on it and a necklace, but distance prevented further detail.

"Yeah, got it. I can go with Mellie."

"Good. Tell her to get some more flyers on the way out the door."

"Yes, Mom."

The younger one darted off behind Eileen, walking quickly to another room. A thought came to the older woman and turned to catch her attention. "Jenny!"

"Yes?"

"Also, check and make sure we've got enough printed copies for tomorrow's lit. drop while you're at it, okay?"

"Okay, will do," she replied, giving a faint salute before returning to her quick travel to the adjacent space. The orders received, Eileen acknowledged Scott. She was initially confused by his presence. He did not look like a volunteer. His tie, slacks, light jacket, and press lanyard showcased this. Then it came to her; she blinked; and her expression went from slight perplexity to full understanding. A big smile came across her face as she walked up to the journalist.

"Oh, hello, you must be Addison with the *Post,* right?"

"Yes," responded Scott as the two shook hands.

"I'm Eileen. A pleasure to meet you."

"Likewise."

"Sorry for the iffy reply about when we could talk. As you can see, all sorts of stuff's been going on with the whole women's healthcare debate in Congress."

"Of course. I understand," commented Scott as Jenny and Mellie walked past him and Eileen. Now that Friedman was right in front of him, Scott saw that her pink shirt had the phrase "I Support Planned Parenthood" in white letters. He also noted the fact that her necklace was a cross pendant. "Where should we talk?"

"Given the subject matter," began Eileen, looking quickly to her side at some of the younger volunteers, "I think it would be best to talk upstairs in my office."

"Fine with me."

"Good," said Eileen with a smile as she turned and went to the nearby stairs, Scott following right behind. The steps were loud, as they lacked cushioning. The two turned left after getting to the second-floor hallway. They passed a couple of rooms with open doors, each one including more people working on laptops or computers. Three of the folks Scott spotted as he walked by were dressed closer to his code.

Finally, they got to what was probably a bedroom before the house was converted to advocacy purposes. It was a large corner room with four windows: one facing the street from which Scott entered the building, two small ones that looked at the street which intersected the initial road, and a fourth facing opposite the first window he noticed. There were four dark green filing cabinets, two placed by the wall with the small windows and another pair to the right of the doorway. A computer, printer, and scanner were situated on two desks in one corner, while a few chairs and a coffee table were on the opposite corner. This was the corner where Eileen and Scott sat down.

"One moment," she said, getting up as soon as she had landed on the chair. Addison saw her close the door. The noises of the activists became muffled by the extra layer. Presumably, it was the same for them. Friedman returned to her seat as Scott took out his notepad, two pens, and a recorder, placing the device on the coffee table. "Sorry about that. I think it would be best to talk away from the others. Some of the young women in particular might be triggered by the talk about Milton."

"That makes sense," said Scott. "Besides, it will make it easier for me to record."

"So, everyone wins. Not bad."

Scott shifted a little in his seat before continuing. There were several political banners on the walls, as well as a few framed newspaper pages. It reminded him of his editor's office and as such, he expected a similar sentiment from the interviewee.

Addison pushed the record button. "So then, just to get started, you've been butting heads with Milton for a long time, correct?"

"Yes, I have," replied Friedman, as though realizing it herself. "Most of the time it's over civil liberties issues, women's health, women's rights. Things like that. I've argued with him more than once on local TV, radio. Not as often as some others, but yes. Plenty of times."

"So, is this why you signed that declaration calling on women to boycott Into Marvelous Light Ministries?"

"I'm sorry?" asked a confused Friedman. Scott paused and then concluded that the confusion stemmed from a lack of specificity.

"Back in 2012, a group of feminist leaders crafted and signed an online declaration calling on a boycott of Into Marvelous Light Ministries because of Milton's sexist rhetoric."

"Oh, I see," nodded Friedman. "I know the petition you mean. But I can tell you with confidence that I never signed that."

"Oh, um," said Scott, "my editor told me that you did."

"Phillips, right?"

"Yes."

"Well, Phillips must have misremembered. I've signed my share of petitions, and I've called for plenty of boycotts. But that was not one of them."

"Oh," said Scott. "Well, um, why didn't you sign the petition?"

Friedman stared at Scott and, with unflinching seriousness, replied, "Because I owe my life to Into Marvelous Light Ministries." The statement and the proceeding explication amazed the journalist.

* * *

She had several streaks of purple hair back then. It was a flavor of the month. Earlier that year, there was pink. Before that, blue. Anything unconventional was worth it. Her outfits reflected this roaring against the norms. No dresses, no pantsuits. Jeans, short-shorts, and revealing shirts. Many of those were tie-dye. After all, the sixties were only freshly buried. The nonconformity remained. Although, in keeping with more traditional ideas, she did have long hair. Her tresses stretched as low as her waist. She often put it in a ponytail, sometimes braided it for special occasions.

There was a group of them sharing a single duplex. People came and went, bringing whatever substances best altered the human consciousness. Alcohol was a mainstay, with beer bottles outnumbering any other liquid container. A Lebanese fellow making his way up to New York introduced them to hookah. They enjoyed it while it was available but switched back to more familiar stuff once he took a bus to Chinatown. Cigarette packs were also prevalent.

The duplex was meat-free—not because everyone there was a vegetarian, but rather because a few were so militant in the diet that the very presence of a former animal in the refrigerator was enough to disgust them. Some residents joked that at the duplex they respected all kinds of grass. She did not identify as any strand of vegetarian, but she also seldom ate surf or turf. Whenever she did, she was eating out. This was a rare occurrence given the expense.

Eileen Friedman did not recall how the people could afford to live there. She knew some folks there had their own money. At least one person was still getting monies from family, apparently in the hopes that he would return home someday. It was not lavish. A few furniture items on the main floor, a television here, and a radio there. Lots of records, lots of music. Residents slept whenever, wherever, and with whomever. There was little tracking of time. It was a little temporal-free society.

"So, wait, wait," began the bearded twenty-something, whose dark brown hair was only a few inches shorter than hers. "You're from Kansas?" He said the name of the state with a faux Southern twang, while carelessly waving around his cigarette-wielding hand.

"Yeah. Kansas," she replied, also holding a cigarette. She put the end of the thin white stick to her lips to ingest more chemicals and blow out more smoke.

"Isn't Kansas totally flat?"

"No, not totally flat," she objected. Her voice was a little louder, successfully speaking over the funky music playing off the vinyl. There were five other people in the room. Three were talking on a couch, a fourth was thinking to himself as the drugs took effect, and the fifth was passed out in a chair.

"But I thought it was totally flat."

"Western Kansas is flat. Eastern Kansas is all sorts of stuff. You know, hills, and, um, rivers, and cities, and waterfalls. All stuff."

"All stuff," nodded the man. "Cool."

"Yeah, cool."

"So Western Kansas is totally flat. But Colorado isn't?"

"No, no," shaking her head in annoyance. "Colorado is flat."

"But Colorado's got the Rockies. Rockies aren't flat."

"Yeah, they've got the Rockies, so people think they're not flat," began Eileen, pausing to take another puff. "But everywhere else is flat. Totally flat."

"Where is it flat, totally flat?" asked the man as he put out his cigarette butt on the floor, adding yet another small burn hole on the abused orange-hued carpet.

"East Colorado."

"East Colorado?"

"East Colorado is totally flat. It looks like Kansas. We hate how no one thinks Colorado is flat when we Kansans know it's very flat."

"So, like, when you're driving through West Kansas and you go into East Colorado, you don't even know you've gone into East Colorado?"

"Yeah."

"Yeah," he said in contemplation. "That's, like, crazy, you know? You can't tell them apart." He smiled as he looked at her again. "Like twins. Colorado and Kansas are twins." He laughed a lot. Soon, the laughter ceased, and the mood turned.

In the days that followed, all the signs pointed to what happened. She was tired all the time, and she was waking up every morning to vomit. Curious, she went to the doctor and had a two-hour Wampole pregnancy test performed. There was little doubt of the results. As a minor, she was able to use her parents' healthcare to pay for the appointment. But everything else was thrown into question when she returned to the duplex, and he was nowhere to be found. Asking around, the others had no idea. It was impossible to find him; she didn't even know his name.

"What should I do?" she asked in tears. Her desperate question was given to a fellow female resident, whom she knew only by the name Gemini.

"Did you try and get an abortion?"

"But that's illegal," replied Eileen, wiping away the water from her reddish eyes.

"So was what he did to you. He basically raped you."

"How do I prove that?"

"You're a minor."

"But where is he? Who is he?"

"I don't know."

"I don't know where to go."

"I know a girl who got knocked up last year. She went to Richmond and got herself fixed up. Of course, it cost money."

"How much?"

"Like two hundred dollars."

"Two hundred dollars?" asked Eileen with widened eyes. "I don't have that kind of money."

"Just a thought."

"Yeah," stated a somber Eileen, looking down at her belly, while holding it with her hand. Her company sat across from her in the living room, looking down in silence before deciding to make the next suggestion.

"Eileen?" she asked, reaching out to grab Eileen's knee and thus getting her attention. "I know of one more place. I don't know if you would want to do it, though."

"What place?"

"Okay, so there's this place near Richmond that girls who have kids go. It's like one of those oldie girls' places. It's run by some Bible-thumpers, but I heard they're helpful. Maybe they can help you put your baby up for adoption?"

"Where are they?"

It was a symmetrical building. There were six windows with black shutters at the front on the first floor and four windows with black shutters on the second floor. The main entrance was covered by an archway, whose gable included the name of the place: "The Ruth and Naomi House." Smaller print below the name noted that it was affiliated with Into Marvelous Light Ministries and was established a few years prior. Nerves and morning sickness made her midsection feel horrible. With a deep breath, she walked to the front and entered a friendly environment. On the wall behind the front desk was a Bible quote: "For whither thou goest, I will go; and where thou lodgest, I will lodge: thy people shall be my people, and thy God my God."[6]

* * *

"How long were you at the Ruth and Naomi House?" asked Scott Addison, while jotting notes on a pad as the recorder continued to tick away.

"Two years," began Eileen. "The first ten months were the toughest. My body didn't like the withdrawal. To say nothing of the rigors of pregnancy. Things got a lot better after Jenny was born. There was a strict religious regimen—you know, curfew, Bible classes every Wednesday, stuff like that. And while Sunday attendance at Into Marvelous Light Church wasn't mandatory, it was encouraged."

"So, you went to Milton's church?"

"Every week," affirmed Eileen. "I didn't consider it a punishment. Services were not boring. I remember they had good music, and Milton's passionate preaching. Say what you will about what he believes; he did a great job of conveying it from a pulpit. He even sang every once in a while. Not often. He was so bashful about it. Not sure why; he was decent enough. On rare occasions, he would join Clayborne and a couple others to do a quartet. Maybe the rarity of his singing made it more precious."

"Going back to the Ruth and Naomi House," inquired Scott, "how helpful were they in getting you back on your feet, so to speak?"

"They were all very helpful. A social worker helped me find a job at a retail store that's now closed. It was open then, and I got to work there full-time. After a while, I saved up enough to rent an apartment for my daughter and I. Since I was so indebted to them, I wanted to give back. I was just breaking even, so money was out of the question. So, I volunteered there. I felt it was the least I could do."

"How did that go?"

"Very well. It was a little strange at first. Seeing young women come in who were just like me only a couple years before. A weird feeling, but also very rewarding as I got to help them."

"That's interesting," Scott replied in sincerity. "Did you run into Milton often?"

"Yes, at least once a week. There were staff meetings he would attend and sometimes give presentations to. We talked a fair amount, even socialized. Never alone, of course. You know about the Billy Graham Rule, right?"

"Yeah, the thing Pence does."

"Exactly. Milton practiced it as well. Whenever we talked, it was always with other people around, in public, etc. Still, we got to the point of first names. He eventually baptized me, as a matter of fact."

"Really?"

"Yup. It was me and five others who joined the church that morning."

"That is something," noted Scott. "I am starting to wonder how you even came to be the way you are now."

"Well," began Eileen with a grin, "for that, you must thank Billie Dietrich."

* * *

It was called a crafts store. That was the simple answer. It was not a convenience store in the traditional sense, as it was closed on Sundays. The size of the building was more comparable to a grocery store, yet the shelves lacked the extensive variety of foods and drinks. Not that there was no food on the shelves. They had a small department with items, and of course, the registers had snacks. Parental complaints led the owner to put the sweet stuff higher up, so little ones could not easily spot them.

Most of the items were craft-related. Pencils, markers, pens, crayons, and a host of other instruments for creating letters and images. Carving knives, clay, beads, string, wicker baskets, thread, needles, and other various things associated with artsy hobbies abounded. Questions on expertise centered on the best kinds of paints, whether this skein of yarn went with that skein of yarn, advice on what tools were optimum for creating Jack-O-Lanterns, and when the next shipment of paints was coming.

Some departments were less centered on that main topic. There was a section focused more on hunting and camping than drawing

pictures or stenciling pieces. That section had pup tents, fishing rods, and even three rows of rifles for sale, ammunition sold separately. There was the aforementioned grocery area, with a short aisle full of milk, orange juice, and assorted fruit drinks intended for family consumption. There was a small selection of frozen foods, cereals, and a few other random products. Another section had a limited supply of generic toys—things like bags of green plastic soldiers, brightly hued water guns, and a small collection of balls for different sports.

Eileen had no specific department. She worked wherever she was needed. On that particular day, she manned the register at the outdoor section. Whenever a question arose about the products, she directed the customer to her male colleague, who, unlike her, was a specialist. Thing is, she seldom recalled being asked such manly queries, as most folk seemed to assume that the man in the department would know more about these matters. She did not mind the stereotyping since, in this case, it was true.

That department was tucked into the far corner, about a hundred feet from the main entrance. There were enough aisles and displays to disrupt a good view of the outside world from her vantage point. Behind their little department were the employees-only sections. Areas invisible to the typical patron. These were the places for storage, bathrooms, offices, and a breakroom with refrigerator and television. Employees were encouraged to bring their meals so as to not be far from the store. During busy times of the year, Eileen worked long shifts, which led to her missing all sunlight in a given day.

She did not mind the excess hours. There was always a bonus for working overtime. The environment was a sociable one, and customers were rarely irritable. Sure, the occasional issue arose, but seldom did they negate the overall eased environment. Many of the folks who came to the store also went to Into Marvelous Light Church, including some who worked at their ministries. Others were local regulars, patrons whom Eileen came to know by name. It was endowed with a small-town wholesomeness.

Eileen was just finishing up a transaction when the store manager showed up. Guthrie by name, his body was rounded, and his head was bald. He often carried a smile, even when addressing serious matters. He rarely raised his voice, and one felt especially wrong in their actions when he did. Like the other employees, he wore a red collared shirt and blue pants. The only real difference was his name tag, which had a golden background versus the beige for sales associates and blue for shift leaders. Eileen detected his presence quickly, for he talked with a few of the customers on his way to her register.

"Hey, boss," she said when he approached.

"Hey, Eileen," began Guthrie in a folksy voice. "Could I have you do a favor real quick?"

"Um, sure. What is it?"

"Follow me," he replied. Eileen walked behind her superior, leaving her coworker behind to look over a department with only one patron looking at the products. Had there been more potential consumers, she would have felt more of an impetus to stay.

"You see out there?" asked Guthrie as the two got a good view of the storefront. There was a woman by the main entrance, passing out papers. "She's some sort of activist or something. Point is, she shouldn't be there. It scares away the customers, and we don't want to scare away customers."

"Yes."

"I would call the cops, but they would probably scare away the customers even more. So, I was wondering if you could tell her to leave. Normally, I would do it, but I feel it would be best if it came from you. Do you see where I'm going?"

"Yes, I do."

"So, if you could please tell her to leave, it would be much appreciated."

"Sure thing. Right on it, boss," nodded Eileen.

"Atta girl," replied Guthrie, who then turned his frame to see to another matter within his store. He was a busy man.

Eileen thought little of the assignment. Occasionally a solicitor or loiterer would show up at their front door. It was a prime spot to perform outreach to the broader community. Sometimes people or groups worked out deals with the store to sit out front and appeal to patrons. Most of the time it was local youth groups selling cookies and cupcakes to raise money for charity. During the Christmas season, the Salvation Army was known to have a red bucket and a constant ringer. The activist was not on the approved list.

As Eileen got closer, she got a better look at the woman. She was statuesque, slender, and had golden brown, frizzy hair. With fine features and a natural energy, the political solicitor could not have been more than a year or two older than Eileen. Most of the people walking east or west ignored her or weakly begged off her handouts. A few took them and looked but seemed only vaguely interested. As Eileen pushed open one of the glass doors at the front, she felt a parallel between her and the activist: Both knew what it was like to upsell something and have most refuse.

"Excuse me, sorry," spoke up Eileen, drawing the attention of the activist. The lady turned to face the retail worker with a look of confused annoyance. "Yes, um, hello. Sorry to bother you, but my boss would like it if you went somewhere else."

"Somewhere else?"

"Yes, ma'am," hesitated Eileen. "Yes, um, you see, this is a business. We are not a political group or something. You see what I mean?"

"Everything is political," declared the stern activist. "The personal, the business, everything. No one minds the presence of politics when they agree with it."

"I mind," countered Eileen. "I think there's a time and place for everything. And not. And I mean, my store doesn't allow solicitors right outside of our entrance. It's the law. We even have a sign, see?" Eileen pointed behind herself, directing the activist to a simple yet visible warning message against unwelcomed solicitation attached to the glass wall.

"How much does your boss pay you?"

"Well, he—"

"Does he pay you as much as your male coworkers?" inquired the activist. "He probably pays you less."

"Ma'am, I don't know what my coworkers make. It's against company policy to talk about wages."

"I bet it is." She cynically smiled. "He pays you less, and then sics you on me. Divide, subjugate, and conquer. Typical patriarchy."

"Ma'am, I really need you to leave."

The activist thought for a moment. Eileen was getting nervous. While she was thinner, the solicitor was taller and feistier. Finally, she spoke up. "Tell you what ... I'll go across the street if you agree to go to a huddle meeting I'm organizing."

"A huddle meeting?"

"Yes," said the activist as she handed the retail worker a single sheet of paper. Eileen looked down at the handout. It contained all the details of time and place. "It happens tomorrow night. If you agree to show up, I'll leave."

"Okay, deal," nodded Eileen, knowing no better course.

"Good," said the activist with a smile. "See you then. And if you have any questions, just use the contact information below."

"Billie Dietrich," read Eileen.

"Yes, that's me."

"Fine. I'll be there."

"Good," noted Billie. "Then my work here is done." Dietrich did as she consented to do and walked across the street. Eileen tucked the sheet into her pants pocket and then reentered the store, holding the door open briefly for a customer to exit.

"Good job, Eileen," said her boss as she walked toward her assigned department. "Much appreciated!"

"No problem, boss."

* * *

A balmy evening in Virginia. No surprise. The humidity thickened the air and welcomed a host of flying insects and long strands of abandoned spider webs. Eileen removed a thin layer of sweat from her forehead as she approached the address for the meeting. It was a house, connected to independent units on either side. Squeezed together. Going up a few porch steps, she saw a little bit of the goings-on behind the pulled curtains. There were two or three young women visible through the curtain opening and the semi-transparent threads. The screen door had a simple paper sign with marker encouraging any to enter. It was not that clandestine an occasion.

Eileen hesitated. Despite the laconic welcome statement, the door was still closed. She did not feel right about simply charging in on those already present. Some of the talk inside sounded confrontational. A potential argument. She was unsure, the perceived hostility adding to her apprehension. After a few moments of pause, she decided to knock. Opening the screen door, she balled a fist and hit it against the hard, wooden barrier. The conversation halted; then two voices briefly said something about the noise. Eileen heard footsteps and then saw the turning of the knob. The loud opening of the door presented a nerdy, petite woman. She was the first to gaze upon the invited retail worker. Eileen briefly smiled.

"You here for the meeting?" she stoically inquired, her eyes, hidden behind glasses, studying the uniform of the knocker.

"Yes," replied Eileen, quickly adding, "Billie invited me."

"Come on in," said the short woman, with a pinch more emotion than before.

Eileen nodded and did so, walking past the door-opener. She heard the portal close behind her as she cautiously walked forward into a circle of women. There were eight of them altogether. They had rearranged the chairs and two couches to form a circle. There were a few small tables between sitting arrangements, with drinks ranging from water to beer positioned on coasters. No one wore any formal attire. Six of them wore shorts, while the other two wore jeans. All wore t-shirts. Five were Caucasian; two were Latinas; and one, the only one wearing a hat, was African-American.

"Ah, Eileen, you made it," said a cordial Billie Dietrich. She was sitting in a rocking chair that directly faced the entrance. "Come and sit down. You want anything to drink?"

"Just water," she replied, while sitting on the empty chair nearest to the door. "It's a hot night. Really humid."

"Tell me about it," said one of the Latina women. "It reminds me of the mother country."

Billie got up to hand Eileen a glass with several cubes of ice. She then took hold of a pitcher of water found on a coffee table at the center of the circle of seats and poured the contents into the glass until it neared the brim. Eileen was only too happy to drink after walking through that weather. Dietrich put the pitcher back onto the surface of the table and returned to her seat.

"Why did you bring her here?" asked the critical African-American woman. She draped her body over one of the plusher chairs, her legs hanging over one arm, while her back leaned against the other. Her unimpressed sentiment seemed perpetual. "I thought capitalist tools weren't allowed."

"Oh, Chiquita, not this again," bemoaned one of the other women. "If she wants to be here, it's her right."

"Rights," Chiquita laughed in cynicism. "Same industries that segregate here and exploit abroad would love to hear us talk about their rights."

"Now, now," said Billie to her peer. "This is a movement for all women. And all women means all women."

"Including the capitalist tools," chimed in Eileen, eliciting a fleeting expression of amusement from Chiquita.

"Anyway, Eileen," began Billie. "We were just talking about what we could do to get the ERA passed."

"ERA? Oh, you mean the Equal Rights Amendment, right?"

"Give the lady a prize," muttered Chiquita, shifting her burgundy newsboy cap.

"And I was just saying that we need to hold a rally," explained the nerdy gal who opened the door for Eileen. "Really show them we want this for Virginia."

"If we could arrange something with NOW and VERA, I bet we could get a lot of people in downtown Richmond."

"So what?" critically interjected Chiquita. As she made her points, she moved to sit more properly in her chair. "Delegate Thomson is on the Privileges and Elections Committee, and he always makes sure to stop the ERA from going anywhere."

"What about protesting him at home?" suggested Eileen, turning five of the eight heads in her direction. "I mean, if you want to lodge a complaint at my store, it's better to go right to the manager than to one of the sales associates."

"It's a thought," acknowledged one of the other women.

"Alexandria is a bit of a stretch, but it could be done in a day."

"Yeah, and DC is right across the river, so we could really get some likeminded people on board. Maybe oust him from his seat."

"Good ideas, everyone," said Billie as she looked at Eileen, who smiled at her ability to provide good advice soon after joining.

* * *

"I was still the greenest member of the group," recalled Eileen to Scott Addison, the recorder continuing to capture the sounds, while the reporter jotted notes. "There were times when what they talked about was above me, little bits of ignorance here and there. But I learned. I got their respect. Even Chiquita came to respect me . . . in her own way, of course."

Addison smiled at the remark, still looking down at his paper. "My life was very busy back then. Maybe even busier than it is now. Whenever I wasn't home with Jenny, I was at Guthrie's, church, the Ruth and Naomi House, or the huddle.

"Most weeks, my schedule was as follows: Sunday morning and Wednesday evening was church and Bible study. Monday through Friday, during the day, I worked my retail job. A couple evenings, I volunteered at the Ruth and Naomi House, and Saturdays I did canvassing and advocacy meetings."

"And you didn't see any contradiction between being active at Milton's home for single mothers and being involved in a feminist group?"

"Not at first, no," noted Eileen, garnering interest from Scott. "To me, the feminist huddle was just an extension of the Ruth and Naomi House. Helping women, bettering women's lives. Same idea, just a little more political. And you have to understand, things were different back then. Milton was different."

"In what way?"

"Well, like a lot of those Southern evangelicals, he didn't really have an opinion on abortion. He never liked it, but he didn't talk about it all that much. When *Roe* was handed down, it didn't even get a mention the following Sunday. Truth be told, I wasn't that passionate about it either. I didn't care about abortion back then. *Roe* was too late for me, and by that time, I was glad I had Jenny."

"So, when did things start to change?"

"1976," Eileen reflected, briefly tilting her gaze upward to verify the date in her mind. "Yes, yes, it was 1976. I remember because Billie and a few others were going up to DC to help with a campaign rally for Carter. Problem is, it meant that we couldn't have our usual Saturday huddle meeting. So the group, without my input, decided to move the meeting to the following Sunday morning. I debated with myself which thing I was going to attend, worship or the huddle. Honestly, it was a coin toss. How different things would be if I had chosen worship! Anyway, I decided to go to the huddle meeting instead."

"And then what happened?" asked Scott, looking up at the interviewee.

"Nothing on Sunday," responded Eileen, her tone shifting into an ominous tone. "Then came Monday morning."

* * *

It was a cold, rainy start to the work week. A layer of gray clouds darkened the morning sky. Large puddles made walking a splashing hazard. Precipitation came and went sporadically. Sometimes, it got pretty heavy, though a few minutes would pass, and it was reduced to fluttery sprinkles. The front door was locked, leaving Eileen at the mercy of the elements for four minutes. Fortunately, it was one of the lesser rainfalls that harassed her during the time of waiting. Through the glass barrier separating her and the interior, Guthrie eventually came to the front and noticed her outside.

He undid the lock and pushed opened one of the two main doors. Business was not to begin for another ten minutes. They exchanged pleasantries, he with his usual big smile. Eileen struggled to recall anything small about Guthrie. His frame, his smile, his personality. He was a big guy. She did her usual tasks in preparation for the regular hours. Eileen tidied up a couple places in her assigned department. Guthrie had taught her how to start up the register for the day, and by this point, she was able to do so with ease. A quick trip to the employee bathroom to make sure her uniform was in good order, and then she returned to her station, just in time for the first customers to arrive.

Mondays were typically a scarce time. Morning and afternoon were usually reserved for employees to clean up the store, stock up on new items, and rearrange products where necessary. One of her coworkers, a woman who worked in that wing of the crafts departments, took to altering the balls of yarn. Eileen's coworker seemed to bear an inherent knowledge of what colors were best put to display at certain times of year. Eileen manned the register while watching her place orange and black skeins near the top and upper middle of the shelves. Red, white, and blue were placed at the bottom, with some of the red and all the green shades placed in the lower middle.

Their particular department had only a dozen or so patrons all morning. This was typical. As noon came, the coworker asked and received permission to go on her lunch break. She went to the back and clocked out temporarily, putting on a raincoat before exiting the store. Eileen was alone in the department. She did not mind. Lunch hour on a Monday tended to be just as scarce, if not scarcer, than morning. Normally, things ticked up closer to the late afternoon, when mothers brought in children fresh out of school or people who left their jobs a little early came for shopping.

"Alright, that'll be $4.76," said Eileen to the customer as she carefully stuffed each bundle of string into a paper bag bearing, in dark red print, the signature of the store owner.

"This should cover it," said the patron, handing Eileen a ten-dollar bill. With the bag standing tall on the counter, Eileen rung up the amount, with the register making a binging noise as it opened. "You know, Eileen, you should tell your boss to switch to plastic bags. They're stronger than paper, and they save the trees."

"I'll let him know, Gretchen," Eileen replied as she closed the register and handed the patron her change. As the customer put the money into her purse, Eileen slowly moved the loaded bag toward her.

"Thank you," said Gretchen as she took hold of the paper handles. "Oh, and Eileen, this weekend some of the girls are going out. I'd be only too happy to buy you your first legal beer."

"Thanks," laughed Eileen, "I'll think about it."

"Okay, take care," said Gretchen, purse slung over her right shoulder and bag held by her left hand.

"Bye," said Eileen as the customer exited. Eileen took to fixing up things here and there in a compulsive manner. A ball of yarn that seemed to jut out a little more than the others? Fixed. A small piece of receipt paper that ended up on the floor on the customer side of the register space? Thrown away. Little things.

After accomplishing another minor repair to the overall appearance to the department, Eileen saw another familiar face perusing the shelves. She was in her forties. Her light blonde hair was starting to gray. She was a little shorter than Eileen and a little wider. The woman had a wedding band, a modest dress, and a small purse. She seemed to make her way specifically toward Eileen, waiting for the department to be as vacant as possible. It was a good time to approach. Eileen met her halfway on the way to the register, happy to see the person and suspecting nothing of concern.

"Hello, Mrs. Milton."

"Hello, Eileen," Virginia Milton kindly greeted. "How are you doing?"

"Doing good."

"How is Jenny handling kindergarten?"

"She's doing good," replied Eileen. "She's making a lot of friends and keeps bringing home drawings of me and animals."

"That's nice," said Virginia. "Well, all three of mine have already gone through that grade. So if you need any advice, I'm here."

"Okay," nodded Eileen, who noticed a faint change in temperament as Virginia went toward a subject that was likely her primary reason for coming to the store.

"You know, we missed you at church yesterday morning," began the wife of the senior pastor. "And I was going to introduce you to a nice young man who started attending."

"Oh, sorry about that," Eileen replied. "Something came up."

"Was it a family emergency?" pried Virginia, keeping an eased outward demeanor.

"Oh, no, no, everyone is okay. You see, I belong to a huddle group, and while we usually meet on Saturdays, it got pushed to Sunday instead."

"A huddle group?"

"Yeah, you know who Billie Dietrich is, right?"

"Vaguely," Virginia cautiously noted.

"Well, we're in a group together that tries to help women. You know, just like your husband's Ruth and Naomi House."

"I see."

"Don't worry, I'll definitely be there next Sunday. I love Rev. Sammy's preaching. And singing, whenever he's willing to do so."

"Yes," briefly laughed Virginia at that last comment. "Well, I need to get going to see about a few things. Have a good day, Eileen."

"You, too, Mrs. Milton."

On Wednesday evening, all appeared as usual. There were seventeen women present for the Bible study at the Ruth and Naomi House. They used one of several simple meeting rooms for the class. In the corner was a table with a coffee machine, disposable cups, napkins, a water pitcher, and two plates of snacks. They sat in a circle, using folding chairs to sit on. Each had a Bible and a study guide, provided by the House. Mrs. Milton was leading the course and had an extra booklet with questions meant to promote conversation among the younger women around her. There were three other classes meeting in other rooms. They were about the same size and likewise comprised of current and former House guests, as well as current staff and volunteers. All female.

Tonight's session was centered on the parable of the persistent widow—the unnamed woman Jesus spoke of who constantly demanded justice from an unethical, irreligious judge. Despite his moral shortcomings, the judge eventually granted justice to the widow due to her constant demands. Virginia did not give a political message for the subject, nor did anyone bring up such a parallel. But it was in Eileen's heart. She enjoyed passages like these, for to her it gave sacred justification for her activism. As the conversation was dying down, Virginia looked at the clock and saw the hour was late.

"Well, if we have no other matters to broach, I would say we can now come together and pray," said the leader. The women got up from their metal seats and drew into a smaller circle, holding hands with eyes closed. Mrs. Milton offered up a brief prayer, shorter than the one given at the start of the class. "Amen," she concluded, with a few of the others saying it after her. "Now remember, ladies, next week we cover the passage when Jesus encounters the Canaanite woman. It is found in Matthew fifteen."

Virginia then approached Eileen, who was saying goodbye to a couple of exiting classmates. "Eileen?"

"Yes, Mrs. Milton?"

"Could I talk to you in private?"

"Sure," replied a confused Eileen. The two waited for the others to leave for the evening. Virginia walked toward the door and closed it. Her younger companion was feeling a bit nervous, as though she was in trouble. "Is there a problem?"

"It depends," replied Virginia, gently drawing close to Eileen. "I just have a few questions. And remember, it is perfectly okay to confide in me."

"Okay," responded an uncomfortable Eileen.

"Have you had a good experience here at Ruth and Naomi?"

"Yes, definitely."

"And you respect my husband and his ministries?"

"Yes," affirmed Eileen, who briefly laughed as she added, "I kind of owe him my life."

"And above all else, you love God, yes?"

"Yes," answered a perplexed Eileen. "Why wouldn't I?"

"I've been looking into this Dietrich woman you said you are working with. This huddle group you speak of. Do you realize the things they stand for?"

"I mean, they support women's rights. Women's health. Things that help elevate women. You know, just like here."

"Eileen, I am afraid you are very mistaken," stated a worried Virginia, holding Eileen's shoulders and staring into her eyes. "Dietrich and her allies are radicals. They hate God; they hate the Gospel; and they hate men."

"That's not true," insisted Eileen, struggling a little under the grip on her shoulders. "I mean, yeah, they aren't very religious, but they don't hate church. A few of them are glad I work here. They see the House as allies. Really, they do."

"Dietrich is a socialist. And she supports murder."

"Murder?"

"That's what abortion is, isn't it? The taking of a human life?"

"Mrs. Milton, please. I don't support murder."

"How about sodomy?"

"Sodomy?"

"Dietrich is a lesbian."

"She is?"

"That is what people have been saying."

"Who said that?"

"She's a feminist. And feminists, without exception, support lesbianism, child killing, and sodomy. They are modern day pagans."

"Mrs. Milton, this is crazy," Eileen insisted all the stronger, getting the older woman to let loose of her grip. "There are plenty of Christians who are feminists."

"Maybe long ago, maybe when I was a child. But not now. Feminism is different now. It has been hijacked by the devil."

"Then maybe someone like me could un-hijack it," declared Eileen, surprising Virginia with her declaration. There was a pause as the class leader collected herself.

"You have two options, Eileen," stated Virginia. "You can either keep going to Into Marvelous Light, or you can surrender your soul to Dietrich."

"Let me think about it," pleaded Eileen. "I've done a lot of stuff with the huddle. They would feel betrayed if I just decided one day to quit."

"You need to."

"Just please let me think about this. I promise I'll know what I want to do soon."

"Okay, okay," gently conceded Virginia. She patted the young lady on the shoulder. "I will pray for you."

Sunday morning began as it always did for Eileen. Her daughter was awake before she was, the noise of the youngster prompting the mother to rise. After some extra effort, Eileen got Jenny ready for worship. A few months before, she had bought a used car from a local dealer who happened to go to Into Marvelous Light. As a result, she got a discount. Its paint job was chipped, and there were some dents here and there. However, in keeping with the claims of the seller, the interior was strong and got her where she needed to go. Jenny sat in the front passenger seat, with Eileen instinctively putting her right arm in front of her child whenever she had to come to a sudden stop.

Eileen did not attend Sunday school. Had she done so, odds are good the young mother would have heard snippets about the sermon from those who attended the early service. With her busy schedule, she felt the Wednesday study was enough. Kind faces greeted her, as well as hundreds of less familiar ones. It was a big congregation that was only increasing in size. Because of her work at the Ruth and Naomi House, Eileen was most familiar with the members who were connected to that charity. She also knew the daycare staff. Sometimes, Eileen had

Jenny sit with her in church; other times, she had her go to children's church instead. That morning, she dropped Jenny off at the daycare center. It was a decision she later agreed was the right one.

Things began as typical for a worship service full of sporadic emotion and improvised messages. A pleasant welcome was given by Beverley Clayborne. Some announcements, and then the music began. It was a fusion of contemporary drums and guitar with traditional piano and organ. Songs ranged from newly released hits on the Christian music charts to old hymns that many had memorized as youths. Many lifted their hands in worship; others swayed to the melody. They stopped short of speaking in tongues, although that was largely because church leadership frowned upon the practice.

For those first twenty or thirty minutes, Eileen was reminded why it was such a hard choice last week to go to the huddle meeting. She was starting to regret the decision. After all, little was actually done at the meetup. Just some procedural stuff and a few minor updates. She could have learned about those things later. The Reverend Sammy Milton was going up to the podium. He had been on the stage the whole time.

"Our Scripture reading for this morning," began Milton, his voice booming throughout the large sanctuary, "comes from Romans, chapter one, verses twenty-one to twenty-seven. Please rise in respect for the reading of God's Word."

The congregation obliged, with all save the very elderly and the wheelchair-bound getting to their feet. Milton read the text from his worn Bible. Some of the golden lettering on the cover had chipped away. His blue eyes glided along the text, periodically popping up to look at his audience:

"Because that, when they knew God, they glorified him not as God, neither were thankful; but became vain in their imaginations, and their foolish heart was darkened. Professing themselves to be wise, they became fools, And changed the glory of the uncorruptible God into an image made like to corruptible man, and to birds, and four-footed beasts, and creeping things . . ."[7]

While Milton read, Eileen struggled to figure out what the sermon would be about. She looked down at the worship bulletin for clues, but the message was simply titled, "Even Their Women." She still suspected nothing as Milton continued to recite the sacred text: "For this cause God gave them up unto vile affections: for even their women did change the natural use into that which is against nature: And likewise also the men, leaving the natural use of the woman, burned in their lust one toward another; men with men working that which is unseemly, and receiving in themselves that recompense of their error which was meet."

Milton solemnly closed the black leather-bound Bible and held it up while looking at the faithful. "This is God's Word." Many nodded at the statement as Milton gently placed the closed Book on the podium and began his preaching. At first, his words did not clearly convey to Eileen where he was going with his message, but then it became all too clear.

"Even their women. Even them," stated Milton. "Friends, we have, as the Roman church of old, a pestilence that threatens the moral and spiritual fiber of even our women. The pillars of our church. The backbone of our charity. God made man and woman. He gave them special orders and made them in specific ways to compliment the family unit which He divinely ordained at Creation. These unnatural ideas that are flooding our culture and even our community must be stopped.

"It has come to my attention that a subversive group is holding meetings and rallying support for its radical agenda here in this city and in the surrounding counties. They come as wolves in sheeps' clothing. Some are already starting to fall because they call themselves 'feminists.'" Eileen blinked in surprise.

She became increasingly fidgety as Milton continued: "Do not be deceived! These are not the benevolent feminists of old—those who under the Christian banner won the right to vote, who demanded equality, and who sought to purge society of the evils of abortion and drunkenness. No! These are the same godless false prophets that tried to destroy our country a decade ago.

"Even as that decade is dead, this plague continues. Feminists are a pariah to family values; their message is hostile to the Bible; and they will stop at nothing to destroy marriage, the church, and this God-blest nation! They promote the same sinful lusts that brought Hell out of Heaven upon Sodom. They demand the murder of babies; they cheer the march of godless Communism; and they seek nothing short of the eradication of men. Stay away from them! Flee them! Run away from them faster than Joseph ran away from Potiphar's wife!"

Milton's sermon lasted for another ten minutes, but Eileen heard none of it. Enraged and saddened, she rose from her pew and stormed out of the sanctuary. Ignoring all else around her, she went to the children's center, took her daughter out, lied about wanting to bring her to the worship service, exited the building, and then drove away.

* * *

"And I seldom returned," recalled Friedman to Scott Addison. "Maybe once or twice a year, I would go. I eventually reconciled with my parents, so they would come into town to visit me and their granddaughter. When they came on weekends, they always wanted to go to Milton's church. They watched him on TV and were big fans."

"So, you quit going regularly after that sermon," said Addison, looking over his written notes. He looked up at the interviewee once again. "You wear a cross."

"Yes," laughed Friedman, who briefly looked down at the necklace and held the aforementioned item in her hand for a few moments. "Leaving Into Marvelous Light didn't mean I left the faith. I still believe. Weeks later, I went to a local UCC church. Their social views were identical to my own, so it was a perfect match."

"I see," observed Scott.

"But yes, from there on, Milton and I were enemies. I purposely fell out of touch with him and his wife. My new friends at the UCC supplanted my old friends at Into Marvelous Light. The hardest part was quitting Ruth and Naomi. I enjoyed volunteering there. But it was still Milton. His presence was assumed. I couldn't stay. I took that time and used it to work at other places, including Richmond's Planned Parenthood clinic. My UCC family was very helpful in pointing me in the right direction."

"And you debated Milton on TV many times, correct?"

"Yes," nodded Eileen. "Sometimes heated, sometimes civil. More civil than heated, really. There was still some respect—a vestige of appreciation from me and a remembrance of better days from him. At least, that is how I think it was."

"Okay," replied Scott, assuming the interview was almost concluded.

Friedman thought for a moment. As Scott was about to push the button on his digital voice recorder, her words stopped him. "You know, there is one more story I need to tell you about Milton. One I think is very important."

"Okay," said Scott, leaning back into his chair, leaving the recorder alone.

"This one happened a few years later ..."

* * *

They were tired but accomplished. For weeks, Eileen Friedman, Billie Dietrich, and a group of other volunteers had pushed to get out the word about voter registration. Clipboards in hand, they ventured out to the surrounding community. They knocked on doors, waited outside businesses, and even met folks leaving church. Inquiries were always the same: have you registered to vote yet in the Commonwealth of Virginia? Some kindly brushed them away; others answered in the affirmative. Yet many said no. These were the ones for which they got the information and filled out the paperwork.

Eileen used up nearly all her accrued vacation time at Guthrie's to spend hours and hours getting people ready for the upcoming election. She was surprised at how many people were not registered. One of the older "Authentic Virginians" in her huddle explained that was due to the once-existing state laws that greatly curbed suffrage. The poll tax, in particular, which was still fresh for many minds, made voting too expensive for the average working-class adult, black or white. Many also felt politics too far removed from their daily struggles. That was usually the biggest objection spoken in response to her work. What's the point? Why bother? Eileen always had responses for those.

While open to anyone, the huddle primarily focused on getting women registered. Many were still convinced that it was not a woman's place to get involved in that traditionally male sphere. However, enough modern sentiment had seeped into the area that changing their minds was not a challenge. The huddle wanted more women voters—not simply because of the benefits of an expanded electorate, the obligations of citizenry, or the sophisticated twentieth century mentality toward gender equality. Billie assured the others that the more women voted, the more progressive society would become.

The need seemed especially urgent for that election season. President Jimmy Carter was dealing with a multitude of problems. His humiliating efforts in trying to handle the Iranian Revolution, coupled with economic recession and the gas crisis, formed a testimony against him having a second term. His support among fellow Southern Baptists, once strong, was visibly ebbing away. The actor-turned-governor was gaining momentum. And the nascent Religious Right was steamrolling into the public consciousness, with Reverends Sammy Milton and Johnny Canker leading the charge. Dietrich and the others stressed the need to vote against this onslaught, to stay the course with Carter. He was not perfect, she insisted, but he was a better ally on various women's issues than the challenger.

"Almost there," happily spoke Eileen to Billie. Both were carrying large amounts of filled-out paperwork. A kind soul held the door open for the two radicals, to which they both expressed a brief thanks. "Where do we go again?"

"That way," Billie spoke with confidence, pointing with her head. Eileen nodded as the two turned right and went down a corridor at the county courthouse. A small sign placed along the side of the hallway directed them further. Turning again, they were in the correct office and before the correct desk.

With thuds, they placed the heavy paperwork on the front desk. They asked the secretary to see the local member of the Board of Elections. She obliged and exited the room. Moments later, a man entered the space. Eileen looked at him with curiosity. He seemed familiar, but she could not identify him at that moment. A balding man with a beard, he wore a pinstripe suit and black tie.

"How can I help you fine ladies?"

"We're turning in some voter registration forms," replied Billie. She knew the routine, as she had done plenty of voter drives in the past.

"Uh-huh," he said.

"So, if we could have these registered, finalized, you know the drill," said Billie.

"And why would I do that?"

"Excuse me?" interjected Eileen.

"These are legally acquired voter registration forms," added Billie. "By law, you have to process them."

"These are not valid forms."

"Yes, they are," declared Billie, turning the head of a person in the hallway who was walking by the open door of the office.

"No, they are not," he said in sinister firmness. "These are brain-washed individuals whom radical feminists like yourself convinced to vote against good Christian morality."

"You've got to be kidding me," said Eileen, who also realized where she knew the man. Not on an acquaintance basis, but as a face, nonetheless.

"Don't you realize that this is the twentieth century?" stated Billie.

"Don't you realize that I'm the only member of the Board of Elections in this county?" he struck back. "Now take your propaganda out of here, or I am calling security."

In angered silence, the two activists heaved their hefty loads and left the courthouse without incident. They did not begin talking again until they left the building when Eileen uttered what had been on her mind: "I know that man."

"Do you know where he lives?" asked Billie. "Because we could get a bunch of people to picket his place."

"I don't know where he lives," responded Eileen. "I know that he is an elder at Milton's church."

"So, we both know who was really responsible for this."

"Yeah," replied Eileen as the two made it to her car and left the downtown area.

Later that day, when politics was thought to be dormant in her mind, Eileen was running an errand. Just a few groceries she needed to buy. Jenny was still at school. A jug of milk, some cereal, and fresh fruit. She broke a ten-dollar bill on it and got some dollars back in change. While a car-owner, she walked to the store. Gas was scarce; if she could walk to a place, she did so. Each arm bore a brown paper bag. They were not heavy, and she made the journey with relative ease.

Then she saw him. Her attention came to his presence when he closed his car door with a thud. Her placid sojourn became enraged as the frustration from earlier welled up within. To see him there, casually going about his business, made her sick. His pudgy frame looked more obese, his smile more sadistic. His sapphire eyes were a pair of putrid lakes. When he saw her, he waved in civility. However, she was having none of it. She put down the two bags on the parking lot asphalt and rushed toward him in indignation.

"You're really something, you know that?" Eileen declared in ire, bringing a confused look on the countenance of Sammy Milton.

"What do you mean? Is this about that one debate—"

"Debate? You know very well what I'm talking about."

"Um, no, I don't," said Milton truthfully, but his words were taken as mere fuel for the fire within Eileen.

"Don't play stupid. You know Dabney. He's an elder at your stupid church."

"Dabney?" replied Milton, who thought a moment and was enlightened. "Oh, yes, Dabney. I know him."

"You must have thought you were so smart, so freaking smart," ranted Eileen. "Have him work at the Board of Elections. Have him oversee voter registration. And then have him reject my forms out right. Sexist pig. Of course, he goes to your church; of course, he'd screw Billie and me over. I bet you're on your way to laugh it up, aren't you?"

"Um, no, I'm not. I have an interview with the radio—"

"I don't freaking care what you have!" shouted Eileen. "You won't get away with this. I'm going to sue Dabney. I'm going to tell everyone about your sexist, patriarchal conspiracy, and it's going to ruin you!"

With that, Eileen turned away and stormed off, nearly forgetting to pick up her two grocery bags that she had placed on the blacktop. Milton was left pondering what Eileen had said. This was the first time he had heard of any of it. Eileen did not look back. She kept walking.

Later that night, she was at the house that Billie and a few others rented. Unable to get a babysitter, Jenny went with her. At this point in the warm evening, she was asleep on one of the couches downstairs.

"Then you walked away?" asked an amused Billie.

"And I didn't even look back," replied a proud Eileen.

"That's so rad."

"I know, right?"

"It's also the highlight of this whole episode," added Billie, the mood of the conversation returning to a dourer climate.

"So, what did your friend at the ACLU have to say?"

"The good news," began Billie, "is that she said the case is an easy one. The Board of Elections is clearly wrong in this affair. They should have processed our registration forms. So eventually, if we sue, we will win."

"But?"

Billie took a deep breath before continuing. "But it will take time. First, we'll need to deliver the complaint to Dabney. Then we need to get it to a judge. Unfortunately, the jurisdiction falls to a man who was appointed by the Byrd Organization. According to my ACLU friend, he's on record saying he still supports school segregation. So if he's bad on race issues, you bet gender isn't going to be much better."

"So, we transfer the venue, right?"

"Which will take time. As will the effort to get an injunction allowing our forms to get processed. And we haven't even gotten into the appeals situation."

"So, we'll miss the deadline? That is the bad news, right?"

"Right."

"So, he won after all," whispered Eileen.

"I keep thinking of what Chiquita told me weeks back," contemplated Billie. "When I told her we were going to help register women, she said it was pointless. She said the system won't allow it. I brushed her off. I told her not to worry, that the laws had changed. But she was still critical, warned me that something would stop us."

"Why do I always hate it when she's right?"

"Because she never had anything nice to say."

"That's probably it."

"Anyway," said Billie, "my lawyer friend should get here early in the morning. We'll all go to the courthouse. Dabney should be there. And when we see him, we'll give him something he can't reject."

"Yeah."

"Since Jenny's already out, if you want to spend the night here, go ahead."

"Thanks," said Eileen, looking down as she continued. "I still can't believe he's going to win. I hate how he's going to win. Milton is behind all this. I know he is."

"Well, maybe taking down Dabney will help take down Milton."

"Yeah, maybe."

* * *

Up the courthouse stairs went the three women, walking side-by-side as though in a line of battle. On the right was the attorney, wearing a blue pantsuit and heels. In the center was Eileen, wearing her best dress, which she often wore for church. To the left was Billie, wearing jeans. In committed purpose, they went through the doors, entering the marble and stone interior. They ventured down the same hallway that the activists had walked the day before. They saw the same sign for where to go and then turned into the office space. They kept up their formation, readied for any resistance.

Eileen was initially surprised to see Milton there. He was talking with Dabney. She could not tell if the lawyer or Billie also were taken by Milton's presence. They kept their walk toward the front desk, where the two enemies were situated. As they got closer, Eileen decided that it made sense for Milton to be there. He was standing in wicked solidarity with his co-conspirator. She was the one who held the legal complaint. She jumped at the chance to serve it to Dabney and, by extension, to strike at Milton. His blue eyes finally caught sight of the trio. He gave a pleasant smile and welcomed them.

"Good morning, ladies," said the preacher. "Dabney and I were just talking about you. Weren't we, Dabney?"

"Yes, Sammy," said the board member, his head bowed in guilt.

"You see, the other day I was informed that my friend Dabney here was not fulfilling his duties as a member of the Board of Elections. This would reflect badly, not just on his secular profession, but also on my church as he is a prominent member. An elder, in fact. So, I gave him a call, and we discussed things last night. For further counsel, we agreed to continue our conversation at his office this morning. We agreed that he had something to say to you. Don't you, Dabney?"

"Yes, Sammy," he said, and then turned to face the three women on the other side of the front desk. "I am sorry for rejecting your voter registration forms. It was wrong-headed of me to not process them."

"And?" Milton egged on.

"And if you can bring them to me today, I promise that I will make sure they are processed and, if found legitimate, will be confirmed by the deadline."

"There we go," said Milton as he patted Dabney on the back. "You see the beauty of contrition?"

"Wait a minute," started the attorney. "You're going to agree to process the forms?"

"Yes."

"And you will not discriminate against my clients again?"

"Yes."

"So sorry to waste your time, ma'am," said Milton to the attorney. "If I had been made aware of this problem sooner, I would have dealt with it sooner. Still, this is a beautiful town, and I highly advise that you see the sights while you're here."

"First and foremost, Rev. Milton, there is still the issue of getting my clients' forms processed. Business first."

"By all means," said Milton in a welcoming voice. "Dabney and I will be waiting here. We are assuming you will be right back."

"That we will," said Eileen with a stubborn confidence not echoed within herself. As they left, she simply felt great remorse.

* * *

"Billie was cynical about Milton's actions," recounted Friedman to Addison. "She was convinced that the real reason for his stepping in was to save face. After all, she later told me, being connected to a blatantly sexist clerk who refused to allow women to vote would have been a PR disaster. But I don't buy that."

"How come?"

"Firstly, you and I both know Milton didn't care about being popular. He stood for what he stood for, hang the consequences."

"And second?"

"Because of the look he gave me. I mean, I bet he was confident. He probably assumed those women we registered would vote for Reagan. And given the election results, he was probably right. But that look.

That look he gave me. Those blue eyes were so expressive. The way he looked at me after we finished turning in the paperwork. It was the same kind of look that a parent gives their child when they've accomplished something. It was like he was proud of me for doing what I did. It felt sincere. It felt like he was rooting for me, that he wanted me to help people, and he was glad I was doing so."

"I think I know what you mean."

"Come to think of it, we were on the same side," Eileen reflected. "Milton talked a lot about getting parishioners to vote. Register to vote, register to vote. He said that a lot more in the last year or so that I went to his church. He had the occasional guest preacher. One I remember— Canker by name—he was all about that, too. He used to really tread closely to that line on church politicking, you know?"

"Yeah."

Something came to Friedman. "You know? All this talk about voter registration, and I totally forgot that I have to get ready for a meeting with some student activists from VCU about the issue. Any other questions?"

"Oh, no," assured Scott as both people rose from their seats. "You have given me plenty. Thank you for your time." Scott collected his things, turning off the recorder and putting the cap back on the pen.

"No problem," said Friedman. "So, my two stories will get into your piece about Milton?"

"Yes, I plan to use them."

"Interesting," noted Eileen. "Years back, your editor did a feature article about me and my battles with Milton. I told him those two anecdotes. My thinking was that he would use them to better flesh out my history with Sammy. But when I read the article, he didn't mention either one. Probably just a word limit issue, right?"

"Yeah, probably," said Addison with a smile, his confidence quietly wounded.

* * *

It was Scott Addison's least favorite part of journalism. Well, save for having to write a correction to one of his stories, of course. He went to transcribing the interview he had earlier that day with Eileen Friedman. Scott was seated by the large window of his motel room, the curtains drawn for privacy. A bright lamp countered the glare of his laptop screen. He typed several words and then pressed play on the recording. After another few seconds of conversation, he paused it again. There were a couple of parts he did not bother to type up, simply reaffirming details he had made in his written notes. Other parts he gave special attention to, as he had marked as important during the dialogue.

When he first began reporting, Addison had a different approach to transcribing. He used to listen to the recording, type what he heard, but then if he was not sure of something, he would start the recording over again and re-listen until he got it right. Eventually, Addison adopted a less anal-retentive method. Instead, he would go through the whole recording once, pausing to write things down. Rather than try to get it all right at the beginning, he would get what he could, and then, after listening through it all once, he would re-listen and make changes where necessary. Scott also came to use the divide button, which meant that he could cut off the minutes he had down and have them as a separate recording. This meant he did not have to listen to the whole thing when something was hard to make out. Scott found this to be a less stressful and more efficient strategy.

While Addison was still going through the Friedman interview recording for the first time, his smartphone rang. It was placed beside his laptop on the circular table by the window. A number came up without a name affixed. He had a pretty good idea of who it was, and so he answered. "Hello?"

"This is Mr. Addison's number, right?"

"Yes, it is."

"This is Johnny Canker. We talked earlier about having an interview tomorrow."

"Yes?"

"I just wanted to know if it was okay that we change the venue."

"Where do you want me to talk to you?"

"I know I said my Lynchburg home, but I think it might be better if we meet at a different location. A more appropriate one."

"Okay."

Canker provided Addison with the name and address for the new location. It was only a couple of miles farther west than Lynchburg. He apologized for the change, but Addison assured him that it was no big deal. The time still worked, and he remained willing to talk. All of this worked for Scott. A fleeting goodbye, and the call was ended. The reporter went back to his transcribing. Thanks to the call, he missed a sentence. However, he agreed with himself to tackle that part on the second run-through.

As he typed up each sentence, he was brought back into the past of Eileen Friedman—the desperate teenager, scared of the future, bearing a child. She had no one to turn to. Addison nearly found it biblical.

To Milton, it would have been. He saw his work as being Scriptural in nature. That looking after the orphan, the widow, the fatherless, the stranger. Addison recalled the many like-minded blogs and partisans. They often bashed Milton for not bothering to spend his time helping the less fortunate. Those blog posts and smart quips now seemed rather ignorant. Addison kept his manifesting doubts about the benevolence of his ideological peers to the side as he continued through the interview. He was getting to the juicy part, the one where Friedman found herself at odds with the Milton family. The missed service, the talk with Mrs. Milton. And then it came to him.

"Three?" Scott said aloud. Eileen told Scott that Virginia Milton had mentioned her three children. Something did not seem right. Something was bouncing in the back of his mind. Addison clicked on the save icon and minimized the document. His internet webpage was already up. Opening a new tab, he searched for an obituary for Sammy Milton. After a couple moments, several came up. He picked a local paper over *The Kensington Post*. He skimmed it for the family part and found it near the end. He read aloud: "Milton is survived by Virginia, his wife of 60 years, his children Helen Edith Moore and Ashley Marquis Milton, eight grandchildren, and two great-grandchildren." His curiosity increased. "That's two. Not three. Why did she say three?"

Addison checked a few other obituaries, including his publication. Those who mentioned surviving family all listed two children, a boy and a girl, Ashley and Helen. He was not fully convinced of a conspiracy. It was possible Eileen misspoke or even misremembered. She was pushing a four-decade old memory. Then again, maybe she remembered it perfectly. Three, not two. Ashley and Helen. Then Scott started to think about his interview with Rev. Jabez Henderson. There was a name mentioned there. Exiting out of the obits, Addison maximized the document where he kept the transcribed interviews. He sped through Henderson's interview, coming across the meeting he and his father had with Milton. The opening pleasantries. The name of the newborn.

"Wallace," spoke Addison. "Who is Wallace?"

JOHNNY CANKER

A WRETCHED SIGHT. IT LOOKED a like a monster, a deformed abomination from the darkest depths. The gigantic beast towered over Scott Addison—both for its overall height and for being atop a large archway that led to the entrance of the theme park. Originally, it had two open arms, each seven feet in their span. One had since broken off. When it was unveiled, the large head was beautifully painted with light pink skin; long, dark brown hair; and a dark brown beard with mustache. These things were chipped and discolored, with a chunk of the face broken off and shattered on the ground. Still, one great eye stared at the parking lot where the lines of people would have congregated. Tilted slightly downward, the distorted cyclops unceasingly examined the journalist.

Addison was intrigued by the image, the creature that held constant guard over the wasteland behind him, never seeing the ruins that he welcomed travelers into. Scott had a fairly easy car trip to the location. While he'd had to drive over one hundred miles from Richmond, traffic between there and Lynchburg was minuscule compared to the slogging mess between Richmond and the District of Columbia. Parking was a simple task. The vast lot must have had ten thousand parking spaces; only a dozen were filled.

Below the damaged statue, upon the joining part of the arch, was a large sign that used to read, "Welcome to JESUS WORLD USA! A

Theme Park With Godly Fun!" The letters were golden and plastered upon a purple background. Many of them had been stripped off. Loads of black spray-painted lines created anarchistic styles of artwork on the structure. Under the arch were customer checkpoints for entering the park. The various crowd control borders were missing, probably removed in the early 1990s when the park finally closed. Addison could make out a few booths, used by security to monitor the throngs of visitors. Beyond the entrance, he saw the first images of a broken land.

"Looks like a scene from the zombie apocalypse, doesn't it?" shouted a voice from behind the reporter, prompting him to turn. Facing the lot, he saw an older man in a long-sleeved checkered shirt, brown belt, boots, and blue jeans. He had bronze skin, the byproduct of a youth spent in work and play under a harsh sun. Adorned with white hair, he had a well-trimmed beard and mustache. He smiled, his expression adding more wrinkles to his aged face.

"Johnny Canker, right?"

"Yup," said the man as he came and shook the hand of Addison. "Thanks for meeting me here. It's a better place for our interview than my home."

"Yes," said Scott as he looked at the archway and the statue once again.

"If you brought a camera, take photos," encouraged Johnny.

"Okay," replied Scott, taking his small gray camera from his coat pocket. He took a few quick shots of the statue, including one zoomed up to the broken face.

"Before we begin our interview, you mind me taking you on a tour of the park? People always enjoyed the tour."

"Sure, why not?" said Scott with a smile. Johnny grinned, walking ahead of the reporter as they went under the archway and into the desolation. To their left was a platform that remained in surprisingly good structural integrity, even as all the paint and banners and accessories had been stripped away.

"Let me give you the official introduction," said Canker with a finger pointed to the air. "The one I gave long ago in better times."

"Okay," consented Scott. Johnny smiled and then made his way up to the podium and onto its creaky stage. The informally-dressed man postured himself well, his arms dramatically moving as he spoke, like a ringmaster.

"Ladies and gentlemen, boys and girls, brothers and sisters in Jesus. Welcome to the greatest theme park God ever gave us. Welcome to Jesus World USA! Here, you and your family can come and enjoy all sorts of fun, all wholesome and kid-friendly. Swim in the pool; race the go-carts; play and ride; and, all the while, celebrate Jesus. For God wants you to be happy; you want you to be happy; and we want you to be happy. So, it's unanimous!" Canker put a stop to the theatrics and looked directly at Scott as he descended the stage. "I must have said that a hundred times during the opening week. Each time, it was met with thunderous applause. Even a few emotional prayers. I bet you a million smackers Walt Disney himself never thought a theme park could be so holy."

"Probably not."

"Now then," said Johnny with a breath of accomplishment, "let's continue the tour."

The two walked around the abandoned park for nearly an hour. The things Scott beheld were tragic and surreal. His guide spoke about the sites as though they were all still functioning. As though tens of thousands were coming and going. Cracked and broken cement. Wild vegetation conquering large swathes of the damaged and gutted structures. The pools had become swamps; the rides rusted; the paint jobs peeled off; the statues shattered or stolen; the windows smashed; and the trash scattered. There was little food to speak of; wildlife had long since eaten it up. The occasional rodent scampered away from the duo, a few birds flying upward as the humans walked near.

"This ride here was our version of the tea cups ride," explained Johnny, standing to the left of the vandalized set. "There were seven of them, and each could hold eight people. They'd spin around and around. Fun fact: we were originally going to make them Communion chalices, but some Catholics on the board complained. They said it would be sacrilegious. So, we conceded and made them normal cups." Scott laughed to himself at the image of the communion chalice ride. "Seems like you agree."

"Yes," said Scott with a smile. "I could see why some folks would take that the wrong way."

They went deeper into the park. Wilderness was all around them. The horizon was obscured by forests, while the foreground included tangles of weeds, ivies, and thick bushes. A large collection of bushes nearly hid a broken-down miniature train. Many of its wheels were missing, and only trace evidence of its once bright-colored paint coating was visible. Johnny walked up to the first car, patting the front of it like it were a loyal dog or a favorite horse. He smiled at it before turning to face Addison.

"This was the motorized train that went around our park. Each car could hold four adults. It was used to ferry people around the park or to the hotel. We called it the 'Jesus Train,'" explained Canker. "No lie, we were originally going to call it the 'Soul Train,' but, well, we didn't want to get sued." Canker laughed, while Addison smiled. The irony of the past worry was not lost on either man.

Canker showed Addison the pool; the slides; and a castle that housed an arcade, a few restaurants, and a wedding chapel. "Yes, a wedding chapel," reassured Johnny. Moving along, they came upon a maze. Its wooden barriers were broken and splintered. One could still make out the overall purpose of the stripped and vegetated square enclosure, though it was harder than when it was in operation. "This was our 'Hell Maze.' The only attraction at Jesus World that was off-limits to kids under the age of thirteen. It was open only at nights and was meant to, well, scare the heck out of people."

"Oh, yeah," nodded Scott. "I've heard of these things. Megachurches still do them, right?"

"Yup," Johnny replied. "And why not? They're lots of fun. It was the most fun I ever had here. Coming up with things for the Hell Maze. I mean, we had laughing skeletons, demons, ghosts, lots of fake blood. And we got political from time to time, too."

"Political?"

"Stuff that modern Hell Mazes don't have," recalled Johnny, looking into the sky as he picked out examples. "We had bloody abortion doctors feasting on dead babies, Muslim terrorists with bombs that shot blanks, all sorts of stuff. No lie, we once hired a Ted Kennedy impersonator, but added horns, a tail, and a pitchfork to his costume." Scott looked at Johnny in judgmental amusement. "What? At the time, he seemed pretty darn scary to us."

"Probably no worse than all those Trump parodies, I guess."

"Exactly!" Canker declared. After a pause for dramatic effect, he spoke in a near robotic tone of voice. "Well, that concludes the tour of Jesus World USA. We hope you enjoyed all the sites, and be sure to tell your friends about us. We will now make our way to the hotel and diner. If you have any questions, feel free to ask them."

Canker returned to a casual tone as the two walked toward the aforementioned spot. "Seriously, you may ask me any questions you have about the park."

"Okay," replied Scott, hastily taking out a pen and notepad from his jacket pocket. "Do you own the property?"

"Yes, I do," Johnny responded. "I know other Christian parks from yesteryear have had to sell off chunks of their land to pay the bills, but not me."

"How so?"

"A few things," began Canker as the two went through more ruins and desolate space. "One was my memoir. Its profits were supposed to serve as restitution for the folks I scammed. But truth be told: the book was such a big seller that I ended up having extra money left over, which I used to pay the bills. I also have the occasional tour group. Film companies come and love to shoot their horror flicks here. For a price, of course."

"Of course," agreed Scott.

"And we still make a profit from our hotel and diner," said Canker, stretching out his arms to present the first well-preserved building Addison had seen since entering the park. Canker walked a little faster to get to the glass door before the reporter. He opened it and held it with one hand while using his other hand to usher Scott in. The journalist said thanks while they entered a largely empty restaurant. Only three human beings were there when they entered, and they were all employees. "I know it doesn't look particularly impressive now; but during the summer months, it's chock-full of people. We get a lot of folks just coming in to spend the night. Thanksgiving and Christmas are our best times. Truth be told, Halloween and winter celebrations do pretty well also."

"I can understand that," nodded Scott as the two walked through the central area, full of empty chairs and pristine square tables. They neared the long counter with three registers, two of which were shut down.

"You hungry? Thirsty?"

"I'll take a soda. Cola."

"Okay," replied Canker, turning to the pimply-faced young man behind the register. "Could I get a medium cola and a bottled water?"

The employee obliged and went to fulfilling the order. He handed Canker the unopened water and the soda, which had a sweating cylindrical frame, a top, and a bended straw. "Compliments of the house," Johnny said as he smiled and handed Addison the drink.

"Thank you," replied Scott before taking a drink through the straw.

"Well, my office is this way," said Canker, pointing down a hallway to their left. "We can have the interview there, if that works for you."

"It does," agreed Scott between straw slurps.

* * *

There was little formality to Johnny Canker. He left his office unlocked and the door ajar. No computer or printer existed within the space. Canker had a laptop, which he usually brought with him to work. The desk was messy, and the walls were crowded with posters and photos, many of which were simply taped to the discolored surface. A couple of shelves and filing cabinets bore their share of unorganized books, papers, and other random stuff. The room was a physical stream of consciousness.

Scott had his choice of three chairs, each rolled to the side. They were each a type of office chair, two black and one brown. One of the black seats was skinny and seemed a little rougher than the other two, with duct tape used on the edges to counter the gradual tearing away of the leather skin. The other black one looked the most comfortable, so he grabbed hold of it and rolled it in front of Canker's desk. Johnny was already seated, leaning backward and drinking from his opened water bottle. The other chair placed where it needed to be, Scott sat down, putting his recorder on the desktop. While many papers abounded, he found a small crevice of free territory. On top of one pile of papers was a familiar political sight: a bright red baseball cap with white letters emblazoned on the front that read "Make America Great Again." Scott could not help but stare.

"I bet you never saw one of those close up, have you?" asked a smiling Canker, breaking the trance of Addison.

"I was in DC during the Inauguration," said Scott, looking up the relaxed Canker. He smiled. "But yes, not this close."

"You know why he won, don't you?"

"Tell me," asked a humoring Scott, who had had plenty of theories explained to him over the past several months.

"Evangelicals," firmly stated Canker. "Millions of evangelicals. Tens of millions. People like me told all the evangelicals to vote for Trump. We told them to look past his obvious moral failings and, remember, that at least he doesn't hate us. Very simple message. Very, very simple.

But truth be told, it worked. It worked big time. Simple messages work in politics. Honestly, they might be the only thing that works."

"Yes, that sounds right."

"So, you're here to do a story about Rev. Sammy, huh?"

"Yes, an in-depth piece for our weekly print edition."

"Michael Phillips is your editor, right?"

"He is."

"I remember Phillips," said Johnny as he looked up to the ceiling. "He hated my guts. He never missed an opportunity to bash me. But that was a long time ago. The past few years, he's left me alone. Pretty much alone. And I know why."

"Why would that be?"

Canker slowly moved forward so that his feet were on the ground and he was leaning forward with his arms on the desk. "Because I'm not powerful anymore. Milton, on the other hand—he was always powerful. Even when we lost, Milton stood firm, while people like me ran away. Or were imprisoned." Johnny cackled at that last remark. "Phillips used to get on my last nerves. So many times, I used to tell Milton, 'Why won't God just strike him dead?'" The comment raised Scott's eyebrows.

"And what did Milton say?"

"He always scolded me. 'Don't say that,' Milton used to tell me. 'He's a sinner, but so are we.' He told me the best way to strike back was to pray for him. 'Pray for Phillips,' he ordered me. No lie, a few times he even tried to invite your editor to coffee or to dinner. You know, just to shoot the breeze. I don't think he ever said yes."

"It would be news to me if he did."

"Off the record, will this be a hit piece?" Canker frankly inquired.

"Off the record," reiterated Scott, with Canker nodding, "my editor would prefer that. For now, I'm just gathering perspectives, and I'm going to see what comes up. If it's more negative than positive, then you can call it a hit piece."

"Sounds fair," admitted Canker, who leaned back and then took a swig from his water bottle. "So, shall we begin?"

"Yes, of course," said Addison, pressing the button on his recorder. "So, first question . . . when did you and Milton first meet?"

* * *

The convention center was abuzz with energy. Music filled the space, stemming from a large stage with a band, chairs for speakers, and several microphones. Twenty circular tables, each occupied by eight well-dressed people, were spread in a square formation of five rows of four. Behind the stage were two large flags: one of the United States and another of Israel. The song drew its lyrics from the Hebrew Bible, with the melody getting gradually faster with each singing of the refrain. Clapping was expected at certain points, the audience encouraged to take part in the festive tune.

It was the concluding song for the event, which featured several speakers from diverse religious and political backgrounds. An elegant affair, men wore suits and women wore flowing dresses. A fair number of invitees wore yarmulkes, with some of their number being rabbis. There were a few Holocaust survivors, with one as young as forty-two. One of them spoke to the audience, dividing his presentation between his harsh experiences in the camps and his disgust at the United Nations' recently passed resolution declaring Zionism racism. Another speaker, a local rabbi, had just returned from a Kibbutz in the Holy Land and described the need for Christians and Jews to come together.

The Rev. Sammy Milton was on the stage. He happily clapped at each point where the song so prompted. He was the most notable speaker on stage. In the advertisements for the event, his name got the highest billing. While not the only Christian speaker at the fundraiser, he was the most ardent in his words. His words stressed the Judaic roots of Christianity, noted with appreciation the prophets and Scriptures brought to him by Jewish writers. At one point, Milton joked that he could not understand why he had not converted to Judaism, to which one sympathetic heckler shouted, "BLTs!"

In the crowd was Pastor Johnny Canker. Sometimes, people called him Rev. Canker, though the appellation was a misnomer. He held no formal seminary degree, having dropped out of a theology school over its modernist slant. Canker taught himself how to preach, to use the Bible, and to speak before large audiences. Milton was a major inspiration. Fifteen years younger than the popular preacher, Canker was raised on Milton's radio broadcasts and pamphlets; and as a teenager, he had the pleasure of seeing him in person at a Salvation Meeting. Canker never heard a sermon from Milton that he did not enjoy.

Brown-haired, slightly tanned, and weeks away from his thirty-first birthday, Canker was on the move. He and his wife of six years drove eight hours to be at that convention center. They sat near to the stage, agreeing that once the proceedings were complete, Johnny would make a dash for the preacher. The song exemplified his drive, the faster and faster melody finally culminating in a long note of lyric. Then suddenly it ended, the systematic clapping transforming into organic celebratory applause.

The speakers all came to the main podium and microphone. A few announcements were made, some reminders of things here and there. A rabbi gave a closing prayer, while the Cankers reverently bowed their heads and closed their eyes. With a strong amen, the event was officially over. Instrumental music played as a wave of scattered conversations were made amongst the many guests. People gathered things, caught up with those at other tables, laughed and chatted, and then gradually left the large enclosed space. Convention center employees in bland clothing waited in the wings for the elegant ones to leave, so as to begin the hours-long process of taking down the set and tables.

Canker kept his attention on Milton, who was laughing and talking with various people on the stage. About thirty folks were there, most having walked up to the stage via one of the two stairways on either flank. Slowly, they exchanged their comments, and when sufficiently socially satisfied, turned to leave for home. Some waited patiently to give a comment, a fleeting remark of some kind. Impatience was possible but slight. As a whole, they left the evening in good and cheerful spirits. Johnny knew no one else at the event, so no one stopped him on his way to the stage. A few utterances of "excuse me" and he got through, ascending the black steps while holding onto a black railing.

"And let me just say," said an aged rabbi to Milton, "I am very pleased to see you here and to know that you are a friend of Israel."

"Thank you for your kind words," replied Milton as the two shook hands and the elderly clergyman walked away. Canker saw his chance.

"Rev. Milton?"

"Yes?" asked Sammy as he turned to see the source of the query.

"Hello, I am Pastor Johnny Canker. From Lynchburg."

"Oh yes, I have heard of you," replied Milton as he offered his hand, and Johnny shook it. "I heard from a mutual friend that you wanted to talk to me about something."

"Yes, I do," replied Canker as the stage and the space was emptying. "Truth be told, this would be a better thing to talk about in private."

"Okay," nodded Milton. "Let me say a couple more goodbyes to people, and then I will be right with you. Just wait right here, and I'll be back. Okay?"

"Yes," said Canker with a smile. He was a little nervous about his proposal, and the extra time waiting did not bode well for his stomach. As Milton made the rounds on the emptying stage, Johnny reminded himself that the worst-case scenario was unlikely to be painful. Just disappointing. A few minutes later, Milton was ready to speak. They went off to the side of the convention center space, several yards away from where many casually-dressed young men were taking down the tables, stacking chairs, and carefully removing pieces of the stage. The following morning, the next shift was going to set up a different layout for a local awards program. The two evangelists sat in unstacked chairs, taken from the stage before the workers began their tasks.

"I understand where you are coming from," said Milton with a breath. "As preachers, we need to guide people."

"Exactly," nodded Canker.

"And things have definitely gotten worse. The sheer number of abortions, the divorce boom, Evolution in the schools, the sex and violence on TV, those awful smut magazines showing up on every corner."

"Yes," said Canker. "And no lie, we both know it's only going to get worse. Which is why you should join me and the hundreds of Christian leaders in the coalition."

"But it's still politics," insisted Milton. "It is not the place of a clergyman to get involved in political things. We have a separation of church and state."

"That is not in the Constitution," Canker firmly replied.

Milton was about to respond. He was going to give Canker the same lecture he had given the Henderson family when they visited his office several years earlier. Then he remembered what happened after he rejected their offer to join the collective action. Years of regret, years of indifference. He had kept contact with the younger Henderson and was thinking of offering a grand apology for his past apathy. They were excuses, he concluded. Petty and unjustifiable. He was not going to repeat history.

"You are right. It isn't."

* * *

They were back in Virginia. Three weeks had passed since their first meeting at the pro-Israel event at the convention center. The coalition welcomed Rev. Sammy Milton with open arms. Many of them were like Johnny Canker, having listened to Milton's messages when children. One of them even came to Christ at a Salvation Meeting. They drew up their agenda items, updating them to include the latest elections and initiatives. One of the more salacious topics was to be debated that night at the county commissioners' meeting. It was the regular monthly session.

The meeting room was a large one. There were three white-painted walls, which enclosed rows and rows of wooden chairs. On one end, the wall was covered with wood paneling. A county seal and the statement "In God We Trust" were placed in the center of the paneling. Two flags, one of the United States and the other of the Commonwealth, were placed on opposite corners of that side of the room. A large counter table was placed in front of the board members, each with a simple placard with their last name placed in front of their seat. On the opposite side of the room was a pair of windowless doors.

The commissioners, all men over the age of forty, stood for the Pledge of Allegiance and a short opening prayer from a local pastor. Sitting down, they faced a gallery with a larger-than-normal audience. Each gentleman on the board knew which of the agenda items brought so many out to the otherwise mundane occasion. They did not feel particularly threatened by the gathering of locals and press. After all, none of them had expressed antagonism toward the initiative. A few of them even felt honored that such a notable public figure as the Rev. Sammy Milton was in their midst.

Milton and Canker waited patiently in the front row of seats. They kept their peace as the procedures of governing parlance went on. There were the voice votes and the brief comments on old business, the mayor prompting ritualized reactions from the others on the board. A few reports on local infrastructure came. Updates on dealing with flooding on a short stretch of main street, a building project that, when completed, would add a couple new businesses to the area, and a report on the state response to a recent power outage. Finally came the reason why the two leaders and their many followers were present.

"And now moving onto new business," began the mayor in a monotone voice, looking down at the docket item. "A proposed ordinance to ban pornographic magazines. As I understand, we have someone from the gallery who will speak on behalf of this proposed ordinance."

"That's you," said Canker as he nudged an already-attentive Milton. He was calm. There were no nerves welling up within. No sense of angst. Milton was fully convinced of his cause. Furthermore, he had experienced greater pressure in front of larger audiences and more hostile ones from time to time than that county board meeting.

"Mayor, commissioners, friends, and citizens of this county," started Milton, looking at each named party with big blue eyes. "Good evening. I am here speaking in strong support for the proposed ordinance to ban smut from your county."

His tone became ever the more serious. "Ladies and gentleman, we live in a very disturbing time. Crime is rampant in our cities. Godlessness abounds in our schools. The Sexual Revolution is ruining millions of American lives. And the Communists appear to be winning, both in Vietnam and on the overall global stage. Many people look at all this and wonder, 'What can we do?' What can anyone do to fix our country, to return it to the Judeo-Christian values that made it so powerful a nation, that led it to spread across a continent?

"I know that this ordinance will not solve all our problems. I know it will not make the plague of pornography disappear from our communities. But it is still, STILL, an important and necessary step in the battle against the immorality and wickedness that seeks to destroy our great country from within."

Many in the audience were nodding in agreement, a few voicing barely heard terse statements of support. Milton got more passionate: "Ladies and gentleman, do not be deceived. Porn is one of the great corrupters of our boys. Through this sexual idolatry, they are taught to treat women as mere objects, rather than the creatures created in the image of God that they are. Porn degrades all involved in it. The watcher, the producer, the models. They are all captive to sin by their consumption.

"The experts constantly debate why so much juvenile delinquency exists in our cities. You want to know what I think?" asked Milton, getting many yeses from the audience. "I think the garbage that the youth of America are seeing on television and in movies and in porn is the source of this delinquency. Porn is like alcohol; it's like drugs. It's like all the other vices in that it poisons both body and soul. Porn poisons the soul by flooding it with perverse, sinful imagery. And porn poisons the body through the objectification of women, through the psychological damage. Tomorrow's criminals are today's porn addicts.

"So, what is to be done? Do we just stand by helplessly as Herbert Spiker's filthy papers turn our young boys into sexual predators? Do we let them do it? Are we going to welcome their trash into our homes?" With each rhetorical question, Milton became more animated. With each statement, a growing number of audience members shouted "No!" in response. The sentiment was entering the board members as well. "What do we do? We fight back. We use not only the pulpit, but also the board. We use not just the sermon, but the legislation. We use not just the church, but the state!"

* * *

"So, things only grew from there, I assume?"

"Oh yes, no lie," nodded Canker. "The ordinance passed unanimously. From there, we went to other counties in Virginia. And then North Carolina. South Carolina. We really put a hurting on Spiker. It got so bad, they tried to smear Milton's reputation. He was always seen as the bigger threat, I guess." Addison smiled while Canker laughed. "Anyway, we did plenty of actions from the local to the federal. We campaigned to get Creation in the classrooms of Louisiana. We railed against SALT treaties. We lobbied to get school prayer back in New

172 A SPIRAL INTO MARVELOUS LIGHT

York public schools. We beat the ERA. We campaigned for Reagan and Bush. We were a force back then. Everyone either loved us or feared us."

As Scott listened to Johnny, he saw the old spark come into his eyes. Still, with the burnt skin and the whited hair, Johnny thrilled within as he returned to those days. It was like the aged Religious Right stalwart was seeing the events anew, beholding throngs of voters and campaign activists. Reliving the speeches and the gatherings. Scott's recorder and notes did little justice to the fiery excitement. "We met the presidents. We shook hands and took photos. Congressmen took their marching orders from us. Both parties pandered to our every demand. No one wanted to be on the wrong side of the coalition."

"What about the federal rules against church politicking?"

"No one cared," said Johnny, brushing off the suggestion. "Truth be told, I don't think anyone in the IRS wanted to be the guy who dared to try and shut down Sammy Milton. No, he was the most valuable asset in all the coalition. No lie. Also, we did have a little nuance. As a nonprofit, the coalition never outright endorsed anyone. We just talked about what we liked about certain politicians, let our loyal following know who supported what. And if I, or Milton, or anyone else offered up an endorsement, our legal team coached us to say 'speaking for myself as an individual citizen and not for any organization I am affiliated with.'" Canker made the statement as though giving a scout's oath.

"A lot of critics said that you and Milton were too political," charged Addison, dimming the nostalgic lights in Canker's eyes. "They said you focused far more on getting Republicans in office and very little time on, you know, helping the poor, preaching the Word. How do you respond to those accusations?"

"I say look at the facts," replied Canker, retaining his pleasant mood. "During the 1980s, when we were so political, Milton did three times as many Salvation Meetings than he did campaign events. I made it a habit to devote no more than twenty percent of my air time to politics. Everything else was the Bible, morality, and begging for money. Lots of begging." Canker laughed at that last comment. Scott withheld acknowledgement of his amusement. "That was just a clever little slight people came up with because they didn't like us. They would have said different if we agreed with them. None of these same people who thought Milton was mixing religion and politics ever said anything when black churches hosted Democrats or Unitarian pastors protested outside legislatures."

Addison wanted to argue the point. However, he lacked any of his own evidences to hurl back at the interviewee. He knew that such an exercise in debate was thus futile. When Scott thought about it, it even sounded a little reasonable. "Tell me about what happened between you two. Because, eventually, you and Milton did part ways. And, unless I'm mistaken, it was not peaceful."

"You're right," affirmed a sobering Johnny. "It wasn't."

* * *

The stage had a blue carpeted surface and a background of large potted plants shipped in from the Holy Land. A large golden cross was on the wall, positioned well above the uppermost tips of the leaves. It was placed high enough that it was not visible during the camera close-ups and yet quite prominent during the distance shots. Plush chairs were on the stage, as well as a podium. To one side was a large black piano. There was theater-styled seating for the audience. There were four squares of chair rows, with aisles that crossed like an intersection.

More seats were found above, with a balcony that stretched along three of the four walls of the room, the stage area being the one without.

Camera crews were positioned at various points in the large, indoor space. Four audio-visual recorders were placed with tripods at the front, with the operators' backs to the audience and their lenses facing the stage. They were equally spread in a semi-circle to catch all necessary angles of the speakers. The two balcony sides to the right and left of the stage each had one camera crew. Another two were placed on the balcony that was directly opposite the stage. These balcony devices were chiefly used for crowd shots, showing viewers across the country the large gatherings. Sometimes, they zoomed into audience members—those driven most by the Spirit during times of worship—the hand-raisers, the tongue-speakers, and anyone else deemed visually inspiring.

At that point of the service, the audience was quiet. Music had already been performed. The audience had a couple of old hymns, the type of sacred songs that they were raised with and their congregations still often used for services. There were some more repetitious and less familiar Gospel selections. Their strength was the emotion that the profound repeating of spiritual truth kindled within the audience. The African-American minority within the crowd were the most familiar with these tunes. There was intense prayer, calls for revival and miracles, petitions for the ill and sinful.

The seats were filled with adults. Most were older, between forty and senior citizenship. A fair number were gray and wrinkled. Very few were in their twenties or younger. Most children were left home with other family. The littlest kids who were at that building were in a daycare center at a recreation room down the hall. Most of the audience wore church clothes. Many women had puffy hair, while many men wore mullets and thick mustaches. Glasses for corrective vision were sizable, with frames that were much larger than the eyes themselves. Wrist watches with three hands were used to tell time, though few bothered as the power of the messenger on the stage commandeered all attention.

The broadcast followed a similar model to previous recordings done by that ministry. The musical director gave some announcements and then led the people in worship. Prayers of various kinds were offered, and even some folks who were drawn by the Spirit were brought on stage and testified before the others. It was an emotionally cathartic series of events, with people pouring out their confessions and their pleas and their joys. Then there was a message from a preacher. About half of the time, a guest preacher gave the sermon. For that broadcast, it was the Rev. Sammy Milton.

Following his preaching, an altar call was made. A peculiar term given that the stage did not have one. Still, a few came and made their commitment to Christ. Milton and the other leadership prayed over the new converts and renewed believers. Some spoke in tongues, speaking what was to Milton garbled gibberish. He refused to pass judgment, just as he refused to judge the occasional Catholic priest with whom he would share a stage at other events who might speak of the Queen of Heaven. Milton always recalled that passage from the Pauline Epistles about how if one believer considers something sacred but another does not, let each man be convinced by his conscience.

Regardless of whether or not there was a guest preacher, the head of the ministry always gave the final comments. The camera lenses all pointed toward Johnny Canker. His eyes were deeply shut, one hand gripping a microphone, while the other was raised in the air. His long, rambling prayer was a homily unto itself. In pathos-laden pleas and declarations, he led the praying of those in the studio and those watching in hundreds of thousands of homes. The piano player brought gentle notes as background for Canker's supplications. The audience was not uniform in its prayer postures. Some, like Milton, simply bowed their heads and clasped their hands together. Others joined hands with their neighbors; still others raised their arms high above, nodding their heads with each point declared by Canker. Many muttered their own invocations as Canker spoke.

"Oh, Lord Jesus," continued Canker, "send Your Anointing Spirit upon us all. Bless us, bless a lot. Let Your manifestation constantly flood our lives. Flood our lives with blessing, O Lord! Give us faith. Faith to move mountains. Faith to drive demons! When we have that faith, that strong faith, we can NEVER fail! Never! The Gospel of our Lord Jesus Christ gives victory and success in all parts of our lives. All of them! Spiritual needs, physical needs, and material needs!" Milton winced at that last statement, but kept his eyes closed and head bowed. "God wants you to be happy. Do this for yourself. Faith is for yourself!" Milton struggled a little more in keeping his reverent stance.

The cameras were off, and the audience was dispersed. Those on the stage were in the back, being tended to by makeup artists. Those who had taken care to put the right lines along the eyes and the edges of the mouth, who rosed the cheeks and powdered the noses, took to removing their work. Milton was a quick project, as he begged off the extra cosmetics for the broadcasts. He stood before Canker, still seated as a smiling young woman removed the last touches. They pleasantly bantered as she finished her work. As Johnny was almost fully cleaned off, he noticed Milton.

"Sammy," he spoke amiably. "I'm surprised you're still here." He turned to the makeup expert. "Milton is usually out the door and on his way home to Ginny by now."

"Could I talk to you privately?"

"I guess," said Johnny, turning back to the woman. "I can get the rest." She smiled in response and exited the backstage area. "No lie, it was a good crowd today."

"Johnny, I am a little concerned about the messages you've been preaching as of late," said a standing Milton to Canker, who leaned back in his seat.

"What do you mean? I am preaching the Gospel."

"Most of the time you are. But every so often, I hear you preaching something else."

"What would that be?" asked Johnny, who stopped leaning back and looked at his company. "I don't recall paying homage to Mohammed or Buddha."

"Wealth," stated Milton. "You were preaching the Gospel of wealth."

"The Gospel of wealth?"

"You said, if I recall, 'The Gospel of Jesus gives you success in all your material needs.'"

"Yes, I did. Glad you were listening," Johnny quipped. Milton remained serious.

"Other times, I've heard you say stuff about God wanting us to be rich. Or God wants us to be happy, and we can be happy when we have money."

"Well, when I am in the Spirit, I say what the Spirit wants me to say."

"Are you sure it's the right spirit?" asked Milton with arms folded.

"Excuse me?" said Canker as he stood up from his chair.

"I am very worried about you, Johnny. Ever since the coalition became mainstream, you've been acting more and more worldly."

"How so?" he defensively snapped.

"Where do I start? The buying of multiple houses. That huge mansion you constructed for yourself. The private jets."

"One of which I gave to you for your birthday," declared Johnny with a raised finger. "It's not like you returned it or anything."

"I use it for business."

"Oh yeah, those debates with that porn king. How many souls have you saved through casting your pearls before swine?"

"More than you have by jetting off to the Caribbean. Or do you do your evangelizing while getting a nice tan?"

"Sammy, you are really pushing it!"

"No, you are," countered Milton. "We've all been seeing more money than we've ever had in our lives. I never thought Into Marvelous Light Ministries would be this in the black. Ever. It's all very tempting. I am telling you, you need to step back and think about how you are living your life."

"I am living just fine. By going to the best restaurants and the finest islands and having the biggest houses and the most cars, I am showing people there is an upside to joining us. Did it ever occur to you that this really is God pouring out His blessing on us? Maybe God is rewarding me for preaching His Gospel."

"A Gospel that has nothing but bad things to say about storing up treasures on earth," calmly retorted Milton.

"Come on, Sammy," said Johnny as he neared his critic. "It's not like I'm taking money out of my ministries. All the charities and missions that I oversee are fully funded. Plenty of souls are saved; mouths are fed; and naked are clothed. To say nothing of my park being profitable. Fun fact: Jesus World USA is the fourth most visited theme park in the entire country. At this rate, we'll be number one by 1988."

"And then you will be further beholden to material things. Greed is swallowing you whole. It is consuming your every thought. It bleeds into your prayers and your sermons. Your belief that our Lord wants us only to be happy, pleasuring ourselves with every worldly good, will lead you to even greater sins . . . if it hasn't already."

That final statement threw Canker into a rage. His teeth gritted, his eyes on fire. He backed away from Milton in seething enmity. Wanting to plaster the clergyman with a flurry of invective, he held his temper and declared simply, "Get out."

"Johnny, you—"

"Get out!" Canker declared with greater force. Milton was lost for words. His mouth was open, but no noise escaped. With great regret, Sammy nodded and turned away from his friend. With his company gone, Johnny took a deep breath and bent over in front of the vanity mirror that the makeup artist used. After a while, he looked up at his own visage. There were still a few touches of makeup. He looked and quickly found a white towel, which he colored when wiping away the last of the markings. Then he smiled. "God wants me to be happy. He wants me to have good things. He wants me happy."

* * *

It was a fantastic structure. The front door was shaded by a large, circular awning with white columns. Each broad side of the edifice had sixteen windows. There were two floors above ground and one below. It had ten large bedrooms, far beyond the number necessary for those who owned it. There were multiple recreation rooms, a couple of offices, a study, a library, a smaller dining room, and a larger dining room. Altogether, there were fifteen bathrooms, ten whole and five halves. The basement level included the garage, where five sports cars, three motorcycles, and two minivans were parked. It was one of many mansions located in that well-off suburb—a community full of businessmen, high level government workers, old money heirs, and music stars.

Among them was one preacher. Johnny Canker gathered up a few things as he ventured down the basement staircase. He had a few places to go before he met his wife at a high-end restaurant for dinner. She drove the sixth sports car, a bright red vehicle that came off the assembly line last year. In one hand, he had some paperwork for the theme park. He was reviewing some of the latest statistics on attendance, as well as some ideas for new rides to add to the massive acreage. One of the board members had advised adding something Lenten-themed to reel in more Catholics. He also had an envelope—a recent donation that a congregant gave him specifically for a charity shipping grain to Africa.

The keys for the various vehicles were placed on hooks attached to a knot board that was nailed to the wall. Under each key was a small, painted sign with the name of the model. After studying the options, he chose the blander, older car his wife typically used when grocery shopping. It was the car that the Cankers used in those rare instances when they did not seek public attention. With the push of a button, one of the two large garage doors opened. Johnny turned his keys to rev up the engine. The basement space was large enough that he could turn around before exiting.

The first part of his journey was a success, though it took a while. The crowds were strong at Jesus World USA. Traffic picked up as he neared. It took him time before he finally got to the backroad that went to the employee parking lot. Once at the office, he had to go over things with management. Things took longer than he expected. No matter, he thought to himself. Johnny mentally reconfigured his agenda, pushing the deliverance of the charity money to later. He had a specific time for one liaison, and there was no way he was going to compromise it, even though it compromised him.

They had some drinks together. They laughed, and they talked. Then they got to the more illicit parts. He was feeling especially frustrated with the stress of managing his empire. And his wife was busier than usual that week. So, the carnal comfort of the makeup artist, who was about half his age, was welcomed. She reserved the motel room, and she bought the wine. It was with his money, though. During the time of pleasure, Johnny passed out. He expected to, assuming that his restful period would not be too long.

Coming to, he saw the cracked paint job of the ceiling. The quarters were not particularly squalid, but they were not five-star elegant either. His head ached. He deeply blinked several times as his head became less fuzzy and his mind was more aware. Beside him in the bed was the cosmetic specialist, also awaking from a rest. Her arms hung over the sheets, which were the only things covering her body. Canker's watch, along with his other belongings and his pants, were discarded on the mantel near the window. The curtains were closed, and the sun was setting. Making his way to the mantel, he sifted through the various items to locate his diamond-encrusted watch. Then his eyes widened.

"Oh, great," he said as he saw the time.

"What is it, Johnny?"

"I'm late!" he said, hastily collecting himself. "I'm freaking late!"

"Late for what?"

"My dinner!"

"Oh yeah, that," she said as she brushed her hair back.

"You were supposed to wake me," he angrily stated as he put his pants on.

"I was tired," she said while seated on the bed, sheets still hiding most of her nudity.

"Can't believe I'm late."

"Sorry, okay?" she said as Canker got his shoes on and hastily went into the bathroom to check his face. No lipstick or other clear marks of infidelity were detected. He rushed out and grabbed what he thought was everything. "Same time next Friday?"

"Maybe," he said as he slammed the motel room door. The young woman left the bed and took to pulling herself back together. As she put on her undergarments and started to pull up her jeans, she looked at the mantel and found the wallet. Finishing up with the jeans, she walked over to the mantel and picked up the item.

"More than maybe," she grinned.

The restaurant was crowded when Canker showed up. Classical music was piped into the dining spaces, and the waiters were dressed in formal wear. He and his wife had a reservation. She was rhythmically tapping the top of the table with her fingers until he came into view. A smile came as Johnny rushed to the table. She rose a few inches from her seat to receive a fleeting kiss from her husband. He immediately pulled back the chair on the opposite side of the square table, catching his breath.

"You're late."

"I know, I know," Canker said apologetically. "Business."

"What's in the envelope?" she inquired.

"Money. What else?"

"Could be a letter."

"Well, it's money," said Canker as the waiter came by. A young man with good posture, he wore the same white bowtie as the others who served tables. One spouse tried something different while the other had the usual. He wrote down the details and then promised to return with their order.

"You've never ordered the lobster before," noticed Johnny.

"I had plenty of time to think about it."

"Sorry, okay?" restated Canker in annoyance. He changed his tone. "So how was your day?"

"Pretty good," she responded. "I ran into Ginny at the meeting. She told me her daughter was getting married next August."

"That's nice."

"She wants me to come. She plans to invite us both."

"Oh, great," replied a dampened Johnny.

"Listen, Johnny," she insisted, her eyes making their own appeals. "It's been almost a year now. I know you don't want to talk to him, but I am good friends with the Miltons. And I don't see why you can't make amends."

"Because he doesn't get it," Johnny stated firmly. "He thinks that we should be ashamed of ourselves for being happy. For being rich. For being who we were meant to be."

"Can't you just agree to disagree?"

"Oh, no," said Canker with a curse as he searched through his pockets.

"Don't take that tone with me."

"No, I mean . . . " Canker completed the search and refocused on his wife. "I forgot my wallet."

"You what?"

"I forgot it. I must have, I must have . . . " Canker knew the answer. "Point is, it's not here."

"Well, I don't have enough on me to cover this," she replied. "You're the husband. You provide."

Canker thought for a moment. It would be very embarrassing to have to explain to the manager that they could not afford the dinner. He envisioned being forced to clean the dishes or spend a day in jail. He saw the headlines in the press, especially those from *The Kensington Post*. Those he hated with utmost enmity. Then he looked down at the envelope. It was full of greenbacks waiting to be spent. He gave a smile and looked up with relief at a woman still making an effort to suppress her fretting.

"Good thing I brought this money," he said as he used his index finger to tear open the envelope and use the charitable funds to pay for the lavish supper for two.

* * *

"Sex and money," observed Johnny Canker, prompting Scott Addison to look up from his scribbled notes. "Sex and money. The two biggest temptations for any minister. And to be honest, I caved in to both of them."

"And it started with the charity money?"

"Yup," sighed Johnny. "So many times—many, many times—I went back to that motel room. Many times in my head, that is. I reenacted it all, and still, I cannot understand how I could have been so stupid as to forget my wallet. And then the money. That envelope over dinner was just the beginning. I started to take out funds on a regular basis. Vacations, lavish catering, fashionable clothes for myself and my wife. Hush money for the young women. More cars and motorcycles to fill the garage."

"Pardon me," interjected Scott with his pen pointed toward his interviewee. "But didn't you say that you had a bunch of cars already?"

"Yes, but they were all older models. You can't keep around old stuff. Not unless it's vintage. Then you take even more money from the poor and give it to the dealer. The whole way through, I felt happy. Not joyful, mind you. There is a difference. But there was nothing I could not get whenever I wanted it."

"Did Milton know about your scam?"

"He had his suspicions. He complained to others," said Johnny as he leaned back once again. "I remember the occasional intercessory. The nervous young man who came to my office to sheepishly give me a message from Sammy. They always included Bible verses about the dangers of wealth. Only now do I realize just how accurate they were. Like the stiff-necked, ancient Israelites, I always had to learn things the hard way."

"Why didn't he tell others?"

"He lacked hard evidence. Besides, Milton and I both practiced the Eleventh Commandment. As Gaylord Parkinson put it, 'Thou shalt not speak ill of thy fellow Republican.'"

"I thought Reagan said that."

"Most people think Reagan said that," nodded Johnny. "Regardless, Milton wanted to have a united front against the secularist agenda. That meant reserving the criticisms and critiques for private conversations. He tried to sway me and other televangelists to stop indulging so much. Sometimes, he succeeded. But he failed with me."

"How did it all fall apart?"

Canker leaned forward. "It all started to go bad in the summer of 1990. There was a big recession. Truth be told, it wasn't as bad as the one we had a few years ago. But it was still bad. Donations went down. So, I found myself with all these luxurious expenses and no way to pay for them. So, I dug even deeper, took even more food out of poor children's bellies and more roofs from the heads of the impoverished.

"Finally, people started to ask questions. They wondered why the books weren't adding up. They wondered why everyone but me had to cut back. So, I started to fire people who asked too many questions. Problem is, they knew people. People who could investigate things. Before you know it, it's all out there. The theft, the extortion, and, most provocatively, the affairs. No lie, I think the affairs got more headlines than the illegal stuff. I remember the night before they hauled me off. After a very brutal argument, my wife stormed out with the kids. I was all alone in that wretched mansion."

* * *

The study was a testament to self-destruction. Books were thrown from their shelves and strewn upon the carpeted floor. A lamp was tossed, its bulb smashed when it struck the wall. A small table meant for TV dinners was overturned. The desk had each drawer removed. They were emptied of their papers and miscellaneous objects, also tossed to the floor. They were likewise scattered, two of them cracking as they were slammed into the wall. The office chair that went with the desk was on its side. Framed portraits that once occupied the desktop and the walls joined the other random, discarded things on the floor.

Amidst the fallout from his tantrum was Johnny Canker. The study was divided from the hallway by three steps. He was seated on the top step, hunched over, facing the panoramic view of disorder. At times, his fingers covered his face. Other times, they were retracted. He looked down. Down at the carpet, down at his legs and feet. The burden pushed him down physically and emotionally. He lost all semblance of time, minutes blurring into one stagnant depression. It was not going to be long. His judgment day was drawing ever closer, with the eventual sunrise promising misery.

He just barely heard the door open. The main entrance was located about two hundred feet from where he was situated, a few walls separating him and the portal. He knew someone was walking into the hallway. It was not the police. There would have been sirens. It was not the press; they were never this orderly. Johnny did not feel any threat, nor any sense of fear about who the intruder might be. In his mind, he would welcome a burglar or a serial killer. He saw no way that such a cruel fate would make things worse. The person got closer and closer, the steps louder and louder. Lifting his head but still facing away from the unknown presence, the suffering man saw a broad shadow.

"Hello, Johnny," said the familiar voice. Canker straightened up a little more, feeling the cracking in his back. He still looked forward.

"How did you get in?" asked Canker in a non-threatening voice.

"The door was unlocked."

"Of course," he said as he hunched forward yet again. "She always forgot to lock the door. Why wouldn't she forget tonight?"

Canker turned his upper body to see Sammy Milton standing above him. His blue eyes had a tender gaze. He was in a suit and had his black, leather-bound Bible tucked under his right arm. Canker noted that its thick layer of pages had a few pieces of scratch paper sticking out as bookmarks. After confirming the identity of the visitor, Johnny silently turned back to face the messy study.

"I have some verses for you," offered Sammy. "Passages from the Good Book that might be of help to you during this time of trial."

"No need to be nice," stated Johnny. "Feel free to gloat. Tell me you were right. Tell me I went too far. Remind me how truly pathetic I am. A fornicator. A thief. A lecherous, greedy hypocrite, who preached holiness and made bucko bucks at every point." He looked back at Sammy in frustration. "Well, what are you waiting for? Skip the Bible study and just lay it on me! Rub it in and leave me like everyone else!"

Sammy looked down as Johnny turned back to face the chaos. There was silence. Milton took a few steps down. He lowered his imposing frame, sitting beside Johnny, who paid him little ocular attention. There was still silence. Johnny was hunched over again, looking down as Milton looked at him. Canker shed some tears, sniffling as he kept his voice quiet. His eyes were already reddish from past bouts of melancholy. He rubbed them once more and tried to think of what to do next.

"God wants you to be happy," Canker said, an occasional tear falling as spoke. "God wants you to be rich. That's how you get to be happy.

I said that. I practiced that. All the material things. They were blessings; they were rewards for good faith. I believed it. They'll call me a liar. But I wasn't a liar. You're not lying when you believe it yourself. It was all for me. Me, me, me. I was preaching the 'Gospel of Me.' And now, now I get my reward. I get to be all by myself. I get to spend this endless night all alone with me."

"You're not alone," said the calm, assuring voice to his left. Canker slowly turned to face the man occupying the step with him. For the first time in hours, Johnny smiled. "Shall I read?"

"It can't hurt," spoke Johnny. Milton nodded and opened the Bible. He flipped through the pages, going across the written names of a couple of grandchildren who were baptized within the past few years. He arrived at the first bookmark, a piece of light blue scratch paper. Milton balanced the Scripture atop his legs and read the text, offering spiritual comfort to the troubled soul.

* * *

"He read Scripture; we prayed; we talked," recalled Johnny Canker to Scott Addison. He was leaning back in his office chair, his eyes looking upward in memory. "There was reconciliation, and there was forgiveness. There was apologizing on my part." Canker laughed a bit. "Actually, there was a lot of apologizing on my part." He laughed a little more. "He stayed with me until sunrise."

"Did he go with you to the jail?"

"No," replied Johnny. "Truth be told, he wanted to. But I told him not to. I explained that things were bad enough without him getting tangled into my problems."

"I see."

"But he visited. During my prison term, he showed up about once a month. More often in December than the other months. It was a similar situation. We would talk, read the Bible, pray together. A real fellowship of Christian brothers. In a way, it was like he was consciously taking me back to the fundamentals of the faith. That personal relationship, that personal accountability."

"What about after you were let out?"

"We continued to meet. He helped me set things up. He even promoted my book to help with sales. Probably wasn't necessary. Knowing that the profits were going to restitution first, plenty of folks were hoping I'd succeed. I think even *The Kensington Post* ran a full-page ad. Might have been the only time in history Phillips ever let me run an ad in his paper." Canker laughed at the memory. Addison smiled in amusement. "We mended those bridges that I so happily burned down."

"So, even the things that you two said about each other? I seem to recall Milton offering some public criticism of your actions," inquired Addison, who initially wanted to say "crimes" but chose to be nonjudgmental.

"That was the past," said a still-leaning Johnny. "And besides, I deserved every bit of it. He could have said far more and far worse, and he still would have been justified. I say 'brother,' but really, he was more of a father to me. The age difference, my heavy reliance on his support. We were not equals."

"So, you had more of a father-son relationship?"

"Yes, but more than that," stressed Johnny, going forward so that his feet were solid on the floor and his words were steadfast. "More than that, Mr. Addison. He was a father figure to me when I was totally useless. When all the others left me. Family, friends, congregants, he was still there. He knew there was no upside to visiting me in prison. He knew there was no upside in ministering to me. Yet he still did it. And, no lie, I'm not sure I would have survived without his aid."

Canker's words were disrupted by a beeping noise. It came from his pocket. The interviewee took out his phone and looked at it. "We're going to have to end this interview now. In fifteen minutes, I need to be ready to go on the air."

"On the air?"

"Yes, I have a weekly radio spot with a local Christian station," said Canker, who then smiled. "What can I tell you? I am good at only two things—preaching the Gospel and making a fool out of myself."

FRANK MOORE

BACK AT THE MOTEL ROOM, Scott Addison was transcribing Johnny Canker's remarks. He ate a free lunch at the diner at Jesus World USA, courtesy of the interviewee. From there, he drove for about ninety minutes back to Richmond. As with the route from Alexandria to the capital, it was full of natural beauty. Endless trees with multicolored leaves, fields and valleys, and some wildlife. The distance was still draining, and it was Saturday, so he rested upon coming back to the motel.

It was menial work, but necessary, going through the recording. The starts and the stops, the typing of a half dozen to a dozen words at a time. He was on his second cola by the time he finished listening to the interview all the way through. At least the motel had a good vending machine selection and plenty of ice. Usually, Addison drank his soda directly from the can rather than dirty a cup. To make it cooler, he sometimes shoved smaller bits of ice into the can opening.

He drank more the second time through. Freed from the burden of constant typing, he paused the audio periodically to fix the quotes. Some parts he did not bother with on exact quotation; he was planning to paraphrase those sections. He was not sure how he was going to use the photos of the park. Canker made little mention of Sammy Milton's involvement in the project. Scott thought about posting them online as a photo album. He might also add a few of them to the admin system for work. That way, if they were ever seen as appropriate, they could be used by him or others for stories. They told a tale all their own—of vainglory being judged.

Scott was intrigued by the comments about Milton and his views on Canker's moral excesses. The journalist had long assumed that Milton was culpable in the scandals of the late eighties and early nineties. Raised on the backlash, as a youth he naturally conflated Milton, Canker, and a host of other evangelicals, Fundamentalists, Pentecostals, and televangelists. They were one great monolith. To hear Milton protest his friend in private, and even denounce him to a lesser extent in public, was surprising. Then again, the whole assignment had been a twisting road.

By now, Scott was able to identify the conclusion of the interview. He stopped the recording, as he no longer needed to listen. Saving the document, he exited out of it. The hour was getting late. While the sun was still present in the skies, it was after 5:00 p.m., and he needed to leave soon. Earlier, he had contacted Pastor Frank Moore through social media. The young man quickly replied. Moore agreed to be interviewed about his grandfather. In his message, he asked Addison if he could meet him Saturday evening after worship. Scott agreed, and Moore sent a smiley-face emoji.

Addison went online and checked the profile of Moore. He wanted to double-check his physical appearance to make it easier to find him at the service. It was not hard to locate images; Moore had scores of them that were publicly visible. As Scott was looking over his profile, Moore posted a new photo. The image was of the worship crowd gathered at the theater for the service. He used some artsy filter to make the image trendy and had uploaded it with hashtags.

Then it occurred to Scott. He was still trying to find more information about Wallace. The mysterious figure that appeared to be the third child of Milton. Yet his internet searches for "Wallace Milton" did not turn up any results that were germane to his quest. Looking over Moore's profile made Addison wonder if the young pastor could unknowingly help the journalist. After all, Moore was a public person on social media and plastered much of his life online.

Scott clicked on the "Friends" tab to see who all Moore was connected to. In the search engine, he began to type the name "Wallace." A few letters in, and the list of over one thousand names rapidly whittled down. By the time he punched in the second *a*, the list was reduced to only those with the exact name. There were eleven results in all. Addison recalled that it was Milton's grandmother's maiden name. Sure enough, ten of the results were either middle or last names.

Then he noticed that one of the results had it as a first name. The fellow was Wallace Smith and was identified as living in Richmond, Virginia. There was an older photo for the profile picture, an image clearly from the days before digital cameras. It was faded and showed a group of people. Given how old they looked in the photo and how old Scott assumed the photo to be, he hypothesized that whoever it was must have been around middle age in the present day.

"It is really going to be this easy?" Scott pondered aloud as he clicked on the name and was directed to the mystery man's profile. There was little to work with on his account. Only forty friends were listed. The newest post was from a year ago, and the one before that was a lone "Happy Birthday" message. It turned out that the old photo was the only photo on the entire profile. Searching the account, Scott found some basic information. A birthdate that occurred when Sammy

Milton was thirty-two. A reasonable age gap between father and son. There was also a workplace listed.

Scott opened a new tab and went to searching the source of employ. He soon found a Richmond-based company with the same name. After getting on their website, he found Wallace Smith listed in the human resources department. A more recent photo, a professional headshot, was there. He was heavy and had graying hair and brown eyes. There was a phone number listed by his name. Scott realized it was the weekend, that the odds of someone answering it were unlikely. Still, he wanted to find out more. This could be the big scoop.

Addison took hold of his smartphone and dialed the number. Raising the item to his ear, he waited through several rings before an answering machine message began. As he patiently heard the voice, readying himself to leave a message, the voice suddenly added that "If this is an emergency, please call Mr. Smith at eight-zero-four . . ." The number went by too quickly for the reporter to get it down the first time. Scott hung up, called the business number again, this time prepared to jot down the information. Hanging up, he then punched in the number and hit the call button.

It rang. Scott was not particularly nervous. Yet he was a bit on edge. He had not conclusively proven that the Wallace he was calling was the Wallace mentioned in the interview with Jabez Henderson. Neither had he confirmed his editor's conspiracy theory that this Wallace was the previously unknown gay son of Milton. A third ring, and he was starting to feel awkward. Scott needed to leave soon for his confirmed interview with Moore. The service had already begun. While Addison was not feeling a particular spiritual need at that time, he did feel that the least he could do for his readers was to describe the environment he entered.

"Hello?" answered a slightly high-pitched voice following the fourth ring.

"Hello, um, is this Wallace Smith?"

"This is he," affirmed the voice. "And who are you?"

"Well, I'm Scott Addison. I'm a reporter with *The Kensington Post*," stated Scott, knowing that he was taking a gamble with his next comments. "I was wondering if I could interview you regarding the death of your father."

"My father?" asked a confused-sounding man. Scott was starting to feel stupid. Yet he soldiered on in his query.

"Yes," stated Scott with a veneer of confidence. "You are the son of the late Rev. Sammy Milton, correct?" There was silence on the other line. The moments felt far longer than they objectively were. Scott was about to say something else to try and further goad the man to speak up.

"You think I'm gay, don't you?"

"Well, um," briefly stuttered Scott, "if that is untrue, you are free to offer any corrections or clarifications. But I would like to talk to you on the record for my story."

More silence, more tension. Then some faint laughter. "Well, I guess one of you news guys was going to find me out some day. Now that he's gone, I guess I have nothing to hide." Another pause. Scott was not sure how to react to this one. Fearing a loss of the other end of the conversation, he spoke up.

"So, does that mean I can interview you?"

"Not now," Wallace said. "When is your deadline?"

"Monday."

"How about tomorrow afternoon at three? I'm free then."

"Okay, good. Should I call you again at this number?"

"How about we meet in person? I would rather talk to a face than a receiver."

"Okay, sure. I'm in town. Where do you want to meet?"

"My place. I'll give you the address."

Scott jotted down the address and recited it back to Wallace, with the future interviewee confirming the written record. "Thank you. Talk to you tomorrow at three."

"Yes, see you then," he said. "Bye."

"Take care," said Scott, a few moments going by before Wallace hung up the phone. The shock of his discovery nearly made Addison forget that he immediately needed to be elsewhere. Snapping out of the partial euphoria, he tightened up his tie, grabbed his light jacket, put new batteries into his recorder, gathered the items necessary for his job, and then left the motel.

* * *

Scott was running late. By the time he pulled out of the motel parking lot, the service had been going on for fifteen minutes. Several minutes later, he was nearing the location. His GPS told him to get onto North Crenshaw. It was pretty easy going, given the residential surroundings. The real delay came when he got to the intersection with Ellwood. Scott was the only one with a stop sign. Cars came from his left and sped by. It was not heavy traffic, but it was greatly annoying in that they came at just close enough proximity in both lanes to make a trek across the street hazardous.

Finally, he saw what looked like a big enough gap and sped across. As it turned out, he nearly got struck by another car. There was no honking, but Addison still felt a little guilty for taking the risk. In his mind, he deserved an angered message from the other vehicle. Addison slowed for the turn into the free public parking garage. He found a space and made the rest of the journey on foot down Cary Street.

Known as Carytown, the stretch had a mixture of shops, stores, and restaurants. On his way to the service, Scott encountered a restaurant with an outdoor upper balcony, a sandwich shop, an eatery that served Korean barbecue, a couple of furniture places, a tanning bed salon, a waxing salon, and a couple of bars. On the street were various pedestrians traveling in groups, the occasional jogger, some musicians plying their talent in return for donations, and beggars attempting to appeal to one's sense of charity. The toy store, the candy store with the pirate statue, and the bicycle places blurred as he got closer to the destination, a historic movie theatre.

It was known as the Byrd Theatre. The building was named after one of the founders of Richmond, William Byrd II. It opened in 1928 and had been showing films ever since. Looking up, Addison saw the signs with the list of movies running at the facility. One of the films had just left the regular theaters, while the other was released years before the reporter was born. He entered through one of the glass doors with golden trim, the vacant ticket booth to his left. No sooner had he gotten inside then he heard rock music. It sounded like a concert was taking place.

Passing the concession stand to his left, a kindly usher opened the door for him. Addison's sense of a rock concert was not shattered when he went inside the elegant theatre space. Much of its upper-class décor was obscured by a dimly lit house and a stage shown in many light shades of diverse colors. On the main stage was a drummer, three guitarists, and four vocalists. There were three screens showing the lyrics, which were the first explicitly religious things Scott saw.

Staying behind the rows of seats, Addison studied the people around him. Those whom he made out through the disorienting mix of dim and light were wearing normal street fashion. They moved around in their stances—many with arms raised, others simply nodding their heads. The vast majority sang at the cue of the large, white words that appeared on the screens. With his tie and slacks, Addison soon realized that he was probably the best-dressed person in the room.

The lyrics gave way to a gentle guitar solo. The song was technically over. A young man, who had been to the side of the stage during the song, walked toward the front, where one of the microphones was located. He was in jeans and a flannel shirt. Bearing blond hair, the man had a style that was unorthodox. The sides of his head were shaved, but the top was long and slicked on one side so that it almost covered his right eye. In one hand, he held a black Bible, while the other hand was lifted up, as though grasping for something. A prayer was uttered, its emotion seeming to feed off of the music. The prayer touched on many topics, contemporary and personal. Addison noted that he stressed certain phrases, getting some amens from the audience. And then he himself gave a single amen, with an organic repeat of his ending from the crowd.

In an odd way, Scott was being taken back to the descriptions Beverley Clayborne gave of Sammy Milton's Salvation Meetings. There was the secular location, the popular music, and the emotional audience reactions. As it turned out, the preaching was also similar. The young man was none other than Frank Moore, the lead pastor Addison had come to interview. He wove contemporary events, happenings and fears, into his preaching. He provided a biblical context; he spoke with conviction, though oftentimes sliding into cute little quips, which received varying levels of laughter.

Addison timed the message to be about twenty minutes long. He admitted to himself that it felt quicker. The band struck their notes again, the screens showed the bold, white lyrics against a dark blue background. Scott became cynically amused when the screens briefly posted the wrong lyrics, but there was little indication of the error among the joyful noise arising. Again, the young pastor went to the front with a musical background for his praying. This prayer was shorter and was followed by an older man sharing the stage to give some reminders about announcements. Things like a charity drive that they were cosponsoring with a nearby congregation, a girls' night out Bible study that was starting soon, and a guys' camping trip to Great Falls. There were jokes woven in here and there during those comments also. To complete the service, they sang the chorus of one of the songs performed earlier in worship.

The lights came on, and Addison finally saw the sheer beauty of the Byrd Theatre's interior. Done in the French Empire style, there were walls of marble, paintings, arches of golden leaf, large red curtains on the stage, balconies, and a giant chandelier. He also saw the demographics of the service. Most of them were college age or mid-twenties. Addison realized that he was not only the most formally dressed person in the room; he was also one of the oldest.

As the crowds gradually funneled out of the ornate theater, Addison made his way toward the main stage. Moore's distinctive haircut and tall frame made him stand out among the others. Scott quickly got a fix on his location once the service ended and kept on it. Sliding past lines of departing worshippers, he saw Moore talking with a few people who had been in the audience during worship. It was all lighthearted. They would say their piece, exchange some words, and then leave in the same direction as the rest of the attendees. Some smiled at Addison as he walked, with him smiling back as a courtesy. They must have thought he was a seeker.

As Scott came within a few feet of Moore, he realized that the young pastor was at least five inches taller than him. Moore was nevertheless a scrawny figure, with the long-sleeved flannel shirt seeming to hang over a much thinner frame. The reporter concluded that running must be a hobby for the preacher. He also found him familiar-looking. Having gotten close enough, he realized that the young pastor had blue eyes. Remembering the photos of Milton, Scott could see the hereditary legacy. The jaw seemed to have a similar rounding; the nose and lips also seemed to fit the same proportions. Moore briefly directed his eyes to Addison. Then he turned to talk briefly with a couple of band members, who proceeded to start packing up their equipment. After a few moments, Moore approached Addison with a smile and an outstretched hand.

"You're Scott Addison, the reporter, right?"

"Yes," said Addison as he got a quick handshake from Moore.

"I'll be with you in just a moment. I just need to talk to a couple more people. You can wait right here," said Moore, getting a nod from Addison.

Scott observed Moore as he socialized with the others. One of them was the older man, who had given the announcements. After their talk, the man exited. Another conversation, some pleasant good-byes to those who helped with the worship service. After the pleasantries and final comments with the others, Moore eventually turned back to Addison. As he did so, a pair of janitors entered the theater space from the back. The young pastor neared the reporter.

"Looks like they're about to kick us out," noted Moore without panic in his voice. "Where would you like to do this?"

"Is there a place at the theater where we could speak?"

"Try the balcony," interjected one of the band members as he walked by. "They usually do them first, so they should be okay now."

"Thanks! That should work."

"Cool," agreed Moore. "Let's go."

* * *

Scott and Frank were both seated in one of the balcony spaces. With the janitors cleaning up the aisles and seats, Addison turned on his recording device. He balanced it on the surface of his notepad. Written on the first page were a few questions he had in mind for the interviewee, whose hands moved as he spoke.

"So, to begin, you are the first member of the family that I have interviewed. Could you state your full name and how you are related to the late Rev. Sammy Milton?"

"Yeah, totally," replied the young pastor. "My name is Frank Milton Moore. I am pastor of Site 20 Fellowship, which meets weekly at the Byrd Theatre. Rev. Sammy is my grandpa. You see, he had three kids: two sons, my uncles, and a daughter. The daughter's name is Helen. She's my mom. She was born in 1965. She met a man named Tim Moore when she was in college. They married in 1988. I was born two years later."

"Okay, interesting," said Scott as he looked back down at the note-pad and jotted a brief note. His writing was limited, since he needed to keep the recorder from falling. "So, obviously, you've known Rev. Milton all your life. Could you explain to me some of what it was like to be raised around a, well, controversial public figure?"

"Yeah, definitely," replied Moore. "I mean, for the first years it all felt normal. When you're a kid, you don't know a whole lot about the outside world. Things didn't come up at family gatherings. And Grandpa never talked about controversial stuff around me. I think he thought that stuff wasn't appropriate for kids. If he did, I don't remember it. He was just your usual, nice grandpa. Bought me cool toys for my birthday and Christmas, played with me when my parents were busy, secretly bought me ice cream when they weren't around. Stuff like that."

"When did you become aware of his public career?"

"Teenage years, like fourteen or fifteen," recalled Frank. "By that time, I was old enough that I could stay up late and watch him on the news programs arguing with people. It was like watching a sports game. I cheered him on, sometimes heckling the other person, claiming they cheated somehow. But, I mean, by that time I didn't see him a lot."

"How come?"

"Nothing crazy. Just that my dad got a job up in Fairfax, working for the federal government. So, we all moved up there. The rest of the family stayed here. So, I went from seeing him a couple times a week to about once a month. What we did was we would all meet in Fredericksburg for brunch or dinner on a Saturday. I must have taken that battlefield tour ten or twelve times," remarked Moore, smiling at the memories. "But again, he rarely talked about politics or stuff like that."

"I see," commented Scott. "What impact, if any, did Rev. Milton have on your decision to become a pastor?"

"A lot," he said with widened eyes. "It all started about a decade ago when I was graduating from high school. You see, not to brag, but I was one of the cool kids. You know what I mean?" Scott smiled and nodded at the query. "I was the star lacrosse player; I got great grades, plenty of dates, and I even won prom king. But then, I was graduating. I was leaving it all. It was all going to disappear. And that totally got to me. I mean, after all that, I was going to have to start all over again. It made me wonder, you know . . . it made me want something that was better."

As he heard the young pastor describe his calling, Addison felt he was hearing a documented instance of history repeating itself. He kept his intrigue to himself behind a professional veil as Moore continued. "So that Thanksgiving, my first Thanksgiving after entering college, I was hanging out with my grandpa. I told him about how I felt and asked him if he ever felt the same way. His eyes got really huge and he said, 'I know EXACTLY what you are talking about!' He told me about his time as a pro-baseball player, which I already knew about. But now, he told me about how he became a preacher. 'You have a calling. God wants you to serve Him.' And I was just so blown away by that. But it made sense. And guess what? It still totally makes sense."

"I see that," commented Scott, looking down at his notes before raising his eyes to ask a question. "And so, how else did Rev. Milton get involved in your, um, calling?"

"A lot of ways," remembered Moore. "He gave me advice on how to preach. He answered every question I had about the Bible. He helped me find the right literature and the right classes. You know, biblically-grounded books and teachers. For my pastoral hours, which is like volunteer hours, Grandpa got me a position at the New Hope Jerusalem Home."

"Is that a church?"

"No, it's a home my grandpa set up to help alcoholics."

"Really?"

"Yeah, my grandpa set up the Home years ago. Before I was born actually. You see, my great-granddad, who I never met, was an alcoholic. So, in his memory, my grandpa opened a home to help people who had my great-granddad's problem."

"Interesting."

"So, I worked there. I did many things, like pastoral care, counseling. A lot of listening, hearing men tell how booze ruined their lives. After working there for a few months, I decided that I was never going to drink. I was twenty at the time and hadn't drank before. But yeah, I'm still a dry guy. To hear what alcohol can do to people, how it destroys lives, I don't want to give my money to something like that. I'll tell you, my granddad was as thrilled about that decision as he was of my calling."

"And did he help with setting up your church, Site 20?"

"Yes, at first," began Moore. "For my twenty-fourth birthday, he gave me a check that would cover our rent expenses for the first three months. From there, though, we supported ourselves through the great generosity of our congregation. And that generosity is still strong, because at the rate we're going, by the end of the year we're going to have enough money to make the first payment on a place of our own."

"That's nice."

"So yeah, he was always helpful. He let me occasionally preach at Into Marvelous Light. I preached my first message there, in fact. I was sweating like you'd not believe. After the service, some folks came up to me and said I must have been inspired, because I had the glow of the Spirit upon me," Moore said with a laugh, with Addison giving a relatable grin. "So, yeah, he was very helpful. Sometimes, we would coordinate our messages. We'd talk over the phone and agree to both preach at our churches on a specific issue. That way, even more people would hear what needed to be said."

"So, with all that in mind," said Scott, looking down at the last question on the notepad page, "how did he take your comments in 2015 about how churches shouldn't be involved in politics?"

At the question, Frank's eyes went big, the blue orbs shining in his emotion. It was not anger, but great excitement. "And I am so glad that you mentioned that. Because let me tell you that I was totally misquoted." The comment jarred Addison, nearly causing him to lose his grip on the recorder. "Everyone quoted me as saying that I opposed my grandpa's coalition work and tackling the social issues and stuff. Thing is, I never actually said that. Like, at all. What I had really said was that I was opposed to churches endorsing political candidates. You know the whole thing about the IRS rules? I explained in my interview with *The Kensington Post* that I still thought it was okay for pastors to take public positions on political issues. I mean, if anything, they should be the first people to comment on the controversial stuff."

"Your comments were made to *The Kensington Post*?" asked a baffled Addison, who knew he had never interviewed the young pastor before. "Who interviewed you?"

"I don't remember his name, but I just remember that when I saw my interview in the Friday edition, I freaked out," Moore said, his eyes still wide with expression. "I mean, I had people calling me up asking why I said that. And I had to explain over and over that my words were misinterpreted. I posted statements all over social media. It was a crazy time, let me tell you. Worst moment of my whole career as a pastor."

"Did you try contacting our editor?"

"Oh yeah, a bunch of times," explained Moore while Addison looked down in contemplation. "I emailed him, called him. At first, he said he'd look into it. Then he said he was busy. And then, he said something about how it was too late to issue a correction and that no one cared anymore—or something like that."

"Timeliness?" asked Scott, struggling to look up.

"Yes, that! That was what he said. After a while, I quit trying. But hey, if you're going to write about our interview, you'll mention it, right?"

"Yes, of course," nodded Scott, aware that he could not guarantee such an inclusion.

"Great, that's awesome."

"Well, um, anyhow," noted the reporter, finally looking up at his interviewee, "that covers my questions. Thanks for talking to me and sorry for your loss."

"No problem, thanks," said Frank as the two rose from their respective seats in the balcony. "Before you go, would you mind if I prayed over you?"

"Um, sure, that's okay," replied Scott. He bowed his head while the taller pastor had his eyes closed and placed hovered hands just above the reporter.

"Dear Lord Jesus, thank You for this evening and for the worship. Thank You for the life of Rev. Sammy Milton, my grandpa. Thank You for bringing Scott here safely. You have given him an important job. You gave him the job of telling the truth. Give him strength, O Lord, to tell facts, to correct wrongs, and to speak truth to power, no matter how risky or dangerous the task. Bless his efforts and his article. Thank You for bringing him here to learn the truth and to fix problems. In Jesus' Name, Amen."

"Amen," lightly added Scott.

"Well, take care, brother," said Frank as the two shook hands. "And if you're ever in the Richmond area again, let me know. I'd love to see you come back here."

"I'll think about it," smiled Scott.

* * *

They were gathered at one of the bars in Old Town Alexandria. They were off of King Street, its trolleys going back and forth outside. The sun had set, and the creatures were out, enjoying the company and the drinks. Loud music blared from the dance floor, which was moderately occupied. Mandy Salver-Jones' husband had reserved the booth and was seated beside his wife, one arm draped over her shoulders and the other gripping a mug. Sitting on the opposite end of the semicircle was Katie Nicholson, bearing a dark brown beer bottle from which she took occasional swigs. An acquaintance from the marketing department was also there, seated in the center of the booth. To his right and to Katie's left was the guest of honor, Tyrone Spearman.

"It was beautiful, simply beautiful," he stated while gripping his third drink for the evening, poured into a mug. "The layout was nice.

And those last-minute edits helped a lot. The printer let me get a few copies for family."

"That was nice," commented Katie.

"You deserve it," stated Mandy. "You wrote an excellent article that made the front page of the weekly edition proud." Tyrone smiled at Mandy, who slightly altered her tone. "Yet you still came up with the worst title for any article this week, if not the worst title for this entire calendar year."

"The best title," corrected Tyrone before taking another drink.

"What is this about?" sincerely inquired the husband to his wife.

"Let me set it up first," said Mandy to Tyrone, who was about to speak up. She directed her attention to her spouse, his arm still around her. "Earlier this week, Tyrone was assigned an article about a book coming out about the Christian beliefs of Donald Trump. It's one of those books about a president's devotions and stuff. So, what you had was a story on a book about Trump, Christianity, and reaching out to that evangelical base. So, what did Tyrone decide to call his article?"

"'Grab 'Em by the Faith'!" declared Tyrone, proud of his creation. While the coworkers smirked and shook their heads, the husband busted out laughing.

"Don't encourage him!" said a quasi-amused, quasi-annoyed Mandy.

"Are you kidding me? That's hilarious," said the husband as he tapped mugs with the creator of that headline.

"The divorce papers will be on your mantel tomorrow morning," dryly quipped Mandy, who smiled the moment her husband kissed her on the cheek.

Katie was amused by the exchange and then noticed that her phone was lighting up. Upon seeing it, she quickly took hold of it and saw the name Scott Addison on the screen. She was not concerned, but more disappointed. Katie took hold of the device and tapped the screen to begin the conversation.

"Why, hello there, Scott!" she said loudly enough to get the whole booth's attention.

"Hey, Katie," said the voice on the other end.

"You know, Scott, Richmond isn't that far away," began Katie, the others amused by the tone taken. "You could have driven up for this."

"I'm sorry. I had to do a couple interviews today. One of them was in Lynchburg. I am totally drained."

"Well, we all miss you, don't we?" she asked the booth's occupants, who gave various lighthearted and insincere responses.

"Katie, could I talk to you alone?"

"Of course. Let me get somewhere quieter," she told the voice and then turned to her immediate company. "I'll be back soon. Watch my drink!"

"Don't we always?" lightly asked Tyrone as Katie got up and headed for the bathroom. As she got away, Tyrone puckered his lips multiple times to impersonate the noise of kissing, to the amusement of those still seated in the booth.

Katie made her way through the space, navigating around tables, booths, customers, and waiters alike. She found the door without a knob, the black icon of a woman wearing a dress, and pushed the portal open to enter the tiled space of privacy. There were only a few others in the restroom, and they were uninterested in the phone conversation. Walls muffled the sound waves of music and banter. A large mirror reflected the reporter as she talked with her concerned coworker.

"Are you alone?"

"Pretty much."

"Are you away from the others?"

"Yes," answered Katie, who was beginning to get worried.

"Good. I need to talk to you alone. Away from them. Because right now, I feel like you're the only one I can trust."

"About what?" she asked as she instinctively stroked away some strands of her hair that swung in front of her face.

"Let me ask you," started a serious Addison, "did you know that Sammy Milton created a charity that helps unwed mothers?"

"No," casually responded Katie.

"Did you know that he once gave a speech urging Southerners to quit flying the Confederate flag?"

"No."

"Did you know that he was good friends with Herbert Spiker—the same Herbert Spiker who battled Milton in the courts?"

"I didn't know that."

"Did you know he has a home that helps alcoholics?"

"Okay, you got me," she stated in annoyance. "I didn't know any of that. What's your point?"

"My point is, none of us knew that. None of us journalists, the great sources of information, knew that," stated Scott, his aggravation disturbing Katie. "I was assigned this story, thinking I was going to remind the world how much of a jerk Sammy Milton was. But right now, all I have are a bunch of people, including his biggest enemies, who thought he was great. The more I work on this story, the better Milton looks as a human being."

"Listen, Scott," replied an assuring Katie, "what you're going through is completely normal. Remember when I had to do that obit for Margaret Thatcher? For a while, I found myself kind of liking her."

"This is different, very different," strongly insisted Scott.

"How so?"

"Because . . . because not only is Milton starting to look good, but our editor is starting to look bad."

"Phillips?" asked Katie, her look of surprise reflected against the bathroom mirror.

"Person after person I've talked to all mention Phillips refusing to cover things that Milton did right. You know, stuff like those charities, his friendships with people, his helping out a feminist friend with her voter drive, his apology to the black community for past wrongs, his bashing of televangelist greed," continued Scott, his tone getting increasingly somber with each point. "My story was supposed to be about how evil Milton was; now it's about how good he was."

"Scott, this happens from time to time," assured Katie. "You know that every so often we get a certain lede; but as we gather the evidence, the lede turns out to be wrong. As professional journalists, we both know that when that happens, we have to adjust our lede to reflect the evidence."

"Don't you see, Katie? There's no way that can work."

"Why not?"

"Because Phillips hates Milton. And if I submit a story that portrays Milton as this misunderstood good guy, how do you think he's going to react? How do you think he will feel when he realizes that I spent a whole week on one story just so that it could be something he despises? What do you think will happen to me? What do you think will happen to our future?" That question hit Katie hard. "What do I do? You have to help me, Katie. You have to."

"Well," said Katie, who took a breath before continuing. "Do you have any more interviews to do?"

"Yes, one more."

"Who is it?"

"Maybe my only hope," began Scott. "Turns out Phillips was right about one thing: Milton has a gay son."

"For real?"

"Yes," responded Scott with some excitement. "It was hard to find him at first because he changed his last name."

"No doubt shamed out of the family."

"Exactly, yes, exactly. Best of all, he's willing to talk to me tomorrow afternoon."

"Well, then, problem solved," said Katie with encouragement. "Interview him; record all his grievances against his homophobic father; and make that your lede. You can include the other stuff, but people won't care. They'll only remember all the bad stuff that he did to his son just for being who he was."

"Yes, yes, that's exactly my thinking," said a relieved Scott. "Thank you so much, Katie. You're an inspiration."

"I try."

"Anyway, I better get to work preparing for the interview. Good night!"

"Good night," she said as the call ended, already beginning to second guess the ethics of her guidance.

WALLACE SMITH

SCOTT ADDISON WAS ON THE highway leaving Richmond proper. He was not done with his task, but rather was headed toward his final interview. Sunday afternoon traffic was surprisingly light. Addison had his share of bad memories trying to travel on the interstates between Sunday lunch and Sunday dinner. For its part, I-64 offered a fairly quick sojourn, with the reporter spending only seven minutes on it before making the turn to Exit 178-A. From there, he found himself on Broad Street, surrounded on either side by countless stores, restaurants, shopping centers, and car dealerships. Via the GPS, he found the left turn onto the minor road. A few small streets later, he was there.

The house had a quaint appeal. Basic brick work, two stories plus an attic, and two cars in the driveway. Addison parked in front of the tacit suburban domicile, its door closed, windows shut, and curtains drawn. He followed the brick walkway up the front lawn, having yet to see a person anywhere near the property. The whole community was quiet. Rain was in the forecast, and clouds were slogging overhead. Perchance, the weather prognosticators had scared the families inside. Regardless, Scott checked his phone to verify the time. He was early, but only by a few minutes. Surely, someone was there.

Scott pulled open the screen door and took hold of the brass knocker. He pounded it five times, each thud feeling louder for want of extensive outside noise. Then he waited. Addison wondered in those seconds why no one was answering. He worried that some hostile neighbor was going to ask him why he was bothering the block. Ignorant of a better strategy, Scott knocked the brass against the door five more times. He waited again. A few seconds after the second round of noise, the journalist heard movement from behind the door. Someone was walking toward the portal. Scott took a pair of steps backwards, while his left hand kept the screen propped open.

A bolt was undone, the knob turned, and then the door swung inwards. The sight was unexpected. He was a medium-sized, light-skinned, African-American male. He looked to be in his fifties and wore khakis with a sweater. For a moment, Scott thought that he had uncovered a very different scandal within the Milton family. The man was reserved, seeming to take a defensive posture. Scott was a stranger, after all. He then spoke up in a soft voice: "Can I help you?"

"Yes, I am a reporter with *The Kensington Post*. Does Wallace Smith live here?" asked Scott, who was starting to think he might have the wrong address.

"What's your name?"

"Scott Addison. I talked with Smith over the phone yesterday about meeting."

"Wait here," he said, placid in speech, yet issuing a command. He pushed the door forward, obscuring nearly all of Addison's view of the inside hallway and staircase. Through the opening, Scott was able to hear the muffled exchanges of a conversation—not quite the words, but the fact that two people were in communication. One of the voices sounded familiar. Scott was pretty sure it was Wallace.

He did not have to ponder the theory for long, as he heard more steps coming toward the door. As Scott continued to hold the screen door, the main divide between outside and in was pulled back once again. Swinging inward, Scott saw the African-American man standing before him and then another figure next to him. A heavyset white man, he had brown hair and brown eyes. Yet the face, the face looked familiar. Despite the beard and mustache, despite the lack of blue eyes, he nevertheless resembled his father.

"You wanted to talk to me?" he asked.

"Mr. Smith?"

"Yup."

"Yes, I do."

"Okay," said Wallace with a breath. "Come in."

"Thank you."

Scott nodded as the two men inside the house backed up so the reporter could enter the hallway. Closing the screen door behind him, Scott saw a basic layout for the space. A mirror and mantel on one end with a bowl containing keys. Light purple wall paper with white painted trim on the entranceways for the three rooms that the hall led to. The stairs had white carpeting, and the bannister was painted as the arches. It looked so conventional for what was an unconventional domestic situation.

"Do you need anything while I'm out?" asked the African-American man of Wallace.

"No, I should be okay," replied Wallace, getting a quick peck on the cheek from the man before he exited the house. Scott noticed the brief display of affection and felt more confident. His theory was holding up nicely. "Let's go to the living room."

"Okay," agreed Addison as the homeowner led him to the room on the right. It had the longest threshold. Scott walked into a regular-looking place, with two couches and a few chairs, a coffee table with a glass top, and a television in the corner. There were photos hung on the wall, including a professional portrait featuring Wallace and the first man Scott met. In the portrait, they were smiling, arm-in-arm.

"Go ahead and take a seat," offered Wallace, with Scott obliging. "Do you need anything? Coffee, tea?"

"No, I'm okay."

"So, you found me," commented Wallace as he plopped down onto the plush couch facing opposite Addison's chair. "How'd you do it, if you don't mind the question?"

"Interviews with other people," Scott said. "They hinted at your existence. And then it all came together when I searched your nephew's friends list."

"Frank, right?"

"Yes."

"Thought so. He's fixing to be the next Sammy Milton. He has a very public life. That's okay with me. I never wanted to be famous. Guess I will be now, won't I?"

"Most likely."

"Well, congrats on the scoop," said Wallace with a well-meaning smile. "We can start whenever you want."

"Okay," agreed Scott as he turned on his recorder, which was gently positioned on the glass top. "What was it like to be the gay son of Rev. Sammy Milton?"

* * *

It was a community-wide event. Into Marvelous Light Ministries invited not just members, but all who could make it. Not just evangelicals, but mainline Protestants, Catholics, Orthodox, and other branches of the Christian tree. There were also non-believers, like Orthodox Jews and even a few Muslims. Nearly all of the attendees belonged to Into Marvelous Light, though. Still, it was a large gathering; only the balcony had empty seats. Quite impressive for an event held on a Friday.

No singular happening birthed the event into existence. There were no referendums pending, nor campaigns running. Neither the Republican nor the Democratic parties had hotly debated the topic for their platform. At that time, institutionally speaking, they were safe. The Democrats held the White House, but their man was a devout Southern Baptist. Meanwhile, the GOP was making more overtures to men like the Reverend Sammy Milton, who waited on the main stage to give his remarks. Still, the culture was starting its long turn toward that movement, inciting responses like the event.

"This debauchery, this abomination, is spreading like the plague," proclaimed Johnny Canker, getting many nods from those gathered in the sanctuary. "It is a disease that destroys the individual, and then the community." He paused for dramatic effect. "Homosexuality is a vile cancer within this country. It spreads through night clubs, through mass media, through the willful actions of radical activists, and through the quackery of the science, falsely so-called, of postmodern atheist psychologists. The homosexual has no interest in family values, no interest in God, and no interest in human civilization. Rather, the homosexual is a predator, hoping to spread his false gospel to young, vulnerable children!" There were gasps by some, not by the vitriol of his words, but by the imagery his rhetoric created.

Wallace was in the crowd. He sat two rows from the stage where Canker, his father, and a handful of other speakers were situated. Each inflammatory phrase stuck to him, slapping him with a fierce wind.

His core shook in terror, less for his immortal soul and more for what might happen to him should his secret impulses be made public. No one else was cognizant of his thoughts, his uncomfortable status. Other family were seated around him. His younger sister was at home, studying for a test. A sitter was there, although as a middle schooler, she needed only basic adult supervision.

"With all their fornication, their constant sleeping around and giving in to perversion, should any of us be surprised that now they drop like flies?" asked Canker, with some in the audience saying no in agreement. "I am not. For I worship a just God, Whose wrath is now being visited upon the wicked." Applause broke out. "If we want this wrath to spare the rest of the country, we must advance good family values," stressed Johnny in a speech that was made about five years before his first affair.

Wallace looked around the audience as Canker spoke. He looked for reactions. Not the usual impassioned support. He wanted to know if there was anyone else. There was no way he could be the only one dealing with this guttural dissent, this thorn in the flesh. Surely, most surely, someone else was suppressing the urge to leave, frightened of where these bombastic words would lead. A face, here and there, that was all. Maybe four or five of them amidst the hundreds to low thousands in attendance. It was all interpretation. Theirs might have been a stomach ache or bad news received earlier that day. He was too afraid to investigate the matter then or right after the event.

"Thank you, Johnny, for those inspirational words," said Milton as he shook Canker's hand before the fiery preacher returned to his seat. Milton was at the podium, his old, black, leather-bound Bible resting upon its surface. He looked over the crowds before giving his remarks.

"Regarding homosexuality, the matter is biblically simple: it brought Hell out of Heaven on Sodom. Homosexuality is condemned in both Testaments, which means both Jews and Gentiles are to recognize it as incompatible with holy living. No matter what the modernists may say, with their pointless compromises, what God's Word says endures. For the generation of Moses, the generation of Paul, and unto the last generation. To say nothing of ours. Of course, our generation and the last generation might be one and the same." The comment garnered some guffawing from the audience.

Wallace took more comfort in his father's speech. He felt relief when Milton said that he would love his children, even if one of them turned out to be gay. He appreciated the call to ministering, the call to compassion. Each moment of mercy was balanced with a call to condemn unrighteousness. Flee immorality, reject perversity. Do not turn America into another Sodom, much less another Gomorrah. His words were less intense, and, to Wallace's expectation, the crowd was less intense in response.

"Make no mistake, though," continued Milton. "We must fight them. We must stop this movement from getting control. They claim they simply want to live and let live. But I warn you, this is their greatest lie. If these homosexual activists take control of our country, they will steer us into dark paths. They will try to change the very definition of marriage to include their unions. They will force schoolchildren to read books claiming that being gay is acceptable. They will force businesses and churches to cater to their every wants or face severe government-sponsored punishments. They will trample on our rights of speech, of thought, of conscience, and of religion. They will attack our basic liberties. And while they persecute us through state and mob rule, they will claim that they are the tolerant ones. So be vigilant! Take every ethical action you can to stop this movement from corrupting America!"

* * *

After grace was said, the breaking of bread commenced. Ginny made her much beloved tuna noodle casserole. There were warm rolls with sticks of butter, as well as plenty of plastic containers of cottage cheese for the topping. Sammy did the initial round of distribution, cutting rectangular chunks of the casserole and carefully placing the crumbling slices on dinner plates. Spoons dug deep into the cottage cheese, lathering the top of the casserole like vanilla ice cream on apple pie. The way the family ate the meal, it might as well have been dessert. The two sons drank water with their meal, while the daughter had a coke. House rules limited each kid to one soda a day, two if they did extra chores. Wallace and Ashley had already indulged earlier that day and had not earned a second one.

"So, how is Algebra going, Ash?"

"Still not good," the son admitted. "My teachers want me to go to a different class, Algebra I, part 1. They say it would be better for me."

"And what did you say?"

"That I need to talk to my parents."

"Well, I think it's worth considering," chimed in Ginny. "If Ashley needs help, then we should do it."

"Can you stay on the team if you drop down?"

"I don't know," replied Ash. "I was too nervous to ask."

"Well," began the father, "ask them about how it will affect your standing. You know if you go too far down in your GPA, you can't play."

"Yes, Dad."

"And we want to know their answer," stressed his mother. "Don't agree to something without us looking over it, okay?"

"Yes, Mom. I won't do anything stupid."

"Like Algebra?"

"Helen Edith!"

"Oh, mom, she's right," said Ashley. "Algebra is stupid."

"Ash, you can come to that conclusion after you pass it."

"Yes, Dad."

The family had a few more bites of their respective meals. Wallace and his father both took seconds from the rectangular dish. Helen was almost done, picking at the remaining bites and their cottage cheese topping while sipping her soda.

"Remind me, Helen, when is your recital?"

"Next week."

"When?"

"Friday at seven," she replied. "My dance team will do two numbers. One before the intermission and one after."

"So, we can't duck out early, like last time?" asked an annoyed Wallace.

"Nope, you're stuck there," replied Helen with a fake smile.

"You know, I heard from the other mothers that they were planning to leave early, and the production caught wind of it. Apparently, the new performing arts director doesn't like people not watching the whole show."

"Hmmm . . . " Sammy contemplated, tapping the top of his fork to his chin. "You know, that night is a little awkward for me. I have a meeting with Pastor Canker."

"You're not going to miss it again, are you, Sammy?"

"Yeah, Daddy. You missed the last two."

"I know, dear. I'm sorry," said Sammy, who noted in self-reflection that his crusade for family values was often the bane of being with his own family. He looked at her sincere face, her big eyes doing all the pleading. His armor was no use against such a weapon. "Tell you what, I'll call up Canker and tell him to push our meeting back. Whatever strategies he wants to tell me about can wait a couple of hours."

"Thanks, Daddy," she said, smiling with braced teeth.

"Be glad she's not on the other side," quipped Ginny to her husband. Sammy smirked in response as the dinner gradually came to a close.

Later that evening, things wound down. Wallace's siblings were already upstairs preparing for bed as he watched the one television in the entire house. His parents rejected the children's request to have smaller sets in each bedroom. Ginny was especially contemptuous of the technological device, believing the claims of some that watching too much TV caused cancer tumors. During the summertime, she ruled that no child could watch more than three hours of television a day. She eventually compromised to allow for more than three hours if a child did not watch any TV the previous day. Since that evening was during springtime, the restriction was not enforced.

Wallace had already done his homework. He was a good, slightly above average student. He preferred the news and sometimes watched pro wrestling with his older brother. When he was younger, he enjoyed the Saturday morning cartoons. However, with teen years, he got over the habit. If nothing else, middle school peer pressure had helped him with that decision. The same pressure kept him inside the closet. He knew there was no way a gym full of heterosexual boys, whose only knowledge of homosexuals was derogatory in nature, was going to let him live in peace.

Yet there was no peace on the television screen. The network news program was showing rioting in California. The jury ruled that former San Francisco Board of Supervisors member Dan White was guilty of voluntary manslaughter, rather than first degree murder, when he shot Harvey Milk and Mayor George Moscone. A demonstration that started out as a nonviolent show of anger descended into rampant destruction. Police cars were burnt; buildings were vandalized; and tear gas was used. Many were injured, with the station reporting that some police were retaliating against the community.

Wallace looked at it all and discerned these matters in his heart. They were him, and he was they. Their orientation was the same, their passions identical. Both were disturbed by the light sentence for White, the ridiculous legal argument, and the sense that every institution, from law enforcement to the Church, was against them. Wallace soon figured that there was one key difference between himself and those standing firm in the face of hatred: he was on the sidelines. He cowered in the corner, afraid to even acknowledge his own self, let alone march in solidarity and brave the forces of bigotry.

"What are you watching?" asked Sammy with innocence, breaking the concentration of his son. Milton found his answer as he got closer to the screen. He only caught the last part of the segment, a quick glimpse of LGBT activism before they turned it over to the weatherman for the forecast. "Looked like increased moral decay."

"Dad?" asked Wallace, turning to his father. "Is it okay to kill someone?"

"Of course not," replied Sammy. "'Thou shalt not kill,' says the Good Book."

"Even if they're gay?"

Sammy was confused by the line of questioning. He had not yet figured out what Wallace was getting at. "Gay or straight. Black or white. Christian or not. Born or unborn. Murder is murder, plain and simple."

"Okay," said a sedated Wallace. "I just wanted to know because those people were really angry about a gay man getting murdered. They think his killer got off easy."

"He was found guilty, wasn't he?"

"Yeah," admitted Wallace. "But they wanted more."

"A bloodthirsty mob, then. I should expect no less from the same people who want to bring Sodom to America."

"Maybe they're afraid."

"Afraid?" asked Sammy, who took a seat on a chair to the left of the screen, his son seated on the couch directly facing the TV. "Afraid of what?"

"Maybe they're afraid that they'll be next. Maybe they think the cops will keep destroying their homes. Maybe they think more people will kill them and then get off, or get a couple years, and then be free." Wallace closed his eyes as though to cry, but no tears escaped. The next sentence slipped out. "Maybe they're afraid their dad won't love them anymore if he comes out to him."

Sammy was about to say something. Then he stopped. He became filled with angst when he realized what his son was getting at. Milton started traveling back to past years. Random bits of information swirling about his consciousness began to harden into a narrative. The lack of interest in girls. The still high-pitched voice. Even his watching of wrestling, featuring the clash of muscular, scantily-clad men. Wallace knew that his wrestling watching had nothing to do with erotic interest; however, his father's thoughts were unaware of the nuance. He remained calm, attempting to suppress his suspicions. His wife was still cleaning up, oblivious to the deepening discourse.

"Why would they believe their father would reject them?" asked Sammy to his son. Wallace was beginning to think that his father was figuring it out.

"Because his father is a religious man. He has a reputation. He's famous. He despises homosexuality. Calls it a sin, a mental disorder. And he lets . . . and he lets people say worse than that from the pulpit of his church."

Sammy silently gasped. His son was shaking, turning to him with glassy eyes. The father stared at the son; the son stared back and nodded. Sammy took a deep breath and slowly blinked his blue eyes. His head tilted with three of his five left-handed fingers touching his face. There was silence for an emotional eternity. Wallace was terrified to say anything else; Sammy was trying to gather his thoughts.

"What's going on in here?" asked Virginia, oblivious to the conversation.

"I need to be alone with God," Sammy stated calmly. "Wally, tell your mother what we were talking about." The patriarch of the family rose from his chair and walked to an adjacent room he used as a home office. He closed the door behind him, with mother and son alone in the living room. Wallace surprised himself by being frank with his mother; telling his father must have made it easier somehow.

If Wallace had any confidence, it was fracturing as he heard the muffled shouts from the office room. His father was lifting up his frustrations, his anger at the news. The argument sounded intense; Wallace never understood how it did not wake his siblings. Maybe it did, but they were too frightened to venture downstairs to learn the reason for their father's rage. Virginia struggled to keep her composure. Wallace was apologetic, but also gathering a slow firmness to his professed identity. He was not going to try not being gay; he was not going through a phase. This was not a joke. He answered all the accusations, all the clichéd queries of his distraught mother.

After several minutes, the shouting halted. There was a tranquil monologue faintly audible through the closed door. Wallace wondered if his father was going through some series of stages for grief. Maybe he was on the acceptance level. Mother and son sat together on the couch as Sammy emerged from the room. Both kept quiet, fearful of disrupting the stable mood he heftily bore as he lumbered forth. Wallace saw that his father was holding his aged, black, leather-bound Bible. It was the same Scripture Sammy used to read from when he put Wallace to bed as a child. Sammy held it to his chest as he walked forward, his dominating frame casting a shadow on the two seated family members.

"Ginny, I want to be alone with my son," said Sammy in monotone. She nodded and exited the room, keeping her composure until she went upstairs. Wallace stayed seated, his stomach giving him much anguish.

"Am I in trouble?"

"You have a problem," said Sammy, looking down at Wallace. "I talked to God about it, and He gave me an answer. Tomorrow, I will make a phone call and set something up. Things will be better soon enough." He got closer to his son and patted him on the head. He even smiled. "We will get through this. I know the solution. We will deal with it tomorrow. It's late. We are both tired. Good night, son."

"Good night, Dad," said Wallace as he rose from the couch, cautious. The two embraced, Sammy still gripping the Bible as he put his arms around his son. Wallace felt better, relieved. That was, until morning.

* * *

"I don't want to do this," declared Wallace.

"You have no choice," replied his father, speaking while looking at the road.

"No shrink is going to change me," he insisted as the vehicle stopped before a red light.

"Now that is no way to handle something. Dr. Seznack comes highly recommended from parents at my church whose kids went through exactly what you're going through."

"Dad, I did my homework. The APA just voted to take homosexuality off their list of mental disorders. According to them, I'm healthy."

"Healthy," disputed Sammy as the light turned green, and the car accelerated. "A bunch of political hacks storm a meeting and shout the experts down, and that's considered science. As if Evolution wasn't enough of a crock."

"But Dad—"

"There is no debate here, Wally. There are not two sides to this argument. You have a problem, and Dr. Seznack has a solution. It's that simple."

"If it's so simple, then why don't all those people in San Francisco go to this doctor guy?"

"If it's so healthy, why are all those people in San Francisco dying of that plague?" asked Sammy, receiving no response from his son. There was silence for another minute, an old Christian hymn playing on the radio. "We're almost there. You will do this, or you're grounded."

"Dad, please . . . "

"Wallace Smith Milton," declared an angered father. "I am not asking you to do this. I am TELLING you to do this. Is that understood?"

"Yes, dad," murmured the teenager as they turned into the parking lot.

Father and son talked little between the turning off of the vehicle and the arrival at the office. They entered a generic office building, simplistic in outward décor and containing twelve floors of assorted companies and professions. Wallace pouted alongside his father as they found the correct floor for the doctor's office, went to the collection of elevators, pushed the up button, and eventually got a lift to the eighth level. It was an unassuming space, with bland black print on the door describing the professionals in practice. There was no mention of the specific psychotherapy they engaged in.

"Hello," said Sammy to a kindly, red-haired secretary. "My son and I have an appointment with Dr. Quincy Seznack at ten o'clock."

"Yes, of course, Rev. Milton," said the woman behind the desk. "Go ahead and have a seat. Dr. Seznack will be with you soon."

The waiting room was also unsuspecting. There were a bunch of secular kids' magazines and news magazines piled on the small tables dividing up the chairs. Instrumental classical music played in the background, loud enough to be heard, yet soft enough to not disturb any conversations. The wallpaper had lightly painted texture, with the occasional positivity-themed posters framed and placed on the wall. The two Miltons were the only people in the waiting room. Sammy read one of the news magazines, while Wallace slumped into his chair in annoyance and dread.

Six minutes after ten, the father and son were disrupted by the opening of the doctor's door. Seznack and a client were laughing as they exited the room. Banal chatter ensued as he went to the smiling secretary and signed out, having filled out paperwork in the waiting room before the Milton family arrived. As the man said his goodbyes and left the office, Sammy rose from his seat and placed the magazine on one of the tables. Wallace grudgingly followed his father to meet the therapist.

"Dr. Seznack," said Sammy as he shook hands with the professional.

"A pleasure to meet you, Rev. Milton," said the doctor, who turned with big eyes to the teenager. "And you must be Wallace." Seznack extended his hand, and after an awkward pause, Wallace shook it. "Well, let's go ahead inside, shall we?"

"Yes, doctor."

"I'm sorry I kept you waiting," said Seznack as the three entered his office. "You can sit on the couch." Sammy and Wallace obliged, situating themselves on the comfy dark blue furniture. Wallace looked around the space as he heard the door latch shut behind him. There were three diplomas posted on the wall, an office chair directly opposite the couch, and a desk in the corner that had various files and papers on it, as well as a few family photos. To his left, Wallace saw a small collection of kids' toys and several academic publications on a shelf. Seznack had a cranial balding head and large, thick-rimmed glasses. To Wallace, he looked like a therapist. "Okay then, should we begin now?"

"Yes, doctor."

"So, what exactly happened?"

"My son, um, came out to me earlier this week."

"Yes," nodded Seznack, who took out a pen and jotted down notes as Milton spoke.

"Since then, he's told me that he feels homosexual. That he has never felt any other way."

"It's the truth," interjected Wallace.

"Wallace, I am talking to an adult now," scolded Sammy before returning his attention back to the doctor. "Anyway, Dr. Seznack, I was told by the parents of former patients of yours that you can cure this."

"I see," observed Seznack. "Well, first of all, I am going to tell you upfront, this will not be an easy process. It is going to require months of counseling with your son. Possibly years. You understand?"

"Yes," Sammy replied, with some disappointment.

"Some people claim that it is a simple matter of flipping a switch. That is not the case. Like any psychopathy, same-sex attraction is something that has to be deconstructed and treated over a considerable period of time."

"Okay."

"Dad, I really don't want to do this," stressed Wallace, tugging at his father's arm.

"Wallace Smith, you are really pushing it. Dr. Seznack is a professional therapist. With his help, you can be normal again."

"I was never normal," whispered Wallace.

"Wallace, I'm not telling you again . . . "

"Rev. Milton, if I may," began the doctor, "I would like to talk with you alone."

"Um, I guess that's okay."

"Okay," said Seznack, who turned his attention to the youth. "Wallace, if you don't mind, could you wait outside of my office for a few minutes?"

"Yeah, whatever," said Wallace, getting up from the couch. He looked at his father and gave a parting, "I don't want to do this," before exiting.

He returned to a moment in elementary school. Wallace was thinking of that one kid, a big fellow, who picked a fight with him. He did not remember why, but he recalled swinging. A teacher saw them and sent them both to the principal. Waiting there, back in grade school, the brutal wait was consuming him in his mind and midsection. It was the same feeling, the same sense of inevitable suffering. The boring waiting room was so horrid. He struggled to stop himself from running.

Wallace jumped up as the noise of an opening door beckoned. His father and the doctor walked out, exchanging a few words at too low a volume for him to understand. "Thanks for listening to my concerns, doctor."

"No problem," he replied. "Let me just say, it was an honor to finally meet the Rev. Milton."

"Thank you," responded Sammy with a faint smile. "What do I owe you?"

"For you, Reverend, consider it complimentary."

"Thank you," said a pleasantly surprised Sammy. The two adults shook hands, and then Milton turned to the receptionist to sign out.

"What did he say?"

"Are you ready to go?"

"I don't have to come back?" asked Wallace excitedly.

"Are you ready to go?" restated Sammy with aggravation. Wallace simply nodded, and the two exited the facility.

Wallace still held on to dread as they drove back home. His father had said nothing since turning on the engine. The boy was afraid to repeat his question. He studied his father, whose eyes stuck to the road. There was a solemnity in his expression, a sense of intractable annoyance. Disappointment seemed to drench his attitude. Wallace wondered what would happen next. He thought about houses he could stay at, friends who would let him in. That same kid he picked a fight with back in elementary school acted amiable toward him in high school. He thought of how to tell his siblings, his mother. He readied for a lonely journey, hoping that his separation would be fairly painless.

"You don't want to go back, do you?" inquired Sammy, stoic. Wallace pondered how to respond, fearful of entering a trap. Then he decided to be laconic.

"No. I don't."

Sammy paused, waiting until he slowed to a stop at a red light before continuing. "And if I sent you to another therapist, you would reject his help also, right?"

"Yes. Yes, I would," said Wallace while looking down. He was waiting for the blow to hit, the ultimate harsh finisher from his angered parent.

"Then we won't go back."

Wallace perked up. "What?"

"We will not go back. We won't go to another doctor."

"Okay."

"Wally," began Sammy, speaking the name with fragility. "I talked with Dr. Seznack. He told me he refuses to take on a patient who is unwilling to be treated. He told me going to a doctor who would treat an unwilling patient was a bad idea. So until you change your mind, I won't send you to another therapist."

"Thank you," Wallace said, barely above a whisper. The car stopped in front of the house. Sammy put it in park and turned off the engine.

"But make no mistake; there will be rules," stated Sammy. "As long as you live here, there will be no dating men. And that is non-negotiable." Wallace grudgingly nodded. "Wally?" The son looked up to see the father and beheld large, blue eyes. "I want you to know that you are still my son. And I want you to be joyful and to succeed. There is nothing you can do to make me forsake you. Now, that's not a call for you to try and find something that will," laughed Sammy, his son faintly smiling, "but I wanted you to know that."

"Thanks, Dad."

"Anyway," said Sammy as he unfastened his seatbelt, his son doing the same. "You have some school work to catch up on, and I need to write my next sermon."

"Yeah," began Wallace. "That history test won't pass itself."

"Exactly."

* * *

"And that was the last of it," said a much older Wallace Smith to Scott Addison, jolting the journalist from his note-taking.

"Wait, that was it?"

"Yup. We barely talked about it after that."

"So, wait, it never came up again?" asked Scott with more prodding. "Like, you never brought a boyfriend home?"

"No, I followed the rules," answered Wallace. "He said no dating while I was living at home, so I didn't date." Smith pondered a moment. "Come to think of it, I didn't date through college either. It took me awhile."

"But why?"

"You forget, I grew up during the AIDS outbreak. 'The gay plague,'" said Wallace, acting overly theatrical for that second sentence. "No pun intended, but I was kind of scared straight. I didn't meet Benny, that is Benjamin, until a few years ago. He didn't like my dad at all, so he was okay with staying away from family gatherings."

"If things were so great, why the name change?"

"That was my decision. I didn't want any attention; and I knew that it would hurt my dad's public career, so I thought it best to keep it all in the closet, so to speak. You've got to understand, Scott, I don't really care about politics. All I know is that me being a headline was going to be used to hurt someone I care for."

"So, you were never angry at your father for being so unaccepting of who you are?" asked Scott at the peak of desperation.

"I was at first. I kept my anger to myself, but yeah, at first I didn't like how he felt about my sexual orientation. But then, ironically enough, that all changed when I moved out and got to know other LGBT folks," said Wallace, his tone getting darker. "When I heard all those stories. Parents kicking them out, relatives constantly telling them they're going to Hell, former friends beating them up, being turned away at Christmas and Thanksgiving." He laughed briefly. "Here I was complaining about how my dad thought I was wrong. Do you realize how petty my complaints were when put next to theirs? All my dad wanted was for me to take some talk therapy. There were people I ran into who were electrocuted in order to 'cure' them. So, yeah, I appreciated him even more after hearing those stories. So, he thought I was wrong. Fine. I thought he was wrong. And yet, we made it work."

"I see."

"I know he wanted me to take therapy. I know he never really got over that. It was inside him, wanting to scream at me. He once told me that he wasn't surprised I turned out so stubborn; he knew I got it from him. The stubbornness, that is," clarified Wallace with a smile.

"Of course," replied Scott as he nodded, the light moment barely phasing him.

"That's just how he was. My dad, he never gave up on people," said Wallace, pausing for a brief laugh. "I don't think he knew how to give up on people. He never stopped loving me." Wallace noticed that he was becoming choked up, and his eyes were watering. "I'm sorry, I didn't mean to—"

"No, no, that's alright," answered Scott with encouragement, pushing the button to end the recording. He rose up to gather his things as Wallace regained his composure and rose up also. "Thank you very much for the interview. And, again, I am sorry for your loss."

"Thank you," nodded Wallace with a recovering smile. "I have to say, I never thought anyone was going to find me. I thought I was going to keep this secret to the grave. Then you called."

"I apologize if I—"

"Oh, no, don't be sorry," assured Wallace. "Now that my dad has passed, I think it's okay to come out with this. You're a good journalist. I'm glad you are going to tell this story."

"Thank you," said Scott. "If all goes according to plan, the article should be in this coming Friday's edition of *The Kensington Post.*"

"I'll be sure to look for it."

MICHAEL PHILLIPS

"MY DAD, HE NEVER GAVE up on people." Scott Addison pushed the pause button on his digital voice recorder and quickly typed up the sentence. He pushed the button again. "I don't think he knew how to give up on people." The button pressed, the audio paused, and additional hasty yet accurate typing. The sentence completed, Scott pushed the button once more. "He never stopped loving me." Again, he put it on pause to produce the spoken statement in written form on his laptop screen. Knowing that little else came next, Addison stopped the recording and turned off the device.

The journalist took a deep breath, massaging his forehead. He rose from his seat, stretching his back and legs. Another long session of transcription, another interview that went against what he was ordered to discover. Scott paced around his motel room and then decided to get some more coffee. The room had its own machine. He had drunk two cups by the time he finished his research. His laptop shared the table space with several pages of handwritten notes, a couple of sticky notes with key phrases and names, and a basic outline for his story. He knew what he had to write and how to write it. He knew where to place the quotes, divide up the material, and format the photos for inclusion in the document to create a decent article.

It was the actual doing that scared him. He stood by the television, several feet between himself and his work. Business on the bottom—he was wearing a pair of slacks and a belt with dress shoes. Comfort on the top—he had on only a white undershirt. He did not bring jeans on this adventure, instead wearing the same three sets of business casual wear the whole week. Only the socks and underwear were new every morning. His mind wanted to wander, his mentality seeking a break from the unenviable task.

"What am I doing? What am I doing?" he lamented to himself. Another swig of the coffee, and he made his way back to the table. There was no way his editor was going to like this article. Yet, Scott knew that even a hated submission was better than no submission at all. Maybe Michael Phillips could simply heavily edit the work, fashion it to fit his own narrative. As Scott had found out over the past several days, it would hardly be unprecedented. Then he thought of the people he interviewed—person after person who were counting on him to convey truth. What would they think of this brutally revised version being released? Scott could already hear the complaints and the disappointment, especially from Wallace.

Scott sat down in front of the laptop. Carefully setting the coffee mug to the side, he minimized the document with the transcribed interviews. He found the document in his files that was destined to be the article. A double-click, and the first draft was before him. He let out a brief snicker at the title that appeared: "A Tunnel Into Darkness." Tyrone Spearman would be proud if Addison kept the name. However, it was incompatible with what the story had become. Scott did not want to delete outright, though. He looked at his things, the many notes and comments. Into Marvelous Light Ministries, First Peter 2:9. Sammy Milton's favorite verse. The name of his church.

Addison moved the cursor to the end of the title and began to hit the backspace button until the word "Darkness" was removed. With all the notes in mind, he typed the phrase "Marvelous Light." Scott quickly concluded that "Tunnel" would not work either. He moved the cursor over to that word and erased it. Thinking of church spires and rapture, he replaced it with "Spiral." He looked over the title with accomplishment.

"A Spiral Into Marvelous Light," he read aloud. "Top that one, Tyrone."

Scott saw the preliminary opening to the article: "Bigot. Racist. Homophobe. Sexist. Hate-Monger. All these are words associated with the recently deceased Rev. Sammy Milton. Those who fought against him the longest share their stories about the worst of his actions." He was about to delete it all. Then he a thought a moment and deleted most of the last sentence. The blinking cursor awaiting his command, Scott took a hard breath and got to work, typing the new thesis: "Those who fought against him the longest and knew him the best, however, reject these labels. For them, Rev. Milton was a civil and even welcoming enemy. He helped unwed mothers, recovering alcoholics, and feminists trying to register voters. He even loved his once-unknown, openly gay son, who chose obscurity rather than be used to hurt his father . . . "

Scott continued to work on the introduction, toggling with the phraseology. It was the shortest section, yet the most important in grabbing the attention of his readers. Only the title mattered more in this capturing. He went through it all again, beginning with Beverley Clayborne. Scott chose the order in which his interviews came. Detailing the baseball career, the decision to become a preacher, the changing views on civil rights, the move toward politics. Frequently, he halted his key-punching to copy and paste a quote from his transcribed materials. Sometimes, it remained a block of interesting information straight from the source; other times, he chopped down the quote to paraphrase, keeping as best he could the spirit of the comments made.

Nearly two hours and three cups of coffee later, the first draft was mostly completed. Only the conclusion was unwritten. He reviewed what he had so far to check for grammar mistakes, of which there were several. Many sentences were rephrased. Scott took to adding photos to various sections. He had many from interviewees and the internet. Scott did not bother to post a main photo like he did for most stories. Being a feature article, Addison expected *The Kensington Post*'s resident cartoonist to illustrate something to encapsulate the fullness of the article's message.

Going through the text, adding things here and there, inserting the photos, Scott found himself within the fabric of the testimonies. The baseball player, the young man longing for greater meaning, the preaching, the charisma, and the converts. Charity, judgment, music, and proclamation. Rallies and demonstrations, services and revival. Family, friends, enemies, confrontation, compassion. The decades rolled around in his mind, the aging yet ageless figure ever marching onward.

"For many reading this article, they might perceive that the Rev. Sammy Milton was a living contradiction," spoke Scott while he typed. "How could a man have so many amiable ties to the communities he so often opposed? A possible explanation . . . " Scott paused and deleted that last word. He continued to talk and type: "A possible theory can be found with the phrase, 'Hate the sin, love the sinner.'" Scott nodded at his wording. "The phrase is often derided . . . " He shook his head and removed the sentence, now only typing. "Critics often bash the phrase as mere apologia for bigotry. And yet, as seen by those who knew him, Rev. Milton appeared to embody the cliché. Being right, at least in his own mind, did not prevent Milton from making friendships the other." Scott went back and added a "with" where it was needed. He started reading aloud once again, remembering that such a practice helped hinder errors. "It might be the case that the biggest difference between Milton and mainstream America wasn't his views on science, women's health, or gay rights. Rather, it was his boundless capacity for relationship. In an era where people are constantly unfriending, blocking, and boycotting those who are different, Milton dared to reach out. 'My dad, he never gave up on people,' recalled his gay son. 'I don't think he knew how to give up on people. He never stopped loving me.'"

Scott typed a few words after the Wallace quote. Then he stopped, thought for a moment, and decided to erase them. The son's quote was too good an ending. Again, he went through the lengthy piece and made some more edits. There always seemed to be something new that was wrong. It was like the errors were self-replicating. Addison felt more pressure than usual to get the grammar correct. He knew this story was going to get a harsher critique than his other pieces.

Saving the document for a final time, he moved the cursor to the upper righthand corner and exited out. The screen showed the transcription document open. Scott closed that one also. He had a few web pages up already. Scott clicked on the tab that took him to his work inbox. Opening a new email, he typed up a laconic message to his editor. He put the email title in all caps to help Phillips see his work amidst the many messages he got on a daily basis. File attached, message written, email address added, Scott paused to behold what looked to be the end of his journalism career.

"Send it," he whispered to himself, hesitating to click on the proper button. "Send it," he repeated, confident something was wrong with the email. "Send it!" With a jolt, he finally got himself to click the button, and the email was transmitted to his boss. He took a breath when he saw the "Sent!" statement pop up.

Then he waited. He looked at his social media accounts; then he clicked the refresh button on his work inbox to see if any new emails came. There was a new one, but it was a press release from some advocacy group. Addison got a lot of those from different organizations. Sometimes, they were valuable for story pitches or, at the least, perspectives on a major development. He paced around the motel room for a little while and clicked the refresh button again. Nothing new. He left to get lunch and brought it back to the room. He refreshed the page, and two new emails emerged; neither was important. Television on, he struggled to eat his meal. Barely halfway through his lunch, he went back to his laptop and clicked refresh. Nothing.

Despite finally eating his meal, Scott was worn. All the travel, the interviews, the fear of backlash. He turned off the TV and laid down. To ponder. To think. Maybe to fall asleep. He was getting there. The night before, he had struggled to lose consciousness. He yawned. Attention was directed to the ceiling. It was a basic plane. Something calm about its basic image. Nothing ornate to arouse the senses. Just there, a pleasant indifference. Scott wondered how many appreciated the simplicity.

Then his phone rang. Scott broke his mellow mood and went for the device, which was in his pocket. Taking it out, he saw the name

Michael Phillips on the screen. He did not want to answer. However, there was no other option. With a breath, he tapped on the answer icon, and the conversation began.

"Hello?" asked Scott as though he did not know who was calling him.

"Hey, Scott, it's Phillips."

"Hey."

"Just wanted to let you know that I got your article, and I read it."

"Okay," replied Scott.

"Gee whiz, Scott, you don't need to act so nervous. We're going to publish it," declared an amused voice.

"Uh, okay, um, good."

"I mean, really, Scott. You haven't sounded this antsy since your job interview."

"Well," hesitated Scott. "Usually when you call, it's because there's a problem."

"True, true, there is that," conceded Phillips. "But there is no real problem. A few grammar issues here and there, but nothing that can't be fixed by Friday."

"That's good."

"The reason I called you, Scott, is because I wanted to talk to you about your article."

Scott was unsure how to react to the statement. He was a little concerned about what his superior was going to say. Yet Phillips had already explained that Scott's article was going to be published. He simply replied "okay" and listened as Phillips tried his best to convey his thoughts.

"I have spent my whole life fighting the Sammy Miltons of the world. When I was a student, I used to attend protests, shout down speakers at town halls, stuff like that. After college, I became a reporter. I dedicated my career to writing up articles that attacked them for any and all wrongs. When I became an editor, I assigned those articles, often giving my help.

"It was always the same strategy, the same plan, the same ethic. Overplay the bad, downplay the good. Now, now, there were times when it was very easy to stress the bad. And there were times when it was very hard to ignore the good." Scott listened intently, waiting for the pause to conclude. He was unable to see his editor, but he felt that something was struggling within him. A great emotional burden had to be lifted. "When we, you know, when we started to win, I felt like it was worth it. It was great to finally see them pushed to the margins, shrinking away from all the corridors of power. Like everyone else, I was thrilled. I thought America would be better off. 'Love wins' and all that junk.

"But then came the new enemy. That void in the American political discourse wasn't replaced by progress; it was filled with vile hatred, the likes of which we thought had died in the 1960s. Soon we found our own tactics used against us. Now they were the ones shouting people down, bashing people on social media, and worse. These glorified fascists rose up, at times violently. If these had been the last gasps of some monster, it would have been one thing. But they weren't. These . . . deplorables . . . won. They won. Over and over. Now we're the ones being pushed away; we're the ones being threatened with destruction. We're the ones wondering if we'll survive."

Scott nodded at the analysis, agreeing with it fully. It was a somber reminder of what both were going through.

"Throughout my adult life," continued Phillips, "I never questioned what I did. I never really thought that I stood for anything other than for good. And if I misquoted someone or ignored a story that might have made my enemies look good, so be it." Phillips paused to compose himself. "And then I read your article. I got to relive much of what I once had. I got to see things I either never saw or refused to see. And . . . and now, I . . . now I . . . " Phillips gave an embarrassed laugh. "I can't believe I'm even going to say this, but I'm thinking it. So, I might as well say it . . . " There was silence for a few seconds. Scott briefly wondered if the connection had been lost. Then his editor said something that stunned them both.

"I miss Sammy Milton. I actually miss Sammy Milton! I really, really miss him. I never thought I would. I never thought it possible. But I do. I really, really do! I am sad that he is dead. I miss him, and I even miss what he stood for." Phillips was beginning to choke up, but he fought well and continued. "I miss the days when my enemy still prayed for my well-being. I miss the days when my enemy believed I was created in the image of God. I miss the days when my enemy wanted to be friends with me.

"There were so many times that Milton invited me to lunch or to some social gathering. I ignored or rejected every request. As far as I was concerned, there was no way I was going to be friends with him. I used to think that he was the worst thing that could happen to this country. But right now, Scott? Right now, right now, I *wish* he was the worst thing that could happen to this country. I *wish* he was the worst-case scenario. Because right now, right now I would take a thousand Sammy Miltons over any one alt right extremist, and that's a fact.

"I can't help but wonder what I did wrong. What we did wrong. Maybe, maybe when we were winning, maybe we should have been more merciful. Maybe we should have left a part of America for Milton and his kind to have for themselves. Maybe we should have done more to incorporate them into our movement. They wouldn't be the only community in the movement that disagrees with us on things. I don't know. But it is something to think about. And that is why I had to talk to you as soon as possible.

"The best kind of writing is the kind that makes you entertain ideas you wouldn't have otherwise entertained. Scott, your writing does that. And so, I have decided to have your article be the front page story in Friday's edition."

"Really?" Scott was exuberant. "Wow. That's awesome."

"People need to read what you have written. Our readers especially. We need to start figuring out what we can do to fix things. More importantly, we need to figure out who we can trust to help out. We need to understand these nuances more than ever. Not only will it be showcased on the front page, but I will write a foreword basically outlining what I just told you. The more eyes that see this story, the better."

"Thank you, thank you!"

"Oh, now, now, don't thank me," said Phillips as he returned to a lighter mood. "You're the one who wrote it. I'm just giving it a bigger audience."

"Well, either way, I'm grateful."

"As you should be. But just so you know, this changes nothing. I still expect you in the office tomorrow morning. Your working vacation is over."

"Yes, sir."

"It's still early afternoon. You'll have little traffic coming up, and I know how fast you drive."

"Of course," said Scott.

"Anyway, see you tomorrow."

"See you."

A beeping noise prompted Scott to look at his screen. The phone call was ended. Overflowing with happiness, Addison hooted and hollered. He punched the air in celebration and laughed in relief. He again took to pacing, but not in fear but rather excitement. Sitting on the bed to take it all in, he turned his head upward to look through the bland ceiling and toward Heaven.

"I guess You liked what I did after all, huh?" he said with a relieved smile.

* * *

Traffic was scarce on Interstate 95 that afternoon. As soon as Scott Addison exited the ramp to get onto the three-lane road, he floored it. Few stood in his way as he motored northward toward the Washington, DC, area. Large trees bearing multicolored leaves upon their many branches blurred along either side of the highway. Knee-high railings on the flanks came and went, as did several right-lane vehicles. He preferred the center lane, giving him more options should he need to switch from his current status. Left lane was too fast, even for him, and the right lane had the slow pokes and the mergers.

Scott had an old CD playing that he knew would complete its last song in about fifty minutes. It was an optimistic measure working under the assumption that he would get north of Fredericksburg as it ended and thus be able to tune in to his preferred stations by the CD's end. The volume was turned higher than usual to account for engine noise; it was always louder on the highway. He liked the increased speed limits, as it meant he could go even faster while being less than fifteen miles above the limit. That was his preference, being told as a teenager that more than fifteen miles per hour above the limit meant a tougher penalty if caught.

Through the rapid transportation, Addison was still able to appreciate the beauty of the drive. Devoid of the skyscrapers and the shopping malls, central Virginia had a natural attractiveness full of green valleys and thick forests. Wildlife occasionally came into view or silently tread between the trees by the road. While Addison focused on the center of the road and planned out what all he was doing upon returning to his apartment, he failed to notice a pair of deer cautiously walking onto the pavement. They, apparently, failed to notice him also, casually sauntering across the open area. Then Addison saw them, slammed his brakes in a panic, and veered off the road.

His car swung around as he hit the nearest light gray guard rail, which grated one side of his vehicle as it came to a rough halt in a ditch. The CD played on as Scott breathed heavily. Fearful of a gas leak or something like that, he turned off the car. He was still trying to gather himself as he undid his belt and got out. The driver's side did not look too bad. He thought about starting up the automobile and continuing on like nothing happened. Then he walked to the passenger side and saw the severe lacerations inflicted when he hit the railing.

More frustrated than hurt, Addison went about finding his insurance information and calling the proper authorities to report the accident.

"Are you okay?" asked a kindly male voice. Addison looked up from the ditch to see a rustic fellow with blue overalls and a gaunt figure. A few yards away was his much older car, with faded coloring and several noticeable dinks.

"I think so, yeah."

"I saw what happened. Crazy stuff."

"Yeah."

"You need any help?"

"No, that's okay," replied Scott as he leaned against his battered vehicle. "I'm insured, so a truck should come soon."

"Okay," nodded the man. He studied the journalist. "You know, it doesn't look like you have a single scratch on you."

"No, I guess I don't," agreed Scott, quickly looking over himself to confirm the accurate claim of the local.

"God must have a plan for you."

"You know something? I'm starting to think He does."

"Take care, now."

"You, too."

Less than an hour later, the various emergency personnel arrived. An ambulance with a physician came to check on Addison. After a basic examination, the specialist concluded that Scott was healthy. He noted that the crash victim did have a slightly accelerated heart rate, though both agreed this was probably due to the trauma of having just endured an accident. A patrol car came as well. Addison agreed to take a sobriety test and successfully followed the prompts to stretch out his arms, touch his nose, and walk in a straight line. The officer officially charged him with reckless driving. A court date was scheduled for December the third of that year. Formalities concluded, the police car drove off. A few minutes later, the pickup truck arrived to tow the vehicle.

* * *

"You almost hit a deer?" asked an amused Katie Nicholson over the phone. She had completed the last of her articles for the day when Scott called.

"Two of them, actually."

"Wow," laughed Nicholson. "So where are you now?"

"I'm near an exit for Ladysmith," explained Scott as his ruined car was loaded onto the back of the pickup. "But the pickup truck is going somewhere else. One moment." Scott directed his attention away from his phone to ask the middle-aged, baseball cap-wearing man where his vehicle was headed. "Um, where is your repair shop located?"

"Bowling Green," replied the man. "Billy's Auto Repair."

"Okay," nodded Scott as he returned to his phone call. "Billy's Auto Repair. It's in Bowling Green."

"Kentucky?"

"Virginia."

"I know. I'm just kidding you."

"Do you know where to go?"

"Is it the Billy's off Main Street?" inquired Katie after doing a quick internet search, phone tucked between her head and shoulder.

"Let me check," replied Scott, again turning away from the phone. The man was securing the wrecked car to the back of his truck. Scott looked up to ask. "Is your repair shop off Main Street?"

"Yes, sir. That's where we're going."

"Thanks," Scott said, going back to the phone. "Yes, you're right. It's the Billy's off Main Street. So, can you pick me up soon?"

"I was about to leave early anyway, so why not?"

"Thank you so much."

"No problem," Katie said. "By the way, I heard the good news from Phillips. Congrats on getting top billing in the Friday edition."

"Thanks."

"He couldn't stop telling us how much he liked your work."

"Then I guess it's grounds for a celebration," said Scott, feeling a little courageous. "How's about I take you out to dinner this Friday evening, you know, after work? My treat?"

Katie smiled. "Sounds good."

"You can pick the restaurant."

"And I'll make sure it's metro-friendly."

"Ha, ha," Scott sarcastically replied. "Anyway, see you soon."

"Bye."

"Ready to go?" asked the pickup truck owner to the reporter.

"Definitely."

The truck roared with diesel might as Scott rushed in front of the stopped pickup and got into the passenger side seat. As he entered into the service vehicle, he heard an old crooner on the radio, singing some revival hymn. Scott thought little of the religious background, possibly because of spending days immersed inside a spiritual culture. "You don't mind if I listen to this station, do you? It's my favorite."

"No, go ahead," Scott assured him. As the pickup rumbled onto the highway, Addison began to look out the window, barely attending to the station.

"A lighthouse in an ocean of darkness, this is Christian Values Radio, WRVA, Ashland, Virginia," said a deep voice before a campier person spoke up.

"Greetings listeners, this is your friend, Brother David. As you undoubtedly know, today marks one week since the Rev. Sammy Milton went home to be with the Lord." The comment perked up Scott's attention. "As our regular listeners know, Brother Milton and I go back many years. You see, when I was a young man, I was a worldly person. I did all the vices and lived only for my belly. Then a friend invited me to one of Milton's Salvation Meetings. I was so moved by his preaching, that I immediately committed my life to Christ and turned away from all those vices forever. Years later, I met Brother Milton at a Bible conference. I told him my plans to start this radio station, and he offered nothing but help. Were it not for his advice and support, we wouldn't be on the air today. Over time, I came to call Brother Milton a friend and because of that, I even learned his favorite song, which I now play in his honor. This one's for you, Sammy. Lord-willing, we shall meet again someday."

As the song gently filled the pickup truck, its slow beginning brought by a pair of guitars and the light tapping of cymbals, Scott Addison entered a different state. While his physical body remained within the confines of his place and time, his mentality soared beyond it. He entered into a different world, possibly from the past, possibly from eternity. Maybe it was real; it had to be. The music drove it on, leading him into a setting that was at once beyond his present and yet encompassing that which he knew.

His frame is no longer visible, nor is it shaped. He feels as though he is floating, feeling nothing else of a physical nature. Not pain, not exhaustion. Only sound and sight. This transparent channel of consciousness comes upon a crowded parking lot for some local high school. It seems connected to a small town, but no matter. It is crowded, nearly every space filled, even though it is not a school day. A sign by the three pairs of the gym's double doors explains the matter.

Going through the solid doors sans effort, he is inside a hallway—a typical school structure with cold, hard flooring and students' projects and photos hung on the walls. A few young men and an older fellow are lightly chatting in the hall. They are the ushers. Their banal chatters do not take away from the song, its radiant passion flowing through the open doors to the gym. Without notice, he gravitates toward the spiritual meeting taking place in the profane multipurpose room.

There are two large columns of metal folding chairs. Each one has someone standing over them. A stage was set at the opposite end of the entrance. Few are sitting at this point. One rare example is Herbert Spiker, compelled to do so because of his disability. Flanked by two security guards, he grits his teeth, not out of annoyance but rather of habit. He is enjoying the service and finds the song decent.

A couple of rows up and on the opposite column is Wallace Smith. It takes Scott some time to recognize him, as he is quite young. Smith wanted to sit closer to the front, possibly with family. His friends, members of the community he moved to after college, were more hesitant. Wallace caved in and agreed to be farther back. He also enjoys the service and even his friends feel moved by the righteous pronouncements.

Nearly all present are adults. Several sway; many hold their arms upward in reverence and personal prayer. Some just stand. Two of those standing include a mother and her daughter. Scott looked long enough and then figured out that the mother is Eileen Friedman. Not wearing a political shirt, it is a little harder to spot her. The little girl must be Jenny. She occasionally asks a question, whispering her curiosities to her more informed mother. Eileen nicely responds to each query.

Five rows more and on the same side as Wallace and his friends, Jabez Henderson is there with his wife and eldest son. A tradition continues, with Jabez wanting his son to learn what he learned in the hopes of seeing him take over his ministry. Like many others listening to the song, they gently sway side-to-side. They are in their polished church clothes, making them some of the best-dressed people in the gym.

With the song entering the chorus, Scott nears the front of the meeting. In the first couple of rows in the left column stand the Milton family. They range in age from the preacher's elderly, yet respectable, wife to their youngest grandkids, infants at this point. Scott is unsure if one of the little ones is Frank Moore, but he does not rule it out. Theirs is a pride in the triumph of another wonderful service nearing its end.

Not far from them is a man before his fall. Or maybe it was after, but now more learned, understanding, holy, and redeemed. Johnny Canker stands with six other men in a row between the front of the two columns and the stage. Each of them is proper, and they wear suits. They await what is expected to come, soon enough. There are three, including Canker, in front of the left column, three in front of the right column, and one in the middle. That way, they are ready for the most important part. Canker is the only one who can see Scott, giving him a wink and a nod as he passes by.

Scott is flowing toward the stairs on the side of the stage. He drifts by the guitarists, the drummer, and a few others helping with the audio equipment. Having ascended the stage, he finds himself in front of a quartet of men singing the beautiful hymn. The one on the far left is the oldest of the four. Though his voice was not what it once was, Beverley Clayborne still holds his own. Next to him is the director of music for a local congregation who helped spread the word about the event. To the director's left is the lead singer. He is a bald, mustachioed man with an amazing professional voice.

The quartet concludes the chorus, with the lead singer looking to his left at the final member of the quartet. He is a last-minute addition, the original scheduled singer catching the flu. Still, it is his favorite song, and so the Rev. Sammy Milton is up for the challenge. The leader of the quartet smiles and tacitly cues Milton for the beginning of the second verse. Looking at the crowd with his sapphire eyes, having just minutes earlier given a rousing sermon, Milton begins to sing. He hits each note as a perfect amateur, his performance enjoyable even if not the caliber of the man leading the four vocalists.

Scott listens to his solo, as it is given by the preacher with holy sincerity to every word. And then entering the chorus, he is rejoined by the other three. Each grabs their own microphone, contributing their own part to the euphony. The preaching, the message, the song. Such movement of inspiration, such grand spiritual ecstasy. It fills many within the crowd. As the chorus is sung again, one leaves his seat. Then another. Then another. Then a pair. Then a few more. Then another. Then another. Then two more. Three more. Five more. Then another. Another pair. A few more from the back rows.

Some come out of inspiration, some out of desperation. A few have never known the Gospel. Many took it for granted. Not anymore. They walk down the aisle and fan out to the various men waiting to hear their confessions. They come to be counted; they are going to start their lives anew. Hands are shaken, words are exchanged. There is prayer. There is joyful crying as the supplications are spoken under the canopy of the wondrous chorus.

The lead singer gives the long final note, the other three repeating the final refrain. The song melts into the roaring applause. Cheers, cries, clapping. Clayborne and the other two singers turn to face Milton and give their applause. The admiration is directed toward Sammy, who blushes and tries to beg off the affection. After his meager yet sincere attempt, he looks at the adoring crowd, at those who made the life-changing decision, and at his family. Satisfaction fills him with the ongoing wonder.

Once a vapor, Scott soon finds himself with the ability to applaud, and he does so adamantly. He claps his hands intensely over and over. He cheers like many of the others, offering his utmost support for the contented preacher on the stage. How can he not? For he knew him. He finally knew him.

ACKNOWLEDGMENTS

It has been said that no one ever makes it on their own. I fully agree. *A Spiral Into Marvelous Light* came to be due to the many and they all deserve thanks. Some of whom I list below.

First and foremost, I thank God for all that He has given me, including the opportunity to write this book and have it released to the world.

I thank my mother, quite possibly my biggest fan, without whose support this book would not have been possible.

I thank my family overall, because they all contributed and continue to contribute to who I am and what I do.

I thank John McClure, Director of Research Services with the Virginia Historical Society, who provided me with valuable information on the political history of the Commonwealth, especially its debate over the Equal Rights Amendment.

I thank Todd A. Schall-Vess, general manager of the Byrd Theatre in Richmond, Virginia, who helped with background information on the facility. If you are in Richmond, I highly recommend paying the Byrd a visit.

I thank George Mason University of Fairfax, Virginia, and especially its Department of History & Art History, for providing me with an education in the time periods for which I wrote about.

Inspiration for the Reverend Sammy Milton came primarily through two individuals, the Reverend Jerry Falwell and the Reverend Billy Sunday. From Falwell there is the Religious Right connection, the Liberty Godparent Home for unwed mothers, the Elim Home for recovering alcoholics, support for voter drives, and the friendship with ideological enemies including Larry Flynn (who, of course, was the inspiration for Herbert Spiker). From Sunday there is the professional baseball career, the distaste for alcohol, the notable preaching career, the support for women's suffrage, and issues with his children.

The Southern Baptist Convention's efforts at racial reconciliation and their passing a resolution in 2016 denouncing displays of the Confederate battle flag also influenced the character of Sammy Milton.

It is my hope and prayer that this book has been enlightening and educational, as well as entertaining, for all who read it. Indeed, even fiction can aid in spreading truth.

ENDNOTES

1 Matthew 24:35

2 Matthew 19:16-26

3 Romans 3:10

4 Romans 3:23

5 Matthew 19:26

6 Ruth 1:16

7 Romans 1:21-27

For more information about
Michael Gryboski
&
A Spiral into Marvelous Light
please visit:

www.facebook.com/MichaelCGryboski
@Puritan1986
www.instagram.com/michaelgryboski
www.crossnation.tumblr.com

For more information about
AMBASSADOR INTERNATIONAL
please visit:

www.ambassador-international.com
@AmbassadorIntl
www.facebook.com/AmbassadorIntl

If you enjoyed this book, please consider leaving us a review on
Amazon, Goodreads, or our website.

59750270R00149

Made in the USA
Middletown, DE
18 August 2019